A MATTER
of DIAMONDS

a faith abbey mystery

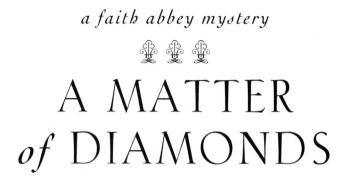

A MATTER
of DIAMONDS

DAVID MANUEL

PARACLETE PRESS
Brewster, Massachusetts

Library of Congress Cataloging-in-Publication Data

Manuel, David.
    A matter of diamonds : a Faith Abbey mystery / David Manuel.
       p.   cm.
    ISBN 1–55725–258–0
   1. Cape Cod (Mass.)–Fiction. 2. Monks–Fiction. I. Title.
    PS3563.A5747 M37 2000
    813' .54–dc21   00-010106

This book is a work of fiction. With the exception noted below, names, characters, places, and incidents are products of the author's imagination or are used fictitiously. Any resemblance to actual events, locales, or persons, living or dead, is coincidental.

Faith Abbey is, however, in spirit quite close to the Community of Jesus, the ecumenical religious community of which the author has been a member for the past 29 years.

10 9 8 7 6 5 4 3 2 1

ISBN 1-55725-258-0

Published by Paraclete Press
Brewster, Massachusetts
www.paracletepress.com

Printed in the United States of America.

To my wife
Barbara
this book is
lovingly dedicated

acknowledgments

There is a reason why so many writers dedicate their books to their wives or husbands; they know how much their spouses have had to put up with. In the case of my wife Barbara, it has been 29 years of crunching deadlines and their attendant emotional roller-coasters. Through it all, she has been loving and supportive, while caring enough to be honest, even when it hurts. So this book's for her.

I would also like to thank series editor Phyllis Tickle, without whose discernment and enthusiasm there would be no Faith Abbey mystery series. And publisher Lillian Miao, for her wisdom and patience. And Fred Leebron, editor of the Norton Anthology of North American Short Fiction, for reminding me that the number one enemy of Best is Good.

Sometimes an author simply has to get away, especially if he or she would prefer to be distracted by the clamor of daily concerns. And so, I would like to thank John and Barry French of Scottsdale, Arizona, for their hospitality and encouragement, as this book and the one before it proceeded from concept to detailed outline. And the Heydon Trust family in Bermuda for providing the ideal solitude for the final draft.

Finally, I want to acknowledge the inspiration of two late writing colleagues and friends: Jamie Buckingham and Carol Sobieski. They taught me to prize the gift of telling.

A MATTER
of DIAMONDS

prologue

THROUGH APPLE-LADEN BOUGHS that swayed gently in a breeze from Cape Cod Bay, the September sun played on the still figure of a white-haired monk. Seated on a bench almost in the shadow of Faith Abbey's new basilica, he had closed his eyes to enjoy the warmth of the afternoon sun.

Another monk—lean and straight, with close-cropped iron-gray hair—approached.

"Ambrose said you wanted to see me?"

The old monk looked up, his blue eyes smiling. "He did? Oh, yes, sit down, Bartholomew." He patted the bench beside him. "You remember when we built this?"

The younger monk nodded. "And planted this orchard—if you can call eight trees an orchard." He sat down and surveyed their handiwork. "Hard to believe it's been eighteen years."

"You questioned everything back then."

Bartholomew smiled. "And you always had an answer."

"They were good questions."

"And they were good answers," replied the younger monk with a smile. "Especially when they turned into stories." He laughed. "I still can't figure out how someone born and raised in Sandusky, Ohio, could be so—Irish."

"Celtic."

"Whatever."

"Well," said the old monk, blue eyes crinkled, "I could claim that my sainted mother was half-Irish, but—" he thought for a moment, "being Celtic is really a state of mind. One worth cultivating, I might add." He looked at Bartholomew. "You're halfway there, already."

"What do you mean?"

"Look how much you've come to rely on your intuition."

Bartholomew frowned. "If you're referring to my helping Chief Burke with that murder investigation last year—"

Columba waved his hand. "I'm talking about the Scriptorium. The way you are learning to see ahead in your illumination work."

"Oh, you mean decorating the opening capital of a chapter? There's nothing particularly—"

"Do not disparage it! You're years ahead of where I was at your age. And I was *good!*"

"You mean, figuring out ahead of time, where those ribbons of light and color are going to wind?"

The old monk gazed out at the bay. "Have you never wondered how they did it? I doubt a computer could devise such intricacy. Yet those simple Celtic monks were doing it twelve centuries ago!"

With a smile, Bartholomew threw up his hands. "I stand corrected. As always."

Columba softened. "I like you, Bartholomew. You make me smile—when it's sometimes the last thing I feel like doing."

From around his neck, he withdrew a small Celtic cross of beaten silver on a silver chain and handed it to Bartholomew. "I want you to have this. A monk in Dublin gave it to me many years ago. It's been a good friend, and now it will be a good friend to you."

The younger monk was shocked and almost didn't take it. "Don't you still need it?"

"Not for much longer. I want you to have it *before* I leave, not after."

"What are you talking about?"

"Don't be alarmed," said Columba, smiling. "Sometimes it is given to us Celts, to know when we will be called home."

"Oh, come on!" said Bartholomew, trying to jolly him out of this strange mood. "You've got years ahead of you!"

But the old monk would not be jollied. "I'm talking to you this way, because it may be our last opportunity. I've had a full life, and by God's grace have been able to accomplish a few things—not the least of which is you, my son."

Suddenly stricken at the thought of losing his mentor, Bartholomew's eyes filled, and he did not trust himself to speak. Seeing what he was thinking, Columba shook his head. "You must release me, if it's God's time for me to go to Him."

He handed Bartholomew a folded piece of paper. "Here's the music I'd like at my funeral. I tried to give it to our Senior Brother, but he accused me of being morbid. So you take it."

Putting the piece of paper in his pocket, Bartholomew asked, "If you really *are* going to die soon, how can you be so—accepting?"

"You remember when I was so ill five years ago? I *wanted* to die then. But it was not my time. I had one more thing to learn."

"What?"

"That the most difficult obedience is not to another's request, but to God's still, small voice within. Many who love Him, can hear Him in their hearts. Especially we Celts," he laughed. "But there's a world of difference between hearing Him and actually doing what you hear Him asking. Because often *that* requires relinquishing what we hold most dear—like our opinions, Bartholomew."

The younger monk nodded.

"To pray without ceasing—is really to listen inwardly without ceasing. And each time there's a choice to be made, to know that there really *is* no choice. That's surrender. And perfect obedience is how you lock it in."

Bartholomew laughed. "So that, O Master, is the secret of life?"

"For us, it is." Columba grew serious. "There's another reason I sent for you: to warn you that you're about to encounter evil."

"I encounter it every day, Brother," said Bartholomew smiling.

"Don't make light of this. I am talking about evil of a magnitude you've never experienced. An encounter that befalls only a few of the faithful, whom the Father, in His infinite wisdom, has chosen."

"I'm not sure I like the sound of this."

"You shouldn't. I'm telling you, so that when it occurs, you will not try to handle it in your own strength. Go to God. And go to Anselm."

"Have you ever encountered such evil?"

"Only once," the old monk shuddered.

1 | the blue angel

(*ANTWERP—SEPTEMBER 29*) AS SHE PRESENTED the identity card to the turnstile scanner, Dorothy Hanson noted the two guards in dark blue, leather-patched commando sweaters and trousers tucked into black jump boots, with Uzis slung over their shoulders. Behind a smoked-glass enclosure, their superior was no doubt observing her carefully. Should he discern anything amiss, with a button he could summon a phalanx of guards to seal all exits, while outside, at both ends of the narrow, L-shaped street of the diamond district, huge stainless-steel cylinders would rise up out of the pavement. They would form a barrier that not even an armored personnel carrier could penetrate.

Passing through the turnstile, she met the nearer guard's impassive gaze—and suppressed an inappropriate smile. It was all so James Bond! An apt analogy, she thought, hurrying to catch up with her long-legged companion. Ever since they'd landed in Belgium five days before, she'd had the eerie feeling she was in a film with subtitles—one of those gritty, on-the-run-in-a-raincoat flicks she used to go to in college.

Down a long, antiseptic corridor devoid of decoration, she and her companion strode. The tall, silver-haired man beside her seemed to be taking two strides to her three, but to ask him to slow down would be to admit she was having trouble keeping up with someone twenty years older. Abruptly he stopped at one of the steel doors—the one with the small brass plaque inscribed *Guertin Frères*—and rang the bell.

"Allô. Oui?"

"Alan Jones, Dickens Brothers Jewelers, and Dorothy Hanson, RKL Investments."

The door opened, admitting them to a small, windowless foyer with another door and a video camera. *"Ouvrez la mallette, s'il vous plaît."*

Alan opened his black attaché case, which contained a set of diamond grading stones, a digital scale, and a ham-and-cheese sandwich assembled from the breakfast buffet at their hotel, just in case.

"Entrez."

The inner door now opened, and they entered a modern office suite adjacent to what reminded her of a well-equipped physics lab. Black leather armchairs faced white Formica counters, on top of which were the precision instruments of the diamond trade—high-tech scales sensitive to a hundredth of a carat, high-intensity gooseneck lamps, and micro photo-monitors that could enlarge any diamond—and its flaws—many times.

Also present, in sharp contrast to the state-of-the-art electronics, were elegant, felt-lined tool cases holding the long-handled tweezers, loupes of varying power, and delicate balance scales that had been the tools of this trade for centuries.

A tall, blonde woman in an elegant gray Ultrasuede suit came forward to greet them. But before she could, Gilles Guertin—portly, jovial, and quite bald—interposed himself. "Ah, Monsieur Jones! We've been expecting you!"

"You have?"

"*Mais, certainement!* One cannot come to Antwerp in search of ten million dollars' worth of diamonds without creating, how shall I say, *un petit bouleversement,* no matter how discreet one tries to be."

He ushered them into his paneled office, where his blonde associate served them coffee and tea from an old silver service. And chocolates. "Try them," urged their host, proffering a mounded silver bowl of delicacies in shades that varied from light cream to almost black. "I think you'll find we Belgians have *un certain, je ne sais quoi, génie,* when it comes to creating nuggets of brown gold. After tasting ours, the only people who still prefer their own are the Swiss and the Dutch."

Dorothy started to reach for one, then withdrew her hand. "Recovering chocoholic," she explained with a sad smile.

"*Quel dommage,*" murmured Guertin. Then noting Alan's dour expression, he gestured to the door and the corridor beyond. "You must understand, we are—" he hesitated, searching for *le mot juste,* "*tous ensemble—comme famille.*"

Seeing her companion nod, Dorothy nodded also, though she suspected that he, too, had only the vaguest grasp.

"In a close family," Guertin explained, "everybody knows—everything. *Alors,*" he leaned back in his chair and tapped his fingers together, "how goes your quest?"

"Suppose you tell me," Alan replied. He was smiling, but his eyes were still cold.

"I believe that you have secured, *peut-être,*" he pursed his lips, "a little over seven million dollars' worth of what you are seeking."

"And what might that be?"

"Investment-grade stones, four carats or larger, F color and VVS_1 or better."

Alan ceased smiling.

"Ah, you are unhappy that despite all your precautions, I should know so much about your mission." Guertin leaned forward. "*Eh bien, monsieur*, which would you prefer? That I feign ignorance like my colleagues? That I let you spend the morning poring over my inventory? And maybe another day or two combing the district? Monsieur Jones, I'll be frank: I would rather have you dislike me but trust me."

The portly diamond dealer got up and went to the window, where he gazed down at the street. With his back to them, he continued, now careful to speak only English. "Everyone in the district knows what you are doing. But I suspect that if you're successful, whomever you're representing will be pleased. And he will tell his friends. And one day you will return on a similar mission."

Now he turned to face them. "When that day comes, I want to be your broker. I will have the stones ready. So that instead of your spending an exhausting week, we can transact your business in a single morning."

Alan stared at him. And then slowly relaxed and extended his hand. "Monsieur Guertin, I think this is going to be the beginning of a beautiful friendship."

Guertin warmly shook his hand and said into the intercom: "Helga, would you bring the parcel I have selected for Mr. Jones?" He paused. "Also, the Blue Angel."

In a moment his associate entered with a small cardboard box that looked like it might hold after-dinner mints. What it held were eleven neatly-folded white papers. Guertin took the first and opened it. It was a crisp sheet of stationery stock, 6" by 7", lined with transparent rice paper and folded four times. Carefully he unfolded it and with tweezers removed the single diamond it contained. This he placed on a black velvet viewing pad in front of Alan who, using his own tweezers and a gold loupe that hung from a chain around his neck, brought a gooseneck lamp closer and examined it.

At length, Alan nodded. "We can use this." With his own scale and grading stones, he determined that the diamond was a D in clarity, and without blemish. Then he weighed it: 4.25 carats. The weight and clarity exactly matched the tiny pencil notation on the edge of the folded paper. It was worth about $170,000.

Guertin excused himself, while Alan went through the remaining stones, giving each the same meticulous scrutiny. Once he thought he'd found a discrepancy between his findings and the notation on the edge of the paper, but on double-checking he determined it was his error.

He explained to Dorothy what he was looking for: "The highest color connotation, D, indicates the stone is devoid of color—perfectly clear. But such stones are extremely rare, and therefore extremely expensive. The same is true of a flawless diamond. Their expense makes them difficult to liquidate, and the whole purpose of buying diamonds as a hedge against inflation is liquidity. That's why I'm not really looking for D flawless stones. An E or F in color is fine; in fact, it would be impossible to tell the difference without a set of grading stones to compare them to."

With his tweezers he handed her the stone he had just inspected. "That's an ideal cut, which means it's been cut for maximum light refraction. There are 58 facets, and the table—the round, flat top facet—is just under 60 percent of the diamond's total width. In the other direction, the sum of the crown, girdle, and pavilion should be around 60 percent of the width. Because some buyers are interested only in maximum size for their money, there's a temptation to cut them shallower than that, to get the largest possible table out of the rough stone."

He had her turn the stone, so that it flashed and sparkled as it caught the light. "But for maximum *inner life* like that, I stick as close as possible to the 60/60 rule."

He passed her another stone. "This is a VVS_1 diamond. That means it has a very, very slight inclusion in the pavilion. A flaw—indiscernible to the naked eye, but," he had her look through his loupe, "visible under magnification. And therefore slightly less expensive—and easier to move."

The process took most of the morning, and Gilles Guertin returned just as he was finishing. Alan rubbed the back of his neck. "This is an excellent parcel; we'll take every one."

Guertin clapped his hands with delight. "You see how much time you can save by trusting me?"

Now Alan smiled. A real smile. "You were right. You've saved me the better part of a day, maybe two. And it would not surprise me, if you could also simplify the shipment home."

"*Bien sûr!* Bring me the goods you've reserved at the other houses. I will arrange for a secured shipment to wherever you instruct. In fact," he checked his watch, "if you can have them here by 2:00, you can watch them leave."

Alan nodded. "I will."

As with the stones at the other firms, these would actually be purchased by the Zurich-based holding company, RKL Investments AG, for whom Dorothy Hanson was the designated purchasing agent. They would be shipped to RKL's offices on State Street in Boston.

"One thing puzzles me," said Alan upon completing the shipping arrangements. "Since you seem to know exactly how much I am prepared to spend, how come this parcel is three-quarters of a million dollars short?"

His host beamed. "At *Guertin Frères*, we do something none of our *confrères* do. My father was in the Resistance. He rescued the son of his best cutter, educated him, and apprenticed him here. The boy—he's a man now—is a true *artiste*. When he finds a rough stone of unusually fine character—with a shape within that is crying to be released—he," Guertin shrugged and smiled, "well, he is Michelangelo, *en miniature*. He asks if he might bring forth the form—a horse's head, *peut-être*, or a rose. And if my brother or I have had an especially fine lunch and are running ahead of the year's projection, we indulge him."

He laughed and patted his girth. "As you can see, we have never refused him. And now our clientele includes collectors who wish to be notified whenever such a piece is available."

From his vest pocket, Guertin now brought a diamond paper, folded like the others, but bulkier. "I will show you something that a certain Saudi prince would be very upset to miss—if he knew of its existence." Unfolding the paper, he placed its contents on the black velvet: It was an angel—wings folded, head bowed, hands clasped in prayer.

Alan and Dorothy gasped. There was a barely discernible bluish cast to the stone, which was about five carats, and seemed to have a fire of its own.

Pleased at their response, Guertin said, "We call it the Blue Angel. By clarity and weight, it's worth approximately four hundred thousand in U.S. dollars. But as the color is so rare, and as we had to lose more than three carats to arrive at its exquisite form, making it like no other diamond in the world," he paused. "We felt it is worth an extra three hundred thousand—at least."

He fell silent to let them appreciate it, and with a gesture invited Alan to examine it more closely. The latter did so, then looked up and shook his head. "In all my years as a jeweler, I have never seen anything like this!" Then he sighed. "But unfortunately I have my instructions, and they do not include. . . ."

Guertin looked genuinely sad. "I guess my prince will not be disappointed, after all." He spoke into the intercom. "Helga, would you bring in the six other stones I've selected for Mr. Jones?"

"Wait," murmured Dorothy. Borrowing Alan's tweezers, she turned the tiny figure in the light of the gooseneck lamp, watching it throw off fire.

They were surprised; she'd not uttered a dozen words all morning. Now she spoke four: "We'll take this one."

2 | the second mrs. armstrong

IN THE MIDDLE OF ANTWERP lay a magnificent woodland park, with a sizable duck pond and a bewildering variety of ducks. Dorothy Hanson drifted along the walk that bordered the pond, pausing occasionally to admire her web-footed friends.

Mission accomplished, she thought, gathering her new black opera cape more tightly against the chill, late-September wind. Though the diamonds would follow on Monday, they were going home tomorrow—three days sooner than Alan Jones had anticipated.

Earlier that afternoon, from the window of *Guertin Frères* they had watched an armored car arrive at precisely 2:30. The moment it had passed through the east guard station, the blocking cylinders had risen behind it: nothing else would enter or exit the district until it was ready to come out. Four guards with Uzis entered the building, and in four minutes they were at the door to *Guertin Frères*. The shipment, in a small strongbox, was signed for and turned over. In four more minutes the security team emerged, and the vehicle departed.

The diamonds—32 in all, each in its folded paper—were contained in two slender cardboard boxes. In their strongbox, they would be held in a central vault in Brussels, and then flown with other high-value shipments by guarded courier to Boston, New York, and Washington. At noon on Monday, the plane would land at Boston's Logan Airport, where it would be met by an armored car that would transport the shipment to the State Street offices of RKL Investments AG. There, they would be held by the bank's president for pick-up by a designated executive of Armstrong & Associates—Dorothy Hanson.

I don't look forward to that part, she thought, as she wished she had a bit of bread to throw to a duck that looked like a mallard. She was to remain in Boston until the shipment arrived, then rent a car, collect the stones at the bank, and drive the shipment 89 miles to their offices in Eastport, on Cape Cod. There would be no escort of any sort. But she would not need one; no one but the bank president would know the nature of her business.

Mr. Armstrong was emphatic that no one was to know of the arrival of these diamonds; they were not to come through Dickens Brothers, or via armored car. There was to be no traceable record of the transaction, no way that the Internal Revenue Service might one day demand its share of the stones' value, in estate taxes. From his numbered account in a Zurich bank, Mr. Armstrong had made a private transfer of bonds to RKL, in exchange for which RKL would transfer diamonds of a similar value to Dorothy Hanson.

When Mr. Armstrong died, his three daughters would receive—or rather, retrieve, for she imagined he'd bury them on his property in New Hampshire—$10 million in diamonds, not $4.5 million.

Including the Blue Angel. Dorothy smiled: they'd have a problem deciding who got *that*. When she'd described it to Mr. Armstrong on the phone, he'd been a little surprised. But he told her he trusted her implicitly and was looking forward to seeing the piece.

She was looking forward to showing it to him.

Meanwhile, she was going to enjoy her last night in Antwerp. Alan was taking her to dinner at the Ritz, where they would probably spend more than it would have cost to stay the extra two nights. But as he said, they had cause to celebrate. He was good company, she thought, as she watched a pair of eider ducks propelling themselves smoothly across the pond like little white boats. But he was married and a member of Faith Abbey to boot. Besides, there was room for only one man in her life—well, two, if you counted Hannibal, her Maine Coon cat.

The thought of him made her smile, and she turned and strode toward the hotel. That was the only bad thing about going on a trip like this: leaving Hannibal. She'd named him that, because he'd come to her over the hills of Truro, the little Cape Cod town where she lived. Last summer, the day after she'd had to put her 82-year-old mother in an assisted living facility, Hannibal had strolled into the back yard of the little cottage. She'd grown fonder of him than she had ever thought possible.

At the moment, however, he would not be pleased with her. Mrs. Thompson across the street had promised to feed him, and he would be all right, Dorothy told herself. But he'd be so angry at her staying away this long, that he would refuse to use his litter box. Which would make her as mad as he was.

But once she'd cleaned the place up, they'd forgive each other, and when she went to bed, he would nestle into the crook of her knees for the night.

She made a mental note to take Hannibal to Faith Abbey this coming Wednesday afternoon. It was the Feast of St. Francis, and the abbey had a Blessing of the Animals, to which all were invited. Maybe a prayer and a little holy water would keep her boy from being so vindictive.

It was growing dark; the lights of Antwerp, like jewels in an evening necklace, were starting to come on. She glanced at her watch: 5:40. It would take her 18 minutes to reach the hotel, and she *would* walk, because she needed the exercise. Besides, she *liked* Antwerp–the clean sidewalks, the quaint buildings, the glamorous shop windows. That would leave her an hour–just enough time to get ready. She picked up her pace, the two shopping bags balancing each other nicely.

◆

At five minutes to 7:00, she checked her appearance in the full-length mirror. And approved. The new gray Ultrasuede suit–thank you, Helga–fit perfectly. It had better! It cost about four times what she had ever spent on herself. But the color was right to show off her blue eyes. And the champagne blouse and burgundy scarf all went together exquisitely. The girl in the boutique may have had stringy hair and ridiculous heels, but she did have an eye for *le tout ensemble.*

Smoothing it over her hips, she promised herself she would wear it only tonight, and not again until the afternoon that she presented the diamonds to Mr. Armstrong.

Thinking of him made her forget the time. She gazed at her reflection, trying to see herself as he might–now. Five-eight, reasonably trim for her age. He'd told her once that he admired her for keeping her figure through the years–and she'd gone home and thrown out the Godiva chocolates and the Ben & Jerry's Heath Bar Crunch.

She had begun working for him back in the dim and misty past, when she had been his assistant at what they wryly referred to as the Ancient & Honorable Trust company. He'd been only 26 and she 21, just out of Katie Gibbs. He looked like Cary Grant, only taller, and possessing every bit of that movie star's savoir-faire. She had been smitten with him from the start.

Dorothy's forte was anticipation. When he would recall belatedly that he should have asked her to book him a flight, she would smile and hand him the ticket. Then he would shake his head in wonder and tell her that she was a marvel, and beaming, she would agree. And remind him that he would need two suits, a blazer–and tennis clothes.

There was only one problem: There was a Mrs. Armstrong. With whom he was deeply in love. When he went into business for himself, as a venture capitalist, the sudden strain had tested his marriage almost to the breaking point. But not quite. It had been tested again in 1981, when he had moved Armstrong & Associates to Cape Cod. (There were only two associates, she and Ed Forester, but who was counting?) Again the marriage had survived.

It was then that she decided that she would rather spend eight hours a day with the man of her dreams (or ten or twelve, if a deal was pending), than find a husband of her own who didn't measure up. (Who could measure up to Cary Grant?)

So she had winterized the family cottage up in Truro, half an hour further out on the Cape than Eastport. It was not much of a commute by Manhattan standards, and she could not imagine anyone looking forward to getting to work as much as she did. For twelve years she had lived happily and had begun to believe it might be for ever after. Then her father had died, and her mother had decided to leave New Jersey and move in with her. It wasn't too bad at first, until she had to take away her mother's car keys.

Five years ago, the unthinkable happened. Mrs. Armstrong had died, drowned while swimming off their beach. Since she had been battling clinical depression and mostly losing the battle, Dorothy suspected she'd deliberately swum out so far that she could not get back.

Mr. Armstrong had been devastated and had never really recovered. While he still seemed to enjoy the venture capital game, he no longer played with his previous zest. It was as if Mrs. Armstrong's depression was a dark vortex that was pulling her husband into it, too.

Recently, though, it seemed as if the dark clouds might finally be lifting. A Yale classmate of Mr. Armstrong's, a man named Trevor Haines, had come to visit for the weekend–and simply stayed. She didn't care for Haines; he put on airs, seeming to fancy himself as the reincarnation of Jay Gatsby. But she had to admit he'd revived Mr. Armstrong's spirits, and she was pleased to see him taking an interest in life.

She turned sideways again and smiled; her new suit definitely flattered her hips. Maybe now, at last, he would also take an interest in her. She refused to allow herself to imagine that one day there might be a second Mrs. Armstrong–who would share his bed, as well as his office.

Goodness, it was ten past seven! Putting the opera cape over her sholders, she swirled out the door.

3 | a drive in the country

DOROTHY SETTLED BACK in the sumptuous leather of the rented Chrysler to enjoy the drive down to the Cape. As arranged, the diamonds had arrived at RKL at 12:30 that afternoon, and she had picked them up at 2:00. Before signing for them, she had examined each one, though obviously no one could have tampered with them. Then she had shifted them from the strongbox to the less conspicuous attaché case that was now on the seat beside her.

It was a beautiful Indian summer afternoon, perfect for a drive in the country. She tuned the radio to the classical music station and opened the sunroof, as the Plymouth exit flashed by. She smiled; in a little less than an hour she would be showing the diamonds to Mr. Armstrong. And WCRB was playing a Chopin waltz—ideal accompaniment for imagining her arrival.

She would go into his office and open the case on his desk. He would start to look through the diamonds, but only cursorily;

he had that much confidence in her. Then he would ask to see the Blue Angel, and he would be so pleased with it and with the whole operation, that he would do something he'd never done before: He would take a bottle of the champagne he kept in the little refrigerator under his desk to celebrate the closing of special deals. And would invite her out on the deck, just the two of them, to sip and look at the sea, while she told him in detail all about her Antwerp adventure. And after a second glass, he might even notice her new outfit. And her.

As the waltz ended, a cloud passed over the sun, and it grew suddenly colder. Reminding herself that it was October 2, not September 2, she reached up to push the button that closed the sunroof. As she did, she noticed that the black Mercedes that had been behind her when she'd gotten on Route 3 south was still there.

Just coincidence, she assured herself. No one—absolutely no one—knew of her mission. Even so, she changed into the far left lane and accelerated to 69, as fast as she dared go on this heavily patrolled stretch of 60 mph, southbound Route 3. When the Mercedes did not follow suit, she relaxed. A little. But she would not take a really deep breath until the diamonds were in Mr. Armstrong's possession.

She was relieved to find no back-up at the rotary leading to the Sagamore Bridge. Another 40 minutes, and she would be in Eastport. And then she stiffened: The black Mercedes was two cars behind her. Well, there was an easy way to check it out. She entered the rotary, but instead of leaving it to go onto the bridge, she continued on around, until she saw the black Mercedes with the two people in it turn onto the bridge.

She laughed out loud. They were just going to the Cape! Like she was, she thought, as she came around again and turned onto the bridge. Mr. Armstrong would laugh, too, when she told him this part. She felt like calling him now, just to tell him she was over the bridge. But he had been adamant about her not making *any* calls, especially not on her cell phone. So she had not even taken it out of her suitcase.

It was good to be back on the Cape! She had grown to love these scrub pines that lined the Mid-Cape, though when she first moved here in '81, she had resented the Royal Navy for denuding Cape Cod of its tall virgin pine and hearty oak. And the Sandwich glass factory for burning most of the rest of the natural timber, to produce their product, no matter how beautiful it was.

And it was still a beautiful day for a drive. She switched the radio to WFCC, which carried WCRB's music on the Cape. They were playing a Mozart horn concerto now, and she was tempted to re-open the sunroof. But more clouds had followed the first, and it had definitely turned colder.

She was approaching Exit 7, when she saw the Mercedes again. *Behind* her. So they stopped for gas at Exit 6, she told herself, so what? Or maybe they just wanted to change drivers or use a restroom. But she had to admit she was shaken. Enough to depart from the plan. "Innovate and improvise" was A&A's motto when a deal started to go south. And that's what she would do now.

At the last second she whipped the big, surprisingly agile car into the Willow Street exit. The Mercedes did not follow her, but continued on up the Mid-Cape. There, you see? she reprimanded herself; it was just your overactive imagination! But her hands were trembling on the wheel, and she decided to continue with her modification of the plan. Mr. Armstrong, when he learned of the Mercedes, would approve.

On Main Street she stopped at the branch of First Colonial, where the company had a safe deposit box. Now, just let the manager, Sumner Watson, be there! Because this would have to be done fast. Thank God, she kept the box key on her key chain!

Watson was there, but on the phone. She could see him in his office through the glass. And he could see her. Giving her a smile of recognition, he indicated that he would be with her in a minute.

But she did not have a minute. Catching his eye, she did something totally out of character: She jabbed her finger at him, then jerked her thumb towards herself. Her gesture was rude and peremptory, and he was mildly offended, nodding that he would be with her as soon as—

She repeated the gesture with more emphasis, and an expression that said: If you don't get off that phone *now* and get yourself out here, not only will you never do business with us again, but Mr. Armstrong, who is a personal friend of First Colonial's CEO, will explain to him exactly why.

Watson got off the phone and hurried out. She apologized and told him what she needed. They went immediately into the vault, where each entered their keys to open the A&A box. Before Watson discreetly left her alone in the vault, she warned him not to get back on the phone, as she would be leaving in less than a minute.

Transferring the cardboard boxes from the attaché case to the safe deposit box, she was about to slide it in and summon Watson, when on impulse she removed the Blue Angel, still in its square of folded paper at the back of the second box. Putting it in the inside pocket of her suit, she called the bank manager, and they closed the box. With her now-empty attaché case, she exited the vault and the bank. The entire operation had taken less than four minutes.

Pausing on the bank's front step, Dorothy looked up and down the street. The Mercedes was nowhere to be seen. She smiled and shook her head, as she got in the Chrysler. This was undoubtedly an unnecessary precaution. But she felt immensely lighter, not having the diamonds with her. She could easily come back in the morning and retrieve them, if Mr. Armstrong didn't want to do it himself.

Back on the Mid-Cape, she was just passing Exit 9, when

the Mercedes reappeared. It was behind her again but coming up fast on the outside. In another hundred yards the two lanes eastbound narrowed into one. With no passing; whatever order cars were in when they entered, they would stay in that order until they got off, or reached the Orleans rotary 12 miles away.

The Mercedes was obviously trying to get ahead of her. But it wasn't going to! She jammed down the accelerator, and the big American luxury car beat the big German luxury car into the two-lane section by about one car-length.

Dorothy kept the accelerator on the floor, as the Chrysler's speedometer needle swept through 70–80–90. She shook her head; the one time you'd be delighted to get a $300 speeding ticket, there're no cops to be seen! Nor was there any traffic visible ahead of her. Where *was* everybody? How often had she been trapped in an endless procession of pokey drivers? How much would she give for just one self-righteous twit to be motoring along at five miles below the 50 mph limit?

When the car reached 110, it was still going smoothly, and she took her eyes off the road, just long enough to glance in the rearview mirror. Her heart sank; the Mercedes was right behind her. Up ahead, she knew from traveling this road countless times, was a rest area, then Exit 10. She would take that exit and find a phone or another car, any kind of help. Forget the no-call procedure; her life was in danger!

Just before the rest stop, she felt a terrific jolt from behind. The Mercedes had hit her! At nearly 120! Were they *crazy?*

There was another jolt, stronger than before, and she fought desperately to keep the car on the road. Screaming, she started applying the brakes. But the car behind her wouldn't let her slow. It was pushing her now, and she could hardly keep it going straight.

Sobbing hysterically, she swerved right, into the rest area— anything to break contact with the car behind! And she did; she could feel her car come free. But the end of the rest area was rushing towards her, and she stamped on the brakes, throwing the car into a skid.

The Mercedes came up alongside her, and almost gently turned into her, guiding her off the paved area and headlong into the woods. Still braking, still sobbing, she managed to miss the first two trees, but sideswiped the third, which headed her straight into the fourth.

Her airbag exploded; it and the seatbelt saved her life. As she struggled to get out, the two people in the Mercedes came running towards her, to help her. Except that, as they got nearer, she could see they had ski masks down over their faces.

Before they got close enough to see what she was doing, she took the safe deposit key off her key chain. Then, taking out the Blue Angel and discarding its wrapper, she swallowed the stone and the key.

They were only fifty feet from her now. Getting out of the car, she kicked off her heels and started running through the woods. But they soon caught her, and while the bigger of the two held her, the other one pressed a wet, sweet-smelling cloth over her nose and mouth. And suddenly everything was fading and echoing, far away.

4 | the message

WHEN DOROTHY REGAINED CONSCIOUSNESS, it was dark. She was on a small powerboat, which was under way and rocking gently. She was down in its little cabin, lying on one of the two bunks. Her hands were tied behind her, and so, she discovered, were her feet. Through the open hatchway, she could hear two people, presumably her abductors, talking in low voices.

She wanted to cry out—or just cry—but bit her lower lip hard. Better to let them believe she was still unconscious. Use the time to think.

Keeping her eyes closed, she reviewed her situation. Obviously they were after the diamonds. Which were not in the attaché case. Or her suitcase. Or the car. Did they know that the diamonds were in a safety deposit box? Not unless they had an accomplice in a second car, who did follow her. Somehow, she didn't think that was the case. She sensed it was just the two of them.

"Wakey, wakey," said a man's voice, as he shook her shoulder.

She moaned, as if just coming around. "What—happened?" She turned over and saw that he was still wearing a ski mask.

"You had a terrible accident," he said, shaking his head. "It was lucky we were right behind you."

"Lucky? You were the ones who ran me off the road!"

"Oh," he said with a disappointed tone, "I was hoping you wouldn't take that attitude. While I know this is not very pleasant for you, I'm afraid that if you continue in that vein, it's going to get more unpleasant than you can possibly imagine."

Dorothy said nothing. Then she muttered, "I need to use the bathroom. Is there a head on this boat?"

"Of course. Right there." He pointed to a small door where the two bunks came together.

"Well, I can't get there, trussed up like a turkey."

"Oh, how thoughtless of me," said the man graciously, and with a penknife, he cut the ropes binding her. And carefully blocked the way to the hatch.

Locking the door to the tiny compartment, Dorothy could feel the boat's engine slow to an idle. Desperately she tried to use the time to think of a plan. She couldn't. She would have to just play along with them, until she could improvise one.

"Are you done in there?"

"Almost."

"Well, done or not," declared a woman's voice, hard and implacable, "get yourself out here—*now!*"

Dorothy waited a moment, then opened the door and emerged. The woman also had a ski mask on, and was wearing black, Euro, pipe-stem pants and a black turtleneck. "Where are the diamonds?" she demanded. "We searched the car."

So they didn't know she'd gone to the bank! They actually *were* out of contact, till she'd gotten back on the Mid-Cape! Slowly, she smiled; for the first time since this ordeal had begun, she felt like she might have the upper hand.

Watching her closely, the woman seemed to know what she was thinking. Suddenly she slapped Dorothy hard.

The latter gasped in shock, the back of her hand flying to her burning cheek. She fought down the panic rising in her.

"We know you didn't tell anyone about them," the woman said. "So you must have stashed them somewhere."

"All you have to do," the man pleaded, "is tell us where."

"And you'll let me go?"

"Of course," said the man. "We're not barbarians! We have no interest in further discomfiting you."

Frowning, Dorothy tilted her head, as if trying to hear something in her memory. She'd heard that voice before. . . .

Observing her expression, the woman turned to her accomplice. "Shut up, you fool! You're talking too much." She turned back to Dorothy. "Where are they?"

Dorothy remained silent.

"Tell me, and I will go get them. When I come back, we'll let you go." She nodded toward her partner. "He won't hurt you. But I *will*, if you don't hurry up."

Why not just tell them, part of her pleaded; it's not as if they can walk into the bank and get them. No, the other part said, but they can force you at concealed gunpoint to go in with them, or the woman can impersonate you. Either way, once they have them, they'll kill you.

Dorothy pressed her lips into a thin line, and seeing this, the woman slapped her again, much harder, back and forth— once, twice, three times.

Dorothy cried out, tears springing to her eyes. In her life, no one had ever struck her that hard! She made a fist and started up, but the man grabbed her and forced her back onto the bunk. "Don't," he pleaded, "you're just making this harder on yourself."

Dorothy said nothing.

The woman said, "We're wasting time. She's determined to

be brave. So you know what we're going to have to do."

The man shook his head. "But you promised! You promised we wouldn't have to! We were only going to scare her!"

"Does she look scared to you?" the woman retorted. "Look at her: she's not going to tell—"

"Let me try," said the man, centering his signet ring. She'd seen that ring before, Dorothy thought, and recently.

With no warning he hit her on the left temple, so hard that her vision went hazy red.

Dorothy screamed and started sobbing.

"Go ahead and scream!" cried the woman. "Make all the noise you want! That's why we're out here, in the middle of the bay."

"Please," the man begged Dorothy, "tell her what she wants to know!" There was a catch in his voice, as if he, too, were about to cry. "*Please!*"

"This is stupid!" exclaimed the woman. "Get the scissors."

"*No!*" wailed the man, who really *was* crying now.

"Do it, you pathetic, whimpering piece of—"

He disappeared up the hatch steps, returning in a moment with a pair of poultry scissors. The woman took them from him. "Hold onto her!" The man did as he was told, pinning Dorothy to the bunk.

And now Dorothy felt icy fingers of fear reach up into her bowels, entwine them, and draw into a fist. Never had she been so scared.

She screamed and screamed, but the woman just smiled. "Go ahead; let it out. There's no one to hear but a few seagulls." She turned to the man. "Hold out her right hand."

Dorothy fought him, but he was just bigger.

The woman bent close to her, her masked face barely an inch from Dorothy's. "You're probably as efficient at typing, as you are at everything else," said the woman softly. "I wonder how many words a minute you'll be able to type without this little piggy," and she grabbed Dorothy's little finger and pulled it out straight.

"*Don't!*" shrieked Dorothy. But that was all she said.

Taking the scissors, the woman cut off the end of the finger, just below the last knuckle.

Blood spurted from the stump, and the pain was so intense that Dorothy threw up. At the smell of her vomit, the man said, "I think I'm going to be sick, too."

"*You are not!*" commanded the woman. "Pull yourself together! We're not done here!"

She grabbed Dorothy's other hand and started to pry it open. "This little piggy wants to stay home, I see. Well, not tonight."

Dorothy sobbed, and the man, himself hysterical, cried, "We're only taking the tips, you know! We're not barbarians! Just tell her what she wants to know, old sport, and it's all over."

"*Will you shut up!*" the woman shouted at him.

But it was too late; Dorothy knew who he was.

And the woman, seeing her expression, knew that she knew.

"Last chance," she said to Dorothy, and when there was no response, she cut off the end of her other little finger.

Dorothy's whole system went into shock, and mercifully she passed out.

When she came to, she could hear them outside.

"She's recognized you," the woman said.

"No, she hasn't!" replied the man frantically.

"Yes, she has. And you know what that means. You just couldn't keep that big mouth of yours shut, could you."

"This is a nightmare!" the man wailed. "I wish I'd never told you about—"

"Stop blubbering. I'll do it. We brought the chains and cinderblocks in case this happened. But first we're going to find out where those diamonds are, if I have to cut off every finger and toe on her body!"

Hearing them, Dorothy felt strangely calm. And resolute. They were not going to let her off this boat alive. But neither would they get the diamonds. Ever.

The wind had picked up, and the idling boat began to rock. Clearly a storm was brewing, and they began deliberating whether to put the boat in gear and start cruising, or wait until they'd finished with her.

Taking advantage of their preoccupation, Dorothy eased herself off the bunk and over to the hatchway. There were three steps up to the deck. She'd have to take them so quickly they would not have time to react.

Do it, she ordered herself. Do it now!

But she didn't move.

"Put the engine in gear," said the woman outside, making up her mind. "But set the throttle low, just enough to keep it moving. I've got the scissors; let's get the job done."

But before they could enter the hatch, Dorothy burst out of it and grabbing the woman, took her over the side.

The water was shockingly cold, much colder than Dorothy expected, but it cleared her mind. She dived down into the blackness, knowing that underwater was the last place the other woman would go. When she surfaced, the boat was thirty feet away, and the man was in its stern calling to the woman: "Lena," he cried, no longer concerned with maintaining anonymity, "where are you?"

"Over here, you idiot!"

It was pitch black. The overcast had blotted out the moon and stars. But the man had found a powerful flashlight; sweeping the water with it, he soon located his partner.

By the time he had gotten her back on board, Dorothy, being careful to swim breaststroke as silently as possible, had put considerable distance between herself and the boat.

Taking a deep breath, she dived again, swimming even further away.

This time, when she came up, the boat was noticeably smaller. And each time they swung the light beam in her direction, she simply ducked.

They'll never find her now. Pretty good improvising—Mr. Armstrong would have appreciated it. Too bad he'll never know.

She had no illusion about surviving now. Even if she knew which way shore was, the water was too cold for her to make it. At least those two would never find her.

She smiled a bit sadly. The second Mrs. Armstrong, it seemed, was about to meet the same fate as the first. But she would be found eventually, and when she was, he would get her message.

And would know at last the depth of her love for him.

5 | not your routine drowning

As he followed his two Springer spaniels, Diana and Felicity, over the wooden walkway to the beach, Banastre Caulfield paused to admire the view. He always did when the flats were out. Stretching north to Eastham and west to Brewster, at low tide the sand flats at the inner elbow of Cape Cod extended out for more than a mile. And at dead low, like now, the channel of the marsh creek running out of Eastport's little harbor was no more than knee-deep.

This morning, just before dawn, the sands were grayish pink, taking on the hues of the high cloud cover beginning to lighten above the trees to the east. When he first came here eleven years before, his favorite times had been when the sky was clear and the colors vivid. But his tastes had changed. Now, he almost preferred the overcast days, with their muted tones and subtle gradations.

Even after all these years he could not get used to the fact that he actually *lived* here. It still felt like he was on some kind of weird sabbatical, and that any day now someone would be demanding to know what was going on.

Which was what he would like to ask his dogs right now. They had veered off to the right, towards the harbor, when they knew that they always went left; it was part of their routine. Diana was 15 now, quite old for a Springer, and he feared she would not last another year. But she was still spry in the mornings, as she bounded after her kennel-mate, Felicity. Seven years ago, when their first Springer, Sandy, had died, Diana had gone into such a decline that they had gotten a puppy to bring her back to life. The plan had worked. But now the two were so close that in a year or two they would probably have to get a puppy to revive Felicity. . . .

What *were* they doing over there? He called to them and whistled. They did not respond, which surprised him, because they were well trained. He went over to see what was so interesting that they were willing to risk incurring his wrath.

As he got closer, he could see that there was a dark form at the edge of the dune grass. Oh, great! A large, dead fish, which any moment they were going to roll in. Which would mean spending the next hour giving each of them a bath, so they could come in the house again.

But he soon realized it was not a fish. He squinted at it, then ran over. A body had washed ashore. The body of a middle-aged woman. Who was staring up at the pink-gray sky with sightless blue eyes.

Getting his dogs under control, Ban Caulfield ran with them to the house, where he called 911. Nine minutes later a white squad car arrived in his driveway, and out stepped Sergeant Otis Whipple of the Eastport Police Department. Ban, taking care to shut the dogs in the house, showed him down to the beach.

Squatting down beside the drowned woman, Sergeant Whipple carefully surveyed her, frowning as his gaze came to her left hand. The frown deepened, as he saw that the other hand was similarly mutilated. And on her left temple was a reddish oval mark.

Standing up, he made a call on his cell phone. "Chief? Sorry to call you at home." He paused. "Well, I'm sorry about that, too. And tell Peg I'm sorry I woke her. But listen: I'm over here at the harbor, and we've a got a drowning. A woman in her early 50s I would guess, about 5'8" or 9", about 150–60 pounds."

He turned to look out at the flats, slowly shaking his head, as he listened. Then, still calm, the sergeant replied: "If that's all it was, I wouldn't have bothered you. But, Chief, this is not your routine drowning. She's been hit in the face and is missing the tips of her two little fingers." Pause. "That's what I said; it looks like they've been removed surgically." Pause. "It's recent, all right; the stumps are still oozing. Chief, I think the woman was tortured."

Fifteen minutes later Chief Dan Burke's old white Bravada joined the squad car in the Caulfield driveway. The Chief, feeling older than his 48 years, yawned and greeted his subordinate perfunctorily. Ban came out with a cup of coffee and gave it to him, before they all returned to the beach.

A couple of early morning beach strollers were standing at the scene, and the Chief bent over and examined the body. He straightened and turned to the sergeant. "Let me borrow your cell phone, Otis; I forgot to charge mine."

The sergeant gave it to him, and the Chief made a call. "Doc? It's Dan Burke. Sorry to bother you this early, but I need you to come over here in your official capacity as medical examiner." Pause. "The beach, just west of the harbor. We've got a dead woman here." Pause. "No, Doc, there's nothing routine about it! And you'll need to get hold of that pathologist down at the hospital and give her a heads-up; we're going to need an autopsy as fast as we can get one."

He ended the call and yawned again, shaking his head as if

to clear it. Then he gave the phone back to his sergeant. "Sorry, Otis."

"For what?"

"For how I acted on the phone. Soon as Doc gets here, notify the county coroner, and get an ambulance over here, to take her down to Hyannis, and get another officer over here to secure the area." He scowled at the onlookers, who now numbered four.

Taking a last look at the body, he peered at her face. "I've seen this woman before," he mused. "She's not from around here, but. . . ." His voice trailed off, as he turned and headed for his vehicle.

6 | lapides vivi

BROTHER BARTHOLOMEW LOOKED UP at the afternoon sky. It was a soft pale blue, with a few brush-strokes of high cirrus at the top of the canvas. Best of all, it was still warm enough to be outside without a jacket—Indian Summer's farewell benediction.

He surveyed the little common which he had finished mowing an hour before. Everything was ready—the plain wooden cross on the outdoor altar, the big Bible, the stack of one-sheet programs with the words to "All Things Bright and Beautiful" on the back. He checked his watch: 4:52. The service would begin in less than eight minutes, but there was no one here.

He smiled. The abbey family, all 350 of them, counting the children, was punctual to a fault. They were never late—but never early. In the eighteen years that he had been a monk in the abbey's friary, it had ever been thus. Five minutes before Sunday Mass, the church would be practically empty. Five minutes later, it would be full. And no one would straggle in late. Well, almost no one; there was always the "cow's tail"—one family which was perpetually late and would probably be late for their own funerals.

Today, October 4th, was the Feast of St. Francis, the day on which Faith Abbey traditionally held an outdoor "Blessing of the Animals" service. It was scheduled for 5:00—late enough so that those who worked in town could attend; early enough to segue smoothly into Vespers in the church at 5:30.

He gazed up at the peak of the west end of their new basilica. Glowing in the late afternoon sun, it looked like the prow of a great sand-colored ship, sailing majestically through a silver-blue sea. He still found it hard to believe that they actually had one of these in their own back yard. Not in Rome or Ravenna; *right here*—a basilica, the crowning architectural achievement of the Church before it split into East and West.

For twelve long years they had worked and prayed for it, struggling to meet all the requirements and satisfy all the objections. They had long outgrown their chapel, and God intended to give them this new home. But not, apparently, without tribulations—each of which He had used to shape them into a spiritual church. What was it Father Horton had called them? *Lapides vivi*—living stones.

Once they'd received the final approval and started building, the church had gone up so fast, that it seemed as if in a single day, like an Amish barn raising. Indeed, of all groups, the Amish would best understand how this church had become the heartbeat of their life together.

At 4:55, the first people began arriving on the common— children with their various pets carefully leashed or boxed. From all corners more and more came, and Bartholomew chuckled. In addition to dogs and cats, rabbits and hamsters, there were birds in cages, and even fish in gingerly carried fishbowls. And here came Brother Ambrose, leading Countess, the milk cow, followed by other brothers escorting goats, with Brother Columba bringing the Scriptorium cat, Pangur Ban.

And now from the convent that faced the common and housed 70 sisters, emerged Sister Melina, the Senior Sister, cradling Celeste, queen of the convent's four cats.

There were townspeople, too, bringing their pets, as the Blessing of the Animals was becoming something more and more people wanted to take part in. The abbey welcomed them all, just as the doors of the basilica were open to all. He looked up at the basilica and smiled; it really was like a mother looking down beneficently on the pageant unfolding in her front yard.

By 4:58, eleven clergy vested in the abbey's cream-colored robes appeared, each bearing a vial of holy water. After the hymn and prayers and the briefest of homilies, they would circulate among the two- and four-footed congregants, praying for each, and if desired, anointing them with holy water.

At exactly 5:00, the service began. They had just gotten to the first chorus of "All Creatures, Great and Small," when the pager on Bartholomew's belt vibrated. He glanced down, at a number he had not seen in at least a year: the personal line of Eastport's Chief of Police.

He frowned. Dan knew they were having this service. He would not be calling, unless it was really important. Slipping away, he went into the retreat house and used their phone.

"Look, Andrew—Brother Bartholomew—I'm really sorry to get you out of all that." Through the phone the Chief could hear the singing outside. "But we've just had another 'hundred-year weather event'—the second in two years."

Among Cape Codders, it was a bitter joke that after a truly horrendous storm, meteorologists up in Boston had a habit of assuring them that this indeed had been of such a magnitude that they would not see its like again in a hundred years. Unfortunately, the forces of nature paid scant heed to such pronouncements. So far, Bartholomew had been through four such events, and he'd been born a generation after the one the old-timers still talked about: the Hurricane of '37.

But his boyhood friend—who'd remained his friend, though their lives had radically diverged since they played varsity soccer together for Nauset Regional High—was not talking about the weather.

"What's up, Dan?"

"Another murder, if you can believe it. Or something that looks awfully close to it." He briefed Bartholomew on the dead wash-ashore who had apparently been tortured. "And frankly," he concluded, "I'd appreciate your help."

The Chief was a proud and competent professional, and Brother Bartholomew knew what this request must be costing him. And they had worked well together last year, sorting out Eastport's first murder in nearly half a century. Even so—he glanced wistfully out the window at the happy chaos on the common. "You really need me to come *now?*"

"Look, I'm sorry. But I've just gotten a call from the pathologist. You know what they found in her stomach? A key. And a blue diamond."

In spite of himself, Bartholomew was intrigued—and resented it. The turbulent events of last year were far removed from the contemplative life he craved, and he had no desire to plunge back into that maelstrom.

"Bart," declared the Chief, tired of waiting, "I'm going down there. Now. I want you to come with me."

His monk friend sighed and acquiesced. "I'll have to check it out." He would talk to Anselm, but he was pretty sure he knew what the Senior Brother's response would be.

"Good," said the Chief, immensely relieved, "you do that. I'll pick you up in ten minutes."

7 | a passing attack

THEY DROVE IN SILENCE down the Mid-Cape. Ahead of them the setting sun was sending out a spectacular array of shafts through the clouds. But Bartholomew merely glowered at it. When he'd spoken to the Senior Brother, he'd hoped he'd be told to remain home. Instead, Anselm had responded: "Is it not a cry for help? From a friend? Of course you must go."

"I'm *not* going to get involved."

Anselm had just smiled. "We'll talk about that when you get back."

The Chief glanced over at him. "Look, if I didn't need you, I wouldn't have asked."

"I'm a *monk*, Dan. Monks don't get involved in murder investigations. They're supposed to spend their days in prayer; even when they're working, they're to do it in an attitude of prayer. While you're out serving and protecting, you know what I do? I prune roses. I spread manure. I mow lawns. I—"

The Chief glared straight ahead. "You think there aren't times I'd gladly trade places with you? When a drunk throws up in the back seat? When I've got to explain to an old widow why she can't drive anymore? When I've got to go before the selectmen and beg for cost-of-living raises for my people, who've been working without a contract for three years?" He shook his head. "What I wouldn't give to just shut out everything and go garden!"

All at once, his monk friend smiled. "It's not really like that," Bartholomew said with a chuckle. "I mean, it's supposed to be, peaceful and all. But it seldom is, when you've got 30 willful, independent, opinionated characters, average age 42, living in close quarters." He laughed. "We have to smile, when visitors are struck by the extraordinary peace they feel as soon as they set foot on the premises. In describing our life, peaceful is hardly the first word that comes to mind."

They lapsed back into silence, now both appreciating the glories of the reddening, sun-shot sky ahead of them.

Abruptly the Chief slowed the Bravada and pulled over onto the shoulder, a look of pain spreading across his face.

"Dan!" cried his friend. "What is it?"

The Chief, wincing, waved him off. "It'll pass," he gasped. Then gradually he relaxed. "That's the worst so far," he murmured.

"You mean—this has happened before?" Reluctantly the Chief nodded. "Have you seen a doctor?" He shook his head. "You've *got* to get checked out by Doc Finlay tomorrow!" his friend insisted.

The Chief scowled, but seeing that Bartholomew was likely to take matters into his own hands, he grudgingly agreed. "Just don't tell Peg, okay?"

Thirty years before, when they were both high school seniors, they'd both liked Peg Foster. Dan had wound up with her, and they'd just celebrated their 25th anniversary.

"Okay, but you let me know by the end of tomorrow what he says."

The Chief nodded and accelerated back into the westbound lane.

Arriving at the hospital, they went straight to the morgue, where they were met by the chief pathologist, Dr. Morton. She took them to the body, still open on the stainless steel table. Bartholomew had to look away. As a Corpsman in Viet Nam he had seen far worse, but it still bothered him.

"The cause of death was asphyxiation by drowning," Dr. Morton reported matter-of-factly. "Probably about two days ago. Those are the clothes she was wearing," she indicated three hangers on a metal rack by the table, "and these," she extracted two Zip-loc sandwich bags from a pocket of her smock, "are the items we told you about."

She passed the bags to the Chief. "You'll have to sign for those before you go," she added, turning to go to her desk. "We checked the stone for hardness, and it appears to be a diamond—in which case, it's worth a small fortune."

She left them, and then came back. "I forgot: it looks like you were right about the torture. The tips of both her little fingers were removed by a sharp instrument. But it wasn't a scalpel; the edges were too rough for that. It must have been some kind of shears or scissors."

Feeling a bit queasy, Bartholomew elected to concentrate on the clothes, while the Chief went over the body. Despite being in salt water for two days, the gray Ultrasuede suit seemed new. And the label appeared to be in French. The blouse was also new, also French. Likewise, the silk scarf. But not the Timex watch or the undergarments with the Hanes label. Ergo? The woman was probably an American who had recently treated herself to an expensive European ensemble. Purchased in Europe?

"Come here a minute," murmured the Chief, peering at the victim's face. "You see this?" He pointed to the oval contusion on the left temple. "I think that was made by some kind of ring.

And look at her other fingers: manicured but with short nails. Whoever she was, she didn't want her nails interfering with her typing."

Bartholomew told him that he thought she was an American, who had recently splurged on a new outfit.

"Oh, she's American, all right," the Chief nodded. "In fact, I think she's from the Cape." He frowned. "I've *seen* her—somewhere." He sighed. "Which means we really don't have much more than we did when we came." He put a hand on Bartholomew's shoulder. "Look, I'm really sorry for hauling you down here. I just thought maybe together we—"

"It's okay, Dan. I'm supposed to be here; I know that now. May I see the diamond and the key?"

The Chief handed him the two bags.

"The key looks like some kind of safe deposit key, doesn't it?"

The Chief nodded. "Heaven only knows what bank."

Bartholomew had removed the diamond from its bag and was studying it. "It's been cut to resemble an angel," he mused, turning it in the glare of the overhead fluorescents. "And it's really hefty. You know, I'd like to show this to Alan Jones. Could we do that?"

"Good idea," nodded the Chief, "and since you thought of it, you get to come with me. What time does he open?"

"Ten—but he's usually there around 9:15."

"Good. I'll pick you up at 9:00, and we'll get coffee at Norma's."

"Whoa, Dan! When I agreed to come with you, I never said I was signing on for the duration."

The Chief looked at him, stunned. "I thought—it was going to be like last year."

Bartholomew shook his head. "That was a one-time deal. Besides, it would have to be cleared with the Abbess, and Mother Michaela's away, in Russia with the Patriarch, planning the choir's next tour."

Abruptly the hurt and anger in the Chief's expression was replaced by a slow smile—like a chess-player who had just seen how to put his opponent's queen in fatal jeopardy. "You know that I respect the call of God on your life. But—aren't you called to be 'in the world, but not of it'? All I'm asking is that you spend enough time in the world to help me get this job done. Then you can go back to your roses."

Seeing Bartholomew hesitate, the Chief said, "Why don't you pray about it."

His religious friend laughed. "You're that confident?"

The Chief just grinned and shrugged. "Let's go," he said, leading the way out.

Dr. Morton looked up from her desk, as they passed. "Aren't you forgetting something?"

"Oh," said the Chief, pausing to sign for the diamond and key, "sorry."

8 | once more, into the world

IT WAS DARK WHEN THE CHIEF dropped Bartholomew off at the friary. The monks had finished supper and scattered to their various pursuits. Bartholomew's stomach suggested that he check the kitchen to see if there were any leftovers. But his stomach would have to wait until he had spoken with Anselm.

First he had to find him. He started down the basement steps, when he heard a *barr-rump oom-pah.* Hmm, trombones—the brass section of the marching band must be having a practice session down there. Smiling, he turned around. He had never known the Senior Brother—or himself, for that matter—to be in earshot of cacophony desperately seeking mellifluence, if he could be elsewhere.

He looked out in the woodworking shop where three brothers were making cabinets for the basilica's offices. Not there. Nor was he in the crafts room, where a brother was working on the cartoon for a fresco for the new basilica, while two others set marble chips in the next section of the mosaic that would run down the nave's center aisle.

Anselm wasn't in the old chapel, where two Brothers were taking their hour on prayer vigil. They knelt in the pew in front of the icon of Jesus, using the light of its votive candle to study the little bulletin board filled with prayer requests for healing and the reconciling of relationships, as well as for global, national, and local concerns.

He finally found Anselm in a corner of the library, in an overstuffed chair that half-swallowed his slight frame. Bathed in a pool of light from the standing lamp next to his shoulder, he was reading Henri Nouwen's *Return of the Prodigal Son*. Bartholomew observed his old friend for a moment. Anselm would read a few lines, then pause, look out the window at the night, and resume.

"You look too comfortable, Anselm," he said, approaching.

The latter smiled. "When you get to my age, you will enjoy just—being still."

"Someday," Bartholomew sighed, taking an adjacent chair. "Not today." He told Anselm what had transpired, and of the Chief's specific request.

But Anselm did not give him the answer he wanted—or any answer. He just asked: "What do you think you should do?"

"I don't know," replied Bartholomew, frustration creeping into his voice. "That's why I came to see you."

Anselm gazed at Rembrandt's painting of the Prodigal Son on the cover of the book he had just put down. "You know," he mused, "I saw that painting. In St. Petersburg. I was with the choir on their first tour, when Russia was still the USSR. We had some free time, and some of us used it to go on a tour of the city with one of the guides from Intourist, the communist agency which made sure we saw only what they wanted us to see."

He smiled at the recollection. "She was a real martinet. We were running late, and so had only 47 minutes to do the entire Hermitage—which could easily take a week."

Bartholomew waited with what he hoped was patience. "Anyway," his friend continued, "we went through the rooms 'briskly,' as the British might say. Almost a dignified trot. But when I came to this," he gestured at the book cover, "I stopped in my tracks. And completely lost sight of her upraised folded umbrella. I must have stood 20 minutes in front of that painting. I could have spent the whole day." He shook his head. "And I still didn't see as much as Nouwen did."

Bartholomew relaxed and smiled, absorbed in the story.

"Suddenly I came to my senses. And panicked. The bus was due to leave in five minutes. If I missed it, I didn't have enough money to take a cab. Worse, I couldn't remember the name of our hotel! I had to get out of there fast—which is not easy in the Hermitage, even when you know how. I prayed and cried, 'Which way out?' And different angels pointed the way." He smiled, reliving the frantic egress.

"A couple of dozen tour buses were parked in a long rank along the east side of the square. I ran towards them, having no idea which was ours. One bus was pulling out as I got there. Then it stopped. Fortunately one of our group saw me and made the bus driver stop." He chuckled. "It was still worth it."

Now he turned to Bartholomew. "But you didn't come to hear an old man's reminiscences."

"No," agreed Bartholomew, smiling, "although listening to that story was about the nicest thing that's happened to me today."

Anselm grew serious. "Let me ask the question you've already asked: What do you think God wants you to do?"

"What's coming to me," replied Bartholomew pensively, "is that He may want me to become involved, but not *involved*, if you know what I mean."

The old monk nodded. "Then what's your problem?"

"I feel—drawn to detective work. And there's a real pull to it—away from my life here."

Anselm tapped his chin. "And this," he waved his arm to encompass the library—and their life, "is what you truly desire."

Bartholomew nodded emphatically.

"Then that is precisely why God can trust you to help your friend, without fear of your losing your spiritual center."

He frowned. "However, that other matter that came up last year—"

"You mean, with Laurel."

"Yes. That *could* have taken you out of your call."

"It nearly did."

"But it had to happen. You had to be tested—and make your final choice."

Bartholomew nodded. And now Anselm closed his eyes—until it looked as if he might have drifted off to sleep. Then he looked up and smiled. "I think you should do this, Bartholomew. And I will tell Mother Michaela so, when she returns. In the meantime, dear Cadfael, proceed under the same stricture as before: at no time can your investigation disrupt your life here. Unless it's an emergency, I want to see you at all meals and services, understood?"

"Understood." Bartholomew got up to leave and then remembered something. "The Chief's got serious angina, and it's getting worse. Could we put him on our prayer vigil?"

"Of course. And by the way, it's good you mentioned that. I've been talking to Dominic, and we feel there should be a formal fitness program for *all* the Brothers. You keep yourself in shape with your bicycle, but I'm concerned about some of the others. I don't want anyone having a heart attack or needing by-pass surgery, just because they've let themselves get out of shape."

"I couldn't agree with you more," said Bartholomew, raising

an eyebrow. He was smiling, but he wasn't sure he cared for where this was heading.

"And so," Anselm beamed, anticipating Bartholomew's reaction, "we want you to organize a fitness program for your Brothers. The young ones can run, the middle ones can ride, the older ones can walk. And they can all do weights. But everyone should be doing something to raise their pulse over 120 for half an hour, at least three times a week."

Bartholomew was not smiling. "When am I supposed to do this? In my free time, between midnight and two?"

"Delegate," said Anselm with a beatific smile, gazing at the ceiling as if the word was a golden feather floating down from heaven. "First, talk to Brother Luke, when he gets home from med school next week. The two of you can interview the Brothers and work out a routine suited to each. Then appoint a Brother to be in charge of each activity, and others to be in charge of each age group. Have them report to you once a month." He looked at the younger monk and raised his hands, palms up, as if handing the project to God. "You see? It's all taken care of."

Bartholomew had to laugh. "Now I see why you and Dominic are so good at what you do. Decades of delegating."

Anselm laughed. "God works in mysterious ways, my son."

That night as he got ready for bed, Bartholomew was relieved to see that the Scriptorium cat, Pangur Ban, had for once chosen to sleep on the foot of someone else's bunk.

9 | a most unlikely suspect

Norma's Café had the best coffee in Eastport. That was the unshakable conviction of the regulars, but others were just as loyal to the Homeport or Nonie's Kitchen over in Orleans, or the Hole-in-One up in neighboring Eastham. As Norma herself was now bedridden, her friend and manager, Isabel Doane, a retired English teacher and Brother Bartholomew's mother, pretty much ran the place.

"I'm not sure your mother's coffee really is the best," said the Chief as they entered Norma's and took a table by the window, "but I've been coming in here ever since I joined the force 20 years ago, and it's a little late to change now."

"I, on the other hand," said Bartholomew authoritatively, "am in a position to offer an objective opinion, having frequented the other establishments when Mother and I were, shall we say, not on the best of terms. And the coffee here really *is* the best."

After his father died, his mother had expected their only child to be—around. And so she'd taken it very hard, when he had informed her abruptly that he was joining a religious order.

By the time Novice Andrew had taken his vow and become Brother Bartholomew, she was reconciled to the fact that her son had become a monk. But it seemed that periodically she forgot that and let her resentment leak out. And her son, perhaps out of guilt for not having been there for her, instead of just taking it, too often responded in kind.

As if on cue, Isabel—tall, gray-bunned, wearing rimless glasses, and looking as if she were still in front of a blackboard—came over with a pot of fresh, steaming coffee. She poured the Chief a mug—then nearly poured coffee on the back of her son's hand, as he covered the top of his mug.

"Andrew! What are you doing? I nearly scalded you!"

"It's Bartholomew," he reminded her, "like it has been for 18 years. And I've told you: I'm on decaf now."

"Well, I knew you'd abstained for a while," she replied, unrepentant, "but I thought it was for Lent, or something."

"Come on, Mother, I quit in the middle of last summer! And it wasn't for Lent; it was for good. And you know it."

She scowled down at her son, as if he was being disruptive in one of her classes. "You used to say that no one ever coaxed as much flavor out of a coffee bean as I did."

Her son nodded. "I *still* say that. Only, the bean was running me, instead of the other way around."

As she left to get the pot of decaf, the Chief, catching Bartholomew's eye, started to grin. Which further provoked his friend. "Dan, if you say one—"

But Isabel had returned. Filling her son's mug, she asked the Chief in a low voice, "Have you ID'd the body of that woman they found down at the harbor yesterday?"

Taken by surprise, the Chief studied her expression. "You got any ideas, Mrs. Doane?"

"I think you're old enough to call me Isabel, Chief. It's been thirty years."

"Whatever," said the Chief smiling.

Returning his smile, she lowered her voice further. "I hear she might be from the Mid-Cape area, though she doesn't live in Eastport."

"*Bandershnoogy* jungle drums," muttered the Chief.

"I beg your pardon?" said Isabel sternly, assuming he had used an expletive.

"This town knows more than it should about everything! And it all comes right through here. As it happens, *I* was the one who said I thought I'd seen her before, but I'd like to know how *you* heard about it."

"Don't you get snippy with me, Dan Burke! You said it in front of a whole bunch of people, down at the beach. If you don't want them knowing what you're thinking, keep your thoughts to yourself." She glared down at him from the moral high ground.

The Chief chuckled. "You're right—Isabel. I'm sorry." He took a sip of coffee. "And I'm grateful for your keeping your ear to the ground, as it were. You were a real help last year," he paused and then continued in a conspiratorial whisper. "And I suspect you're going to be able to help us on this one, too."

Instantly the anger left her. "Well," she whispered back, "I really am proud of you boys, you know that." They both nodded. "I'll keep you posted."

Glancing at his watch, the Chief got to his feet and reached for his wallet. Isabel raised her hand. "Not this time."

"Mother—" Bartholomew started to object.

"It's my coffee, and I'll give it to whomever I feel like! And my decaf, too."

"Thanks, Isabel," said the Chief, smiling and beating a hasty retreat. "Come on," he said to his friend, "we've got a lot of ground to cover."

◆

Though the jewelry in the front windows of Dickens Brothers Jewelers on the corner of Front Street and Bayview changed with the season, there was one constant: a semi-circle of felt caroling characters from Dickens' *A Christmas Carol.* Alan Jones, the tall, seventy-ish owner, had always been fond of that story, reading it aloud over the radio every Christmas Eve. At least, he used to, before there were so many glitzy versions on television that his homey, fireside rendition seemed quaintly archaic, even to him.

Alan Jones had a wry but gentle sense of humor that reminded his older customers of Fred Allen, and the really old ones, of Will Rogers. Since Eastport was rapidly filling with retirees, many of his customers were his age or older and would often drop by to pass the time. That was fine with Alan, as long as they bought something occasionally.

As Chief Burke and Brother Bartholomew entered, a bell on a curled spring over the door announced their arrival, much as the bell over Scrooge & Marley's door must have.

Seeing them, Alan Jones came over. "Well," he said to the Chief, "did she like it?"

"What?"

"Peg," prompted the proprietor. "Did she like the Rolex?"

Explaining to Bartholomew that it had been a 25th anniversary present, the Chief said to Alan, "Yeah, she liked it. Except she won't wear it."

"Why not?"

"She says it's too good for everyday."

Alan beamed. "Did you tell her that's the beauty of a Rolex? You can wash dishes with it on, wear it in the shower, even go in the ocean and–"

"I told her. She doesn't totally believe it."

"Bring her in, and I'll tell her."

The Chief laughed. "Oh, she'll get used to it in time. But for now, she'd rather admire it than wear it." His smile faded. "Alan, what can you tell me about this?" He withdrew the sandwich-bagged diamond from the pocket of his windbreaker and handed the stone to Alan.

Who went ashen.

"Where—did you get this?"

The Chief's eyebrows went up. "You've seen it, haven't you?" When there was no reply, he pressed on. "Alan, what's going on here! What do you know about this diamond?"

The proprietor's face screwed up. "I—I can't tell you, Chief."

"You can't?" There was a definite edge to his tone.

"Client confidentiality."

Losing patience, the Chief leaned forward and whispered: "Do you know where this was found?" Alan stared at him, incapable of speech. "In the stomach of a dead woman!"

"Oh, no!" gasped Alan. "Not Dorothy!" He was trembling now, his eyes filling.

"Dorothy who?" demanded the Chief.

"Dorothy Hanson," groaned Alan. "I can't believe this! I was with her four days ago!"

"Where?"

"In Antwerp."

"Belgium? What were you doing?"

"I—I'm sorry; I can't say."

The Chief glared at Alan, his eyes narrowing. "I'm not sure you appreciate the seriousness of your situation! I'm conducting a murder investigation, and right now *you* are beginning to look like the chief suspect!"

Alan looked desperately to Brother Bartholomew, who shrugged, as if to say, what can I do?

At length, his shoulders shaking, Alan put a hand over his eyes and started to the back of the store. "Come into my office. I'll tell you what you want to know."

10 | fallingwater east

CAPE COD THRUST OUT INTO THE ATLANTIC and bent up at the elbow, as if Massachusetts were signaling for a right turn. In 1961, at the strong encouragement of President John F. Kennedy, a Cape Codder at heart, Congress declared much of the Cape's outer beach from the elbow (Chatham) to the tips of the curled fingers (Provincetown) to be a National Seashore. What had always been regarded as sacred ground by the locals would henceforth be treated with reverential respect by the Cape's many visitors.

A favorite pastime of those drawn to its wild and desolate vistas was to stroll north from Nauset beach to Coast Guard Beach, taking in East Bluffs. (And thanks to USA Today's recently putting Coast Guard Beach at the top of its list of the ten best beaches in America, there were more visitors than ever.) These spectacular sand dune cliffs reached 150 feet into the air and comprised the eastern boundary of the Town of Eastport, according to its incorporation in 1799.

Atop the bluffs stood an assortment of old Cape Cod cottages—modest and sensible in their weathered-gray cedar shingles and white trim, set well back from the precipitous edge of the cliffs. But interspersed among them were the "new houses"—bolder, prouder, and caring little for an architectural tradition that went back three centuries.

But the increasing frequency of "hundred-year weather events"—which attacked the fragile sand cliffs with ferocious savagery and could remove 30 to 50 feet of frontage in a single horrendous hour—had put a moratorium on further construction, radical or traditional. Even so, there were a few examples of owner whimsy that never failed to astonish first-time visitors.

Commodore Peters's home, the deck of which extended out like the prow of a cruiser, had been built by his father, a real admiral, and boasted all the requisite nautical accoutrements, right down to the correct flags, pennants, and running lights. But the jewel in East Bluffs's crown was its neighbor two houses to the north, the home and offices of venture capitalist Clayton W. Armstrong.

The Armstrong home was a mirror image of Frank Lloyd Wright's *Fallingwater*. But while that house with its soaring, cantilevered concrete wings and stone parapets seemed breathtakingly appropriate in the wooded highlands of southwestern Pennsylvania, on the raw, windswept bluffs of Cape Cod, it seemed breathtakingly inappropriate. What sort of man would build such a house? asked countless visitors, gazing up at it.

One who knew exactly what he wanted and didn't care what they or anyone else thought. Clay Armstrong first clapped eyes on *Fallingwater* in 1953, as a Yale freshman under the spell of Vincent Scully. The legendary art historian was lecturing on Frank Lloyd Wright's well-deserved place of prominence in the world of modern art. When the slide of *Fallingwater* came up, there was a stunned intake of breath throughout the auditorium. Pleased at the response, Professor Scully informed them that they were looking at the greatest work of residential architecture ever created. Young Clay Armstrong wholeheartedly concurred—and determined even then, that one day he would live in a house exactly like that.

It was not an unreasonable expectation. He came from a long line of Ohio iconoclasts who were used to getting their way. His great-grandfather, Asa Armstrong, had served on the general staff of William Tecumseh Sherman in the Civil War. Asa's son, William Sherman Armstrong, the first of the Ohio Armstrongs to go to Yale (Class of 1899), had the uncanny prescience to sell short into the Stock Market Crash of 1929. Some said that in so doing, he had exacerbated the Crash, but there was no question that he had trebled the Armstrong fortune. Bill's son, Asa II, (Y '30, LCDR, USNR), became one of the first venture capitalists.

Venture capitalism was a blood sport. Not for the faint-hearted, it required a gift for discerning, a little ahead of everyone else, what the next big thing was going to be. Then find the youngest, brightest innovator in that field, whether he was burrowed away in some research lab or working in the family garage. To a brilliant but penniless pioneer, the offer to capitalize the venture for only 15 or 20 percent of the embryonic company must have seemed like divine intervention.

After the deal was struck, there would inevitably be unforeseen obstacles that would delay the new product—or drug, or system—coming on line. A cash-flow problem would result, which the venture capitalist could smooth over with a few million more—for another 15 or 20 percent.

But the moment that the venture capitalist had acquired 51 percent of the stock, he was likely to take his profit early by breaking up the company and selling off its most promising pieces to the highest bidder. Too late, the broke and hapless pioneer, having signed away his intellectual property rights, would discover there was nothing he could do.

This was the arena awaiting Asa II's son, Clay Armstrong (Y '57, LT(j.g.), USNR), as soon as he got a little seasoning on Wall Street. Through his father's connections, he was able to get an excellent entry-level position in what he promptly dubbed "the Ancient & Honorable Trust Company." After five years, Clay was ready to go into business for himself. The AHTC tried to persuade him to stay, of course, offering to treble his salary and make him assistant trust division manager. But it was too little, too late.

His assistant, Dorothy Hanson, left with him. When the name Armstrong & Associates went on the door of their new office, she was the only associate. But Ed Forester soon joined them, and by the time Clay realized in 1981, that what they were doing could be done virtually anywhere (here, too, he was a little ahead), there were four associates.

For Clay, anywhere meant Cape Cod, where his family had vacationed when he was a boy. Only instead of Chatham, he would locate in the sleepy village of Eastport. And on East Bluffs he would build the house of his dreams. After working on Wall Street, he wanted to spend less than a minute commuting, so his offices would be in one of the house's wings. There would be several to choose from, for he really *was* going to build the house of his dreams.

To create it, he hired one of his classmates from Yale, Charlie Morris, who had gone on to Yale Architectural School. Being a Scully disciple himself, Charlie shared Clay's enthusiasm for *Fallingwater*. But not to the point of obsession. He balked at what Clay proposed to do—until the latter offered to treble his customary fee and agreed to reverse the layout, to avoid it being an exact duplicate. Also, where the stream known as Bear Run ran through the original, a broad flight of wooden stairs would spill out of the house like a waterfall, running over the edge of the precipice and down to the beach far below.

This was the man who had built what he wryly referred to as *Fallingwater East*, or *FW* for short—the man whom Chief Burke was about to confront with the torture and drowning of his oldest associate.

11 | the eye of the beholder

TURNING ONTO THE SMALL WHITE STONES of Armstrong's circular driveway, the Chief smiled at the large bronze statue in the center of the front lawn. Basically it was just drop-dead ugly! The whole house was ugly, if you asked him. The rectangular concrete slabs reminded him of pieces of bread—as if a small child had been trying to make a peanut-butter sandwich and couldn't get the pieces to go together right.

But the statue, surrounded by a reflecting pool, with a fat green turtle squatted in front of it expelling a jet of water from its mouth, was the *pièce de résistance,* he thought, as he got out of the Bravada and paused to study it, before ringing the bell. It was larger than life—a lumpy, blobular form that vaguely resembled a fat and angry old man wrapped in a bathrobe. Good grief, he might as well have stuck a wrought-iron flamingo out there! Shaking his head, he rang the bell.

The door was opened by an elderly man in a dark suit, whom he assumed was the butler or houseman.

"Chief Burke, Eastport Police Department, to see Mr. Armstrong, if he's at home."

"Wait here, please."

"Um, before you go, can you tell me what—*that* is, out there?" He nodded in the direction of the statue.

"Of course. That's Rodin's *Balzac*, a replica of the bronze at the Museum of Modern Art in New York."

"Oh."

The houseman soon returned with the owner of the house. Who was tall, spare, and agile—nobody over 60 deserved to be that good-looking, thought the Chief.

"Chief Burke? Clay Armstrong," said the owner, extending his hand. "I'm surprised we haven't met before, after all these years."

The Chief shook his hand. "I expect we didn't have any reason to," he said smiling. "And I wish we didn't have reason to, now."

Armstrong frowned. "I guess you'd better come in to my office." He led the way over the green marble floor to a corner room overlooking the ocean. In keeping with the house, the room was long and low ceilinged, with a seemingly endless stretch of window above an equally endless window bench.

"This is your office?"

"I use the far end as that. I built the house because I liked the way it looked outside," he said with a wry smile. "I had no idea what it was going to be like to live in."

They reached the end of the room, and Armstrong offered him the end of the window bench, while he took a rigid straight-backed chair behind a green glass table. "My wife always said the house was ridiculous," he smiled, "and she was right. As she was about most things."

The Chief frowned, remembering. "She drowned, didn't she?"

Armstrong nodded. "Five years ago." He gazed out the window at the sea. "Since then, all this," he gestured to the room, which stretched away to a vanishing point, "has been only a place to live." He paused. "Her hand, I'm afraid, was 'the only warm hand in the castle'—at least, it seems that way."

The Chief felt genuinely sorry for him—and realized that, despite the Cary Grant looks and atrocious taste in sculpture, he was beginning to like Clayton W. Armstrong. Which made the next part all the more difficult.

"Mr. Armstrong, I'm afraid I'm here to tell you of another loss."

"Dorothy Hanson?"

"Yes. We found her body washed ashore yesterday over at the harbor. Did you know?"

"Only that she was overdue and hadn't called." The tall man got up and walked over to the window, to look down at the waves breaking along the beach. "Did she—drown?"

"Yes," the Chief confirmed. "I understand she was on a mission for you. Would you care to tell me about it?"

Armstrong turned from the window, frowning. "I see you've talked to Alan Jones."

"There's no reason to be put out with him. He was determined to protect your involvement, until I informed him that with-holding information in a murder investigation was tantamount to obstruction."

"Murder?"

"Yes, and when he still wouldn't tell me what he knew, I informed him that as of that moment, he was the principal suspect." He smiled. "That's when he realized that assisting rather than impeding the discovery process might take prece-dence over 'client confidentiality.'"

The Chief walked over to the window and faced Armstrong. "We'll keep your diamonds, wherever they are, confidential. But since you're the only person, other than Alan Jones, who knew what she was doing, you'd better tell me everything you know."

When there was no response, he declared, "All right, now it's *your* name at the top of my list!"

Armstrong's eyes widened, but he said nothing.

Cool, the Chief thought, very cool. Obviously shaken. But not stirred. I would not want to go up against this guy in a bidding situation, or whatever it is that venture capitalists do.

When he saw that irate wasn't working, he tried affable. "Here's how I see it: it was *your* money, being spent at *your* instruction. It makes no sense for you to hijack your own shipment." He paused. "Unless you stood to collect on insurance. But since you were doing this so 'discreetly,' shall we say, there would be no insurance. No armored car. No heads-up to those of us," he glared at Armstrong, "whose job it is to protect you and your property."

Armstrong said nothing. But he did nod—apparently curious to see where this was going. So was the Chief.

"Other than Dorothy Hanson," he went on, "you told only one person about the diamonds: Alan Jones. And he told," he consulted the notes he'd made in his Daytimer, "two people: the head of *Guertin Frères*, and the manager of the Boston offices of RKL Investments."

The Chief looked up from his Daytimer and smiled. "Of course, there's no telling how many people *they* told." Then he shook his head. "No, forget that: both of them were professionals, in positions of trust. They would give the least possible information to the fewest possible people." He sighed. "There could, of course, be a bad apple in either operation, and I've asked the State Police and Interpol to make discreet inquiries. But it seems very unlikely."

Putting away his little notebook, he joined Armstrong in gazing down at the beach. "Which leaves us with—nothing. Unless you told someone else."

Armstrong shook his head.

"You're certain?"

"Yes."

This was going nowhere. But the Chief had one card left to play that might shake Armstrong out of his composure. He told him the grisly details of what had been done to Dorothy Hanson, before she drowned.

The latter appeared physically shaken. And stirred.

"We don't know," concluded the Chief, "if they—and there had to be at least two of them—got what they were after. One of my officers is sure they did, else why would they stop doing the finger thing? But," he said pensively, "I think maybe she was able to get away from them, before they could find out where she'd stashed the diamonds."

He started to put his Daytimer away, then stopped. "Is there *anyone* who might have known what Dorothy Hanson was going to Europe for?"

Clay thought. "The only other people *in* A&A are Ed Forester and Nigel Rawlings. And they didn't know."

"A&A?"

"Armstrong & Associates."

"Are they here?"

"They're in New York, closing a deal."

"When do you expect them back?"

"In the morning."

The Chief made a note and frowned. "You said they didn't know—how can you be sure?"

"Dorothy was the only other person who had access to my private affairs. And acquiring the diamonds was strictly a private affair; it had nothing to do with A&A."

The Chief put away his Daytimer. "Then there's only one other possibility: Dorothy Hanson herself may have told some-one—perhaps without realizing it."

He asked Armstrong to give him a rundown on her, and as the latter did so, his voice broke.

"You really liked her, didn't you," said the Chief softly, when he had finished.

"Well, of course! We'd been through a lot together over the years." He looked at the Chief and scowled. "But it wasn't like *that*, if that's what you're implying. It was never like *that*. I had too much respect for her, to even think of her in that way."

The Chief nodded and was about to say goodbye, when he remembered what was in the pocket of his windbreaker. He pulled out the two little sealed bags. "These were found in her stomach."

He passed them to Armstrong, who examined the diamond first, carefully removing it from its container. As he turned it, the stone flared in the sunlight.

"The Blue Angel," murmured Armstrong with a bemused smile, returning it to its little bag and passing it back to the Chief. "Incredible! I've never seen anything like it."

"Me, either. But you called it 'The Blue Angel.' That's what Alan Jones called it." He looked at Armstrong, his head tilted. "Have you two talked to each other?"

"No. Dorothy called me from Antwerp, when they'd finished their buying. She mentioned that particular stone, being sure I would want it." He sighed. "And I do—as soon as you're done with it, of course."

The Chief pointed to the other bag. "What about the key?"

"Your guess is as good as mine," Armstrong shrugged. "Looks like a safe deposit key."

The Chief nodded. "Any idea where the box is? Or what bank?" He looked at him very carefully.

But again Armstrong just shrugged. "Haven't a clue," he said, handing back the key in its bag.

"Well, thanks for your time," said the Chief, as Armstrong walked him to the door. "I'll keep you posted."

"I'm sure you will."

As he climbed into the Bravada, the Chief paused and nodded toward the sculpture. "Interesting."

"Oh, come on, Chief!" chuckled Armstrong. "I was in my office—my work office—when you arrived." He gestured toward a line of windows above a nearby slab. "When I heard the car on the driveway, I looked out to see who it was. And caught your expression, as you looked at it." He laughed. "It said a lot of things, none of which was 'interesting.'"

The Chief laughed sheepishly. "I guess you're right about that."

"Well, don't feel too bad. The fact is, when it was first unveiled in 1897, you would have been in good company." He started across the lawn, and the Chief had no choice but to follow him. "At the time, Rodin was considered the greatest sculptor since Michelangelo, and was commissioned to create a monument to the great French writer, Honoré de Balzac. It took him seven years. When he was finished, the critics hated it. One likened it to a sack of flour, another to a colossal fetus. They even made him return his commission. It just about crushed him."

They were standing at the bronze now, looking at the proud, defiant figure.

"But—" prompted the Chief with a smile.

"But it also had its defenders, and in ten years' time, the latter far outnumbered the former. It turned out Rodin was just a little ahead of his time. Brancusi calls this the incontestable point of departure for all modern sculpture."

"Hmm," grunted the Chief, "I learn something every day."

He thanked Armstrong, got in his vehicle, and headed out the drive. Looking at the *objet d'art* receding in the rearview mirror, he revised his opinion. It was definitely a cut above a wrought-iron flamingo. But not two cuts.

Turning onto the road that ran along the bluffs, he had not gone more than a hundred yards before he had to pull over. The vise in his chest was closing again.

This episode was the worst of all, he thought, as he started sweating and swearing. The pain increased, becoming so intense that he stopped using the Lord's name in vain and started using it in appeal.

When the pain finally subsided, he took out his cell phone and called Doc Finlay.

12 | no greater love

AFTER THE CHIEF'S WHITE VEHICLE had exited the drive, Clay
Armstrong turned back to the sculpture. And to a warm fall
Saturday in 1959. Out of the Navy less than a month, he had
already found an apartment on E. 66th between Madison and
Parks and started work at the Ancient & Honorable Trust
Company. Now he was checking out his new neighborhood—
specifically MoMA. On 53rd between Fifth and Sixth, the
Museum of Modern Art was a little far to be considered neigh-
borhood, but it had always been his favorite museum.

After browsing for an hour, he was hungry, and so wandered
out to the walled, ferned sculpture garden, where there was a
little restaurant. Checking the menu, he grimaced: It seemed
designed to appeal to elderly ladies in white gloves, a number
of whom were presumably supporters of the museum. Three of
these ladies were seated on wrought-iron chairs at a little
wrought-iron table. Another table of two sat nearby, and the rest
were empty.

Settling on a chicken sandwich on white bread with its crust removed and some iced tea, he sat down at one of the tables and ate his sandwich, gazing up at the commanding presence of Balzac in housecoat.

And then he noticed her.

There was a girl seated directly in front of the sculpture, wearing jeans and a striped bateau jersey, covered by a man's white shirt knotted at the waist. Her auburn hair was swept back and held in place by a blue scarf. In her lap she held a large sketchpad on which she was working in chalk and charcoal.

She was, without doubt, the most attractive woman he had seen since coming to New York.

Should he just go up and tell her so? No, too forward; this wasn't a cocktail party. He went in to get some more tea. On the way back, he took the circular route, till he stood unnoticed behind her chair. She was good—very good. He'd taken a year of life drawing in college and knew how difficult it was to get the proportions right, let alone the subtleties of shading she was achieving. She was close to being finished; just a little adjustment to the eyes. . . .

All at once, she began to giggle. And peering more closely, he could see why. The eyes she had drawn were not in perfect alignment. First getting them to match, and then to look like the eyes of the subject was, he recalled from his own endeavors, the hardest part. He squinted at the sculpture—and could see her predicament. Could it be that the sculpture's eyes were not perfectly aligned? *Zut alors! Incroyable!* Unthinkable! But then— what of Monsieur Balzac himself? Could it be that the problem began there?

He suppressed a conspiratorial chuckle.

Startled, she turned to see who had entered her world, unannounced and uninvited. And smiled; whoever this stranger was, he seemed to appreciate the delicacy of her predicament. Very well, he could stay.

They returned their scrutiny to the sculpture—and giggled some more.

The group of three ladies taking tea *shushed* them, as if they were in a library, and the two ladies at the other table nodded their approval of the first group's admonition.

Chastened, Clay and the girl fell silent. But mirth was now dancing in their eyes. Frowning, they compressed their lips, fighting to hold in what was welling up inside. Then they made the fatal mistake of catching a glimpse of each other's expression.

Laughter burst forth from them—loud, raucous, hilarious! The ladies at tea were scandalized. Seeing their appalled expressions, he and the girl laughed all the harder. When the manager came over, Clay explained, "It's all right; we were just leaving."

Out on the Street, he shook his head and said, "Sorry to get you tossed out of there."

"It's all right," she smiled, "I was finished anyway—until I can find a photograph of Balzac, to see if his eyes really were a teensy bit—askew."

They started laughing again, and this time, they let their hilarity run its course, oblivious to the people passing by on the sidewalk. The passersby, assuming they were in love, were happy to see them so happy.

"My name's Sheila," said the girl forthrightly, looking him in the eye and sticking out her hand.

"Clay," he replied, shaking it.

She looked at him, her head tilted. "I guess I'm supposed to say: 'Well, I've got to be going.'" She paused. "Only I don't want to."

"Then don't."

"And you're supposed to say: 'Why don't we get a drink?'"

"Okay, why don't we?"

The sun was lower, but it was still warm enough that the places with outdoor tables had them out. They found one—and found that though they were complete opposites, they felt the same way about a lot of things. An art student at Parsons School of Design, Sheila was indeed the freest spirit he had ever encountered. He'd thought Truman Capote had been dreaming, when he'd conjured up Holly Golightly. Now he had met her. And was totally captivated by her.

Three weeks later, they would again be standing in the middle of a busy sidewalk, once more laughing with abandon. And this time the smiling passersby would be correct.

◆

Sheila Dawson of Sewickley, and Clayton W. Armstrong of New York City were married in the spring of 1960. Three years later, they had their first daughter, Samantha. In '65, they had Serena. They would have stopped there, but Sheila knew how much he wanted a son. Whom he would name after his grandfather. (They didn't even pick a girl's name.) When in September of '67 William Sherman Armstrong II turned out to be a girl, her father had left the naming of her to her mother. All he asked was what he'd asked before, that her name begin with S and end with A, like her mother's. In a moment of whimsy, Sheila named her Saralinda, after the heroine in a beloved James Thurber tale from her childhood. And whimsy would become one of SL's (her family's nickname for her) most endearing traits.

Like any newborn business, Armstrong & Associates required the constant care and attention of its founder. Which Clay duly gave it—often to the neglect of his wife and children. Gradually he had become wholly absorbed in A&A, even as Sheila had become wholly absorbed in raising their three daughters. It seemed like there was precious little time for the shared laughter that had brought them together—and eventually for shared anything.

When he moved operations to the Cape in 1981, both of them had hoped that in those most congenial surroundings, they would grow back together again. On their front lawn he had even put a full-size replica of the sculpture that had brought them together.

But it had seemed like there was less time than ever. Once Sheila had said she wished he *was* having an affair; then at least she could understand why he had so little time for her. He never knew what to say when she got like that; whatever he said was invariably the wrong thing. So he simply said nothing. Which only made her angrier. There were long periods now when they didn't speak, not because they were angry, but simply because there was nothing to say.

The girls grew up and went off to Deerfield and Yale like their father. And the silence in the house grew oppressive. Sheila tried to take up her art again, only to find that she had lost all desire to create.

Her depression settled in like a heavy fog that never lifted. She went to psychiatrists. She took medication. There were times when her mood brightened, usually when the girls were home for Christmas vacation or during the summer, and the house was again warmed by her. But then they would leave, and the silence would return.

It culminated on a cool, gray morning in early June, when she had gone swimming—in the ocean. Which she never did, once the girls were too old to play in the surf. It was too cold. When the Gulf Stream which warmed the waters of the Eastern Seaboard reached the elbow of Cape Cod, it wandered off into the mid-Atlantic, leaving the water off the National Seashore in the low 60s, even in mid-summer.

It was ten degrees colder than that on the morning Sheila had donned her suit, gone down to the beach, and struck out for—England? When she had not returned by lunch, James the houseman alerted Clay, who called the police. They checked the beaches, north and south, but at first were not unduly concerned. Each summer, a handful of people were reported to have disappeared off the beaches, only to turn up several hours later with full shopping bags. But this was well ahead of the season, and by 3:00 the police called the Coast Guard. Within an hour a helicopter was methodically scanning several miles of beaches and offshore waters, to no avail.

Three days later Sheila's body washed ashore up in Truro. The coroner recorded her death as accidental drowning. But neither her husband nor her children believed that.

Suicide is a devastating event in any family. If the family is close, it is like a rocket grenade going off in a crowded village square. And despite Clay's obsession with his work, the Armstrongs *were* close. None of them ever fully recovered, and the most severely injured was Clay, who had to live daily with the thought of what might have been, had he made different choices.

With a heavy heart, Clay turned and went in the house. It now appeared that another person for whom he cared a great deal, had met the identical fate—once again, because of him.

He went into Dorothy's office and closed the door. He would have to arrange a memorial service. Probably Monday, so that Ed and Nigel could attend. But other than her mother, they would be the only ones. Dorothy had not had a private life.

Looking at her empty chair, he could almost imagine her sitting there, deftly managing two phones and keeping track of the market information streaming across her monitor. He could not imagine what life was going to be like without her. But he would find out soon enough, as he tried to cope with the myriad details she had taken care of for him, in her tireless competence.

He ran his hand over the back of her old leather swivel chair. He was not obtuse. He knew that her personal feelings for him ran deep. He knew why she'd chosen to spend eight or ten hours a day working with him, even if she couldn't be with him the rest of the time. And after Sheila's death, he could sense her secretly hoping. But he loved the memory of Sheila too much.

And now, in her final act of love, Dorothy had told him where the diamonds were.

13 | the armstrong assessment

ALL AT ONCE HE HAD TO GET OUT OF THERE. *Far* out of there. Stopping at the fridge and the freezer to get something to cook, he went out to the garage, took his tent and camping gear from its shelf, and threw it in the back of the Land Cruiser.

When Clay Armstrong had a particularly knotty problem to sort out, he took to the woods. Literally. As a teenager at a canoe-tripping camp in Ontario, he'd gained a lifelong love of the wilderness. And now he owned some—a thousand acres of undeveloped woodland in northern New Hampshire. At times like this, a couple of days in its solitude was usually enough to restore his equilibrium.

Four hours later, he turned off I-93 and onto 25, and then 25a. A couple of miles east of the Connecticut River, he turned onto the track that led to his property. It was so badly potholed, gullied, and boulder-bound that only the most serious four-wheel-drive vehicles could negotiate it. Which was why he had a Land Cruiser. On safari in Kenya, the guides he'd used had all switched from Land Rovers, because Toyota's version of what was appropriate in the bush was simply tougher. And where he was going now, he thought, shifting into his bottom gear, fording a creek, and picking his way up a steep embankment, not even a "Montana Cadillac"–the Suburbans favored by Bozeman's fishing guides–could negotiate. Coming up the Interstate, it was cumbersome and noisy, although the tape of Mozart Horn Concertos that Dorothy had given him helped. But once he was really back in the bush, nothing could touch it.

And back in the bush was where he wanted to be. So far back that no one could find him, even if they wanted to. The cell phone was switched off and would stay off, until he returned to civilization. The only reason to bring it at all was the remote possibility something might happen.

But nothing was going to happen now, he told himself, except two things: He was going to work through the death of Dorothy, and he was going to resolve the question of going forward with Trevor Haines. It was a weighty decision: What they were planning would radically alter the remainder of his life.

Which was the whole point.

And then something did happen. He was crossing the gully to the campsite he'd carved out atop a wooded rise, with a clear vista of the rolling green foothills descending to the river. It had just rained, and the creek was full, and he misjudged his footing. The Land Cruiser slid and bounced off a large boulder. It wasn't the Cruiser's fault, he told himself; just plain old pilot error.

Well, at least he was here. He got out and surveyed the damage–a nice ding to the right side of his front bumper. Not too serious–he'd get it to the Tinknocker next week.

Meantime, he stretched and inhaled and smiled. It was good to be here. On previous trips he had cleared a campsite–a small one, big enough for one tent. Which he now extracted from his gear and proceeded to erect. In his youth it had taken about half an hour to put up a twenty-pound canvas tent–*after* you'd trimmed out five long, straight saplings for tent poles. Now, it was simply a matter of fitting together flexible aluminum rods joined by shock cord. These suspended a light, igloo-style nylon tent, and just above it, a separate rain fly. The whole rig weighed four pounds and could be pitched in four minutes. Progress.

On his previous visit, he had left a stack of wood by the stones he'd assembled into a fireplace. He soon had a fire going, in front of which he set up his last piece of equipment, a canvas camp chair. That was something else he'd learned on the Masai Mara: If you could just as easily be comfortable, then be comfortable. Putting an extra log on the fire, he leaned back and assessed the situation.

Two months before, a classmate of his, Trevor Haines, had called him, on behalf of the Yale Alumni Fund. Their 50th reunion was coming up, and the class gift committee had decided that Haines was the right one to approach him for one of the "special gifts." Clay had known Haines only peripherally at Yale—he had been Fence Club, while Clay was a Zeta. He vaguely remembered Haines as being charming and amusing, but a bit over the top, fancying himself an F. Scott Fitzgerald character. But things had been even more quiet than usual at *FW*—morbidly quiet. He invited Haines for the weekend.

Clay smiled to recall his grand entrance. At the crunch of the driveway's gravel, he had glanced up from his desk and observed the arrival of his houseguest. Haines's car was an immaculate, midnight-blue Bentley Saloon of late-50s vintage with great sweeping fenders—twice as elegant as the new ones. As he got out, Clay found it hard to believe they were the same age. Haines was lithe and graceful, with long blond hair (how could it still be blond?) swept back like a lion's mane.

Watching this tableau unfold (as its creator must have hoped someone would), Clay had the odd sense that he was watching a pre-war British film. Haines was clad in white, from his Topsiders to his Lacoste polo shirt. He even had a white tennis sweater draped casually over his shoulders, its sleeves loosely entwined on his chest.

"Bravo!" Clay had murmured, getting up to greet him himself, rather than leaving it to James. As he came down the steps, his guest looked up at him, dumbstruck. "This can't be Clay Armstrong! Not the one I knew!" He frowned and looked around the premises. "Well, where is it?"

"Where's what?" responded Clay, nonplussed.

"The Fountain."

"The only fountain is that one," said Clay, indicating the figure of Balzac in its reflecting pool. At its base, a bronze turtle spouted a stream of water that glimmered in the afternoon sun.

"I meant the Fountain of Youth, old sport! The one you must be immersing yourself in daily! I mean, look at you! You haven't aged ten years since I last saw you! Still trim, still debonair. You put us to shame!"

Clay grinned in spite of himself. "And you're as ebullient as ever! Well, come in; let me show you around. James will look after your luggage." He turned to the houseman, waiting behind him. "I think we'll have Mr. Haines in the Burnt Ochre room, James."

He turned to his guest. "Each guestroom is done in a unique color. I'm not sure Frank Lloyd Wright would have approved, but when the then-currently 'in' decorator in New York heard I was building it, he offered his services at half his customary fee."

As they walked down the long hall, Clay pointed out the Burgundy Red, Emerald Green, and Cerulean Blue rooms. At each, Haines nodded appreciatively. "Have I seen these in *Architectural Digest*?"

"No, and only because I didn't want them there. The decorator begged me; it had been over a year since his work had been in *AD*. But the house had already caused enough comment."

Haines smiled. *"Eh bien, le domaine, le bel ensemble, c'est—for-midable! Mais,"* he stopped and faced his host, *"pourquoi?"*

Clay hesitated, then decided to tell him. "Ever take History of Art 12?"

"It was one of my favorites."

"Remember when Scully showed us *Fallingwater*?"

Haines nodded. "Do I! I nearly went to Pennsylvania to see it."

Clay grinned. "Me, too! I determined that one day I'd live in a house just like it."

Haines shook his head in admiration. "A lot of us had dreams like that. You made yours come true."

When they arrived at the Burnt Ochre room, Haines ran a finger over the spare, ladder-backed, wicker-seated desk chair. *"C'est magnifique,"* he murmured, *"mais ce n'est pas guerre."*

"What?"

"I was just thinking: it's all magnificent to look at, but—how comfortable is it to live in?"

Clay smiled wryly. "That's the only problem: All these straight lines meeting at right angles—even the furniture—make a striking presentation. Yet, you've got to wonder, did old FLW actually have furniture like this in his own house? Or did he just think *we* should have it in ours? To complete *his* aesthetic?"

Haines picked up on it. "What did he say to his children, when they asked, 'Why can't we have a squishy-comfortable sofa like all the other kids?'"

"Because you're not like all the other kids!" Clay responded. "Your father is the greatest architect in the world!"

"So sit there," concluded Haines, "and stop that squirming!"

Both men laughed. "The truth is," admitted Clay, "my kids did say something like that. So we compromised: We would have one room that was ours—the library. It would have all my books, and nothing but squishy-comfortable sofas and chairs." He smiled. "Guess which room became—and still is—the heart of this home?"

Haines gave a knowing nod, and Clay said, "You know something? I'm glad you're here."

Between the Dover sole and the veal, Haines came to the point of his visit: "You know the drill, old sport: If our 50th Reunion Gift is going to top the Class of '53's, it will take thirty of us giving six-figure gifts, a dozen giving seven figures, and four giving eight." He paused and smiled. "Guess which category we have you penciled in?"

While Clay appreciated his candor, he had already decided that he was going to disappoint Haines's committee by about two zeros. But there was no reason to go into that now. "I'll think about it." Then he brightened. "And now that you've discharged your obligation, tell me what you've been doing for, what, the past forty-four years."

A sad but knowing smile played across Haines's face. "I see you're going to let us down," he sighed. Still smiling, he looked carefully into his host's eyes, his own narrowing in the candlelight. "By about two decimal places, I would imagine."

Then he beamed. "Well, before I leave, I shall do my best to restore at least one of those naughts."

Clay laughed. "Then you'll have to stay on a while—which would be fine with me, incidentally; I've not laughed this much in—a long time."

As it turned out, Haines had led an exotic life. He came from old Philadelphia money—old *and* heavy: As long as he didn't marry foolishly, he need never seek gainful employment. He had chosen not to marry at all. Though he preferred the favors of the opposite sex, he assured Clay, he saw himself in the John Buchan mold, a confirmed bachelor.

He was, in sum, a dedicated seeker of truth. How dedicated? If truth summoned, he must simply drop everything and pursue it. His quest had taken him to Tibet to study healing and Buddhism, to the Philippines to investigate psychic healing, and to Vienna to learn the intricacies of hypnotherapy.

Over dessert (strawberries with clotted cream), Haines said, "Tell me about the Rodin in the front yard. It looks like the one in the Museum of Modern Art."

"It had better," replied Clay with a smile, "it's an exact copy." He told his guest the story of how he met his wife.

"Sheila? That wouldn't be Sheila Dawson, would it? From Sewickley?"

Clay stared at Haines, his fork halfway to his mouth. "You knew her?"

"Only briefly, alas. I met her at the Junior Assemblies in New York, her coming-out year. I invited her up for the Princeton game. She was enchanting! But so beautiful, I got a bit nervous. After the game I took her to Fence, and a couple of seniors started bird-dogging her. I got into the bubbly—a little too far, I'm afraid." He sighed and shook his head. "That weekend was our first and last encounter. I always wondered who she wound up with."

Clay found his voice. "This is—extraordinary! Now you really are going to have to stay another week!"

And he did.

◆

Clay shivered. It was getting dark, and he was getting hungry. The New Hampshire woods did that to you—gave you an appetite, even if all you were doing was sitting around, watching a fire.

He hadn't thought at all about the death of Dorothy, he realized, as he got up to get supper ready. Haines had taken center stage, as usual.

Yet as he was opening the cooler in the back of the Land Cruiser, he had the oddest thought that somehow the two were connected.

14 | dead cat bouncing

CLAY ARMSTRONG BUILT UP THE CAMPFIRE and took the ground round out of the cooler. It had thawed enough on the trip up to start cooking, but first he fried up a mess of potatoes and onions, and tossed a salad.

As he prepared his supper, his attention was again drawn to the center ring, where Trevor Haines, appropriately attired in red cutaway and black riding breeches, mesmerized him with his ringmaster's spiel.

The days of Haines's visit had passed quickly. Armstrong & Associates had kept Clay fully occupied during the day, while Haines went sightseeing or read or walked the beach. Once, he went up to Boston to visit his sister. The evenings were spent in conversation.

In the middle of the second week (Clay had again invited him to stay on, and Haines had gladly assented), the talk turned to Clay's work. Haines wanted to know how he had gained his reputation. "What did *Business Week* call you? 'An unsurpassed master of entrepreneurial innovation.'"

Clay raised his eyebrows. "You saw that? You people on the Class Gift Committee really do your homework."

"What's your secret?" asked his guest.

Clay smiled. "We Armstrongs have a family trait: In each generation one of us seems to have what we call 'the gift.' I have it—the ability to see a little further over the horizon. I saw satellite communications in '68, fiber optics in '71. And I foresaw the Internet—three years before Al Gore invented it."

"All right, what do you think of the market?" asked Haines. "Is it going to continue downward?"

"Yes."

"You think it's just a correction?"

"No."

"What about last week's rally?"

"There's a saying on the Street: 'If dropped from a sufficient height, even a dead cat will bounce.'"

Haines winced. "Then—?"

"Let's just say I'm not optimistic."

"But the experts are saying there's no reason not to expect a full recovery. The global economy's still basically strong, and the new technology is bound to—"

"I know, I know," Clay waved his hand. "They can still find enough blue sky to make a Dutchman's pants."

"But you can't."

Clay shrugged. "I can remember when the storm clouds were a smudge on the horizon, no bigger than a man's hand."

His guest gazed out at the Atlantic, its breakers smooth and soothing. "As it happens, I'm inclined to agree with you."

Clay pursed his lips. "The plane may yet right itself and go soaring off into the wild blue yonder. But I was in the Naval Air Force, and I believe in parachutes. A chute may cost only a tiny fraction of the plane's value—but it could save your life."

"Then you've taken—precautions?"

Clay looked at him and smiled. "Have you?"

His guest nodded. "I recently acquired one of the Thousand Islands in the St. Lawrence. And 'forty-three paces due north from the old oak tree' I've buried a million in Canadian gold sovereigns." He turned to Clay with an expression that said: I've shown you mine, now. . . .

But his host hesitated. He had taken certain measures as a hedge against a worst-case scenario. Confidential measures. On the other hand, he now regarded Haines as a trusted friend; perhaps it was time to trust him. He told him about the land in New Hampshire. And went a little further: "I have about the same amount as you do, invested it hard currency."

"Gold?"

Clay shook his head. "Too easy to counterfeit. I like old quarters. The ones minted before 1964 were 90 percent silver—and too much work to bother counterfeiting."

"Anything else?"

Again Clay hesitated. His other hedge was a lot more significant. And since it would not be recorded anywhere, he would be able to pass it on to his daughters without the IRS being the wiser. Again he decided to trust his new friend. "I'm putting the bulk of my emergency reserves in diamonds."

"Diamonds?"

"They're extremely portable, easy to liquidate, and can't be counterfeited."

"But if you get them in New York—"

"I'm getting them in Antwerp. Quietly. In fact, someone will be buying them for me in a couple of weeks."

Haines leaned forward and delicately tapped his fingertips. "I don't suppose you'd ever let me use your—source."

"I'd have to think about that," Clay replied.

And now, as he put another log on the fire, he realized that what he'd told the Chief earlier that afternoon was not entirely true: He *had*, in a way, told someone else about Dorothy's mission.

15 | armstrong dreaming

TREVOR HAINES WAS THE MAN who came to dinner—and stayed. But at his host's request. Each time, Clay realized as he built up the fire, it was he who had suggested that Haines stay on. And his friend had become progressively more fascinating.

Two days after the diamond discussion, they were in the library having a cognac after dinner, when Haines commented on the portrait of Sheila over the mantel. "It's a remarkable likeness! It's the way I remember her. A little older, of course, and more thoughtful, but the eyes are exactly the same." He turned to Clay. "You must miss her very much."

"You can't begin to imagine," said his host with deep feeling. "And instead of it getting better with time, it's getting worse."

"How do you mean?"

Clay thought for a moment. "Well, with each passing year, I see more clearly how I drove her to—" He couldn't complete the sentence.

"What was your happiest, most carefree time with her?"

"The most truly free-from-care time? That would have to be the beginning."

Turning back to the portrait, Haines asked, "How would you like to relive that time?"

"I do," said Clay with a sad smile, "often."

Haines shook his head. "I mean, really *relive* it."

"What are you talking about?"

"In my peregrinations, I've done a fair amount of work in hypnotherapy, helping patients to achieve closure on particularly painful episodes in their past."

He paused and gazed again at the portrait over the mantel. Without taking his eyes from it, he said, "If you wanted me to, I could take you back to that afternoon you met. And what followed. In your mind, you would relive it. Everything would be crystal clear, and you would experience it so vividly, with details you've long since forgotten, that you would quite literally be reliving it."

Clay frowned. "Is it—safe?"

"Safe as houses. You'll be in a very light trance, nothing you can't emerge from at any time, in an instant. But you'll experience all the emotions of that first encounter—all the surprise and joy of that afternoon."

Clay remained unconvinced. "Tell me about the first part, the business of putting me under."

Haines smiled. "We can do it in this room. You can stay in that chair. I will act as your guide, making a series of suggestions. If you follow them, you will eventually enter your past. Just remember: You're there simply to re-experience, not to attempt to change anything."

"Let me think about it."

The following evening after dinner he said, "I'm ready."

"You won't have to move," said Haines, drawing his chair closer, so that he could speak softly and still be heard. "Now settle back and put your feet up on the footstool," he continued in a calm, soothing monotone. "That's it. And close your eyes, as if you're about to take a nap."

Clay followed his suggestion, composing himself for sleep.

"Good, now take a deep breath, and let it out slowly. And another, deeper. Good, and one more."

Haines leaned forward. "Now I want you to visualize a mountain meadow, filled with wildflowers—daisies, buttercups, violets. It's a warm, sunny afternoon, and you're standing in the middle of the meadow. You can hear the crickets, and the mountain air is wonderfully fresh—fill your lungs with it."

Clay, eyes closed, completely still, took another deep breath.

"Now, look over there, to your left: Do you see that butterfly?"

"Yes," Clay murmured.

"What kind is it?"

"Monarch."

"Look at the mountains in the distance, so green they're almost shimmering in the sun. Do you like this view?"

"Oh, yes!" Clay softly agreed, his mouth forming a smile.

"There's a path ahead of you, leading down that gentle slope to the wooded glade—do you see it?"

"Mm-hmm," Clay nodded.

"I want you to walk down the path, and let me know when you're about to enter the glade."

In a moment, Clay murmured, "I'm there."

"Good, now go into the glade." Haines paused. "It's a little cooler in here out of the sun, but it's not uncomfortable."

"No," agreed Clay.

"Up ahead there's a fork in the path—which way should we go?"

"To the right."

"Good, we'll go that way." Pause. "Do you hear that? It sounds like a squirrel. There he is, in that oak tree over to the left—can you see him?"

"I'm not sure," murmured Clay, eyes still closed, but frowning.

"He's hiding behind the trunk, about halfway up. But look: He's peeping out at us."

"Oh, yeah," said Clay, relaxing and smiling. "I've got him. Cute."

"Up ahead—do you see that clearing there, where the sun's coming through the trees?"

"Mm-hmm," Clay nodded. "Lovely."

"Why don't you go there—and let me know when you're there."

In a few seconds, Clay said, "I'm here."

"Good. Look to your left: Do you see that little hummock with the soft grass?"

"Yup."

"Why don't you lie down there on the grass and rest your head on the hummock, because you're going to take a little nap."

He waited while Clay, motionless in the chair, got comfortable in his mind. "You're falling asleep now, but it's a light sleep—you'll still be able to hear me."

Clay nodded almost imperceptibly.

"Asleep now?" asked Haines gently.

"Yes."

"Good. You are beginning to have a dream of the afternoon you met Sheila. You can describe it to me, as it occurs. It's going to be the best dream you have ever had. And when you awaken, you're going to remember—everything. Are you looking forward to this dream?"

"Very much," murmured Clay.

◆

When he awoke from the trance/dream that Haines had induced, Clay remembered—everything. And wept. "We were so happy," he murmured.

He looked around the room, trying to get re-oriented. When his eye fell on the grandfather clock in the corner, he gasped. It said 9:48. "How long have I been—gone?"

"A little over an hour," said Haines with a smile.

"I want to go back."

"We'll see," said Haines thoughtfully.

"But not tonight; I'm really tired. I think I'll head for bed."

"Sweet dreams," Haines replied, and both men laughed.

At breakfast the next morning, as Clay read the *Wall Street Journal* and Haines the Boston *Globe*, the former asked, "You mentioned hypnotherapy—what exactly is that?"

Haines looked up from the paper. "It's helping people recover from severe emotional trauma in their past."

"Well, take me, for instance: How would you help me?"

Haines spread dark marmalade on his crisp, cold toast. "I've already begun. Last night was Phase I, leading you back to your happiest time together. That's the foundation on which we will build—that is, if you want to continue."

"I do," declared Clay. "It's incredible; I still remember every detail of that dream. It's as if it all happened yesterday!" He laughed and then added, "Which, in a way, it did."

He looked at Haines, who had turned his attention to the half grapefruit, which James had sectioned. "What's Phase II?"

"Phase II would be to go back to a pivotal episode, when the two of you were—well, at your worst." He lowered his spoon and looked up with a smile. "An incident probably came to mind, when I said that."

"It did," said Clay, wincing. "It was the day she blew up at me and accused me of having an affair. I didn't know what she was talking about and got furious. Then she said that A&A was my mistress, and that her rival lived under the same roof—down the hall, less than a minute away!" He was shaken by the vividness of his recollection. "It was after that, that the depression really got hold of her."

Haines nodded. "Then that will be Phase II."

"What happens?"

"The same as last night: You go back and relive *that* afternoon. Only this time with full understanding of what you have done, and taking full responsibility for it."

Clay shuddered. "I don't think I can handle that."

Haines finished his grapefruit and turned to his shirred eggs. "Well, I'll leave it to you; you can tell me when you're ready. But we can't complete the healing without it."

"Then there's a Phase III?"

"These eggs are perfect!" declared Haines, patting his lips with the white linen napkin. "James is a remarkably accomplished chef, in addition to all his other talents."

But Clay would not be deterred. "Phase III."

Haines looked out the window. "This is where hypnotherapy gets, shall we say, sensitive."

"What do you mean?"

"I mean, that if you were ever to mention Phase III to anyone, it could cause me a great deal of difficulty."

Clay looked at him, mildly annoyed. "I should think, Trevor, that after all the ground we've covered in the past three weeks, you'd be beyond thinking I would ever do such a thing."

Haines threw up his hands in mock dismay. "I stand—or rather, sit—corrected." The smile left his face. "Phase III is the time of forgiveness and reconciliation. I lead the patient—you—into another realm. The Beyond. Where Sheila will be waiting for you. Where you can have the reunion that your heart so badly wants."

Clay stared at him, speechless.

"When people lose loved ones," Haines went on, "the only comfort they have is the thought that one day they will be reunited in heaven." He paused and smiled. "With my help, they don't have to wait that long. I can do it for them now."

Clay was in torment. His rational common sense was screaming that this was too weird, too radical, too far out. But his heart was longing for what Haines seemed to be promising. He found his voice. "Isn't that—a little like a—séance?"

Haines recoiled as if he'd been slapped. "Hardly!" Quickly regaining his composure, he smiled. "Phase III will be no different from what you experienced last night."

"We go to the meadow?" Haines nodded. "And the glade?" He nodded again. "I'll have to think about it."

16 | *in bushmills veritas*

THE SUN WAS DOWN, the pot and frying pan, plate, mug, and utensils were all washed and put away. The fire was burning low. Clay stirred it up, put on another log, and returned to his ruminations.

He never had gotten to the point where he was ready for Trevor Haines's Phase II. But something else had happened at breakfast the following morning that sent everything in a whole new direction. Over Belgian waffles and apropos of nothing, Haines had said, "At 10:35 Eastern, 90-day futures in Chinese copper are going to dip 23 cents a pound. At 10:48 they will start to recover. By 11:00, they'll be fully back, and by 11:15, they'll be up ten cents. If you want to make some easy money," he said with a mysterious smile, "buy low and sell high."

On principle, Clay never did options or warrants. The whole futures market was wildly unpredictable and subject to the unknown—a complete crapshoot. He had better uses for his capital. When he did a deal, the only unknown was what his opponents would do under immense pressure, applied suddenly.

And to Clay, their response was hardly unpredictable. Indeed, he felt at times like a card sharp taking advantage of tinhorns. But he shrugged off such twinges of conscience. While his adversaries might have little experience at the high-stakes table, they were convinced they were man enough to be in the game—and that if someone was going to lose, it would not be them.

Worse, the futures market *could* be manipulated. It was illegal, of course, and in theory, impossible. But Clay had seen it happen, and so had others. He—and the SEC—just didn't know who was jiggering it, or how. Nevertheless, what Haines had said made him curious—enough so that at 10:34, he punched up 90-day Chinese copper on A&A's market monitor. A minute later, the 90-day asking price started down, went down 10 cents, and bottomed at 23 cents down. Thirteen minutes later, after everyone in the world who was holding Chinese copper had had a chance to at least partially divest, or re-set their computer trading programs that had triggered a sell-off, it started to rise again. By 11:00 it had fully recovered, and fifteen minutes later had actually gained ten cents.

Clay stared at the machine. It could have been an anomaly—unusual, but not extraordinary. Except that Haines had called it. To the minute and to the penny. Which was impossible. Unless. . . .

That evening at dinner, he asked Haines how he'd done it. His guest just smiled and said, "Would you like to see me do it again?"

"Sure."

"Tomorrow morning at 11:03, 120-day Venezuelan crude will start dropping from $28.30 a barrel. When it reaches $25.18, sixteen minutes later, buy it. By noon it will have fully recovered. But sell then, because it's going back down." Haines chuckled. "And this time, why don't you actually buy some."

"What makes you think I didn't today?"

Haines wouldn't say. "You really should tomorrow."

"What about you?" responded his host. "Are you going to put your money where your mouth is?"

Haines smiled and shook his head. "Of course not! I never play with my own money! That's why I still have some. But I don't mind making my friends a little richer."

Clay decided that if 120-day Venezuelan crude *did* start behaving as Haines said it would, he would buy fifty thousand barrels. Since a buy that size would obviously affect the market, he would start before it bottomed, then buy in increments along the floor, until it started to rise.

Precisely at 11:03 the next morning, 120-day Venezuelan crude started down. Clay followed his plan, buying as it went down, selling as it went up. He sold the last of it at 12:03, netting around $148,000.

At dinner that evening, he handed Haines a check for half that amount. "What's this?" his guest responded, surprised.

"Your share of today's proceeds."

"But I didn't—"

"It was your information; it's only fair."

"I'm—touched," said Haines. "But I'll tell you what: Let's put it in a war chest for a project I have in mind. In the meantime, we'll simply re-invest it from time to time, as similar 'opportunities' present themselves. Obviously it won't be every day, and perhaps a whole week will go by without a play."

His host laughed. "You see? You're just going to have to stay on longer. But why a whole week with no action?"

"Mustn't be greedy, you know; mustn't go to the well too often. Everyone in futures is going to know something's going on, but they won't know what, or how, or when."

At the end of the week, the move was in Brazilian coffee. On the following Tuesday ("It goes without saying, Trevor, that you'll be staying another week—oh, just stay till Labor Day, and we'll sort it out then") the anticipated fluctuation was again in coffee, this time from Kenya.

david manuel

Haines stayed another month. As they reached the end of September, their war chest was at 6.7 million. And Clay still had no idea how Haines did it. But one evening he determined to find out.

After dinner, instead of cognac, he had suggested they end the meal with a tot of Irish whiskey—out on the terrace, since it was an unusually warm evening. He produced a bottle of 28-year-old Bushmills, which he had been saving for just such an occasion, and they settled back to enjoy the full moon rising out of the Atlantic.

An hour later, as he emptied the last of the whiskey into their glasses, Clay asked Haines how his scheme worked. His guest smirked and said, "I could tell you, but then they'd have to kill me."

They laughed at the cliché, and then Clay asked, "Who are 'they'?" He asked offhandedly, smiling, trying to keep it light.

Haines tilted his head and replied in a heavy brogue, "Sure'n ye have na' been plyin' me with the milk of the Auld Sod to get me to reveal how I make the broom carry water?"

Clay laughed, a little embarrassed; he'd been caught.

Haines wagged his finger. "Sorry, this sorcerer will never reveal the magic incantation."

But Clay suspected the cliché was based in fact: He must be somehow connected with an enormous and extremely well-disciplined cartel.

As if reading his mind, Haines said sadly, "Don't ruin everything, old sport. There are some things you can't—really mustn't—know."

The only trouble with drinking with someone to loosen his tongue was that if you matched him drink for drink—and if the person was as astute as Haines, you pretty well had to—was that it had a similar effect on your own tongue.

Clay found himself telling Haines something he'd not told anyone, even his daughters. Two months earlier, in the course of a routine physical, chest x-rays had turned up two spots on his right lung. Doc Finlay refused to speculate on what they might be; all he would say is that in a couple more months they should take some more pictures. After the second set, Doc had called him in for some solemn news: The spots were bigger, and their growth was rapid. He had scheduled a biopsy for October 3, this coming Wednesday.

Clay had no illusions. He'd been a pack-a-day man—two packs, if it was a tense day, and most of them were. Then on his 40th birthday, at Sheila's pleading, he had quit. Cold turkey. With fierce withdrawal pangs—which only made him the more resolute. His grandfather had once said that a man either ruled his passions, or was ruled by them. Well, nicotine was not going to rule him.

But now it appeared that nicotine was going to have the last laugh. A friend of his who had quit smoking around the same time had recently died of lung cancer—ten months after spots had appeared.

"So, you're scared, right?" Haines had responded, when Clay told him.

"Well—sure. Wouldn't you be?"

Haines shrugged. "Yes. And no."

"What do you mean?"

"Cancer can be healed."

"Not mine. If it is cancer, they will probably have to take the whole lung."

Haines looked up at the full moon, which was now almost directly above them. "There's more than one way to skin a cat, even if it's bouncing."

"What do you mean?"

But Haines's only reply was an enigmatic smile.

17 | chicken soup

CLAY SHIVERED; WITH THE COMING OF NIGHT, the temperature was dropping fast. He got up and pulled on his old leather jacket. Adding the last two logs to the fire, he promised himself that when they were done, he would call it a night.

But instead of returning attention to the center ring, he concentrated on the darkened one in front of him. Whoever had killed Dorothy Hanson knew what she was carrying. But only three people knew: himself, Alan Jones, and the manager of the RKL office in Boston. And now, peripherally, Trevor Haines.

He considered each—and ruled out each. He'd been doing business with Jones for nearly twenty years and trusted him enough to pay him $50,000 plus expenses, for one week's work. As for RKL Investments AG, their entire reputation was built on trust and maximum discretion. And he trusted Haines, who was now closer to him than anyone on earth. Especially now that Dorothy was gone.

Which left him—nowhere.

But he *would* do something for Dorothy, he decided. Now that the diamonds' existence was common knowledge, he would donate the Blue Angel (when the police returned it to him) to the Smithsonian for their rare gem collection: "In loving memory of Dorothy Hanson." Maybe they'd display it near the Hope Diamond; she deserved that.

He poked the fire with the long-bladed machete he'd used for clearing the campsite, and turned back to the brightly lit center ring. Two weeks ago, he and Haines had finished dinner and adjourned to the library, when the latter asked, "How would you like to go to the meadow this evening?"

Clay shook his head. "I'm still not ready for Phase II; I don't know if I'll ever be. But I must admit, Phase III intrigues me. Can't we just skip the middle part?"

Haines smiled. "No pain, no gain, I'm afraid. The healing cannot be completed without it. But you'll be ready soon." He paused. "That's not what I had in mind."

Clay looked at him. "Now I'm *really* intrigued."

"How much do you know about psychic healing?"

"Pretty kooky, isn't it?"

"Some of it," Haines mused. "A lot of it, in fact." With thumb and forefinger, he rubbed the bridge of his nose. "But science is only beginning to understand the mind's ability not only to see what can't be seen, but to project—power."

"You mean like—spoon-bending?"

"Psychokinesis is one aspect," admitted Haines, smiling. "I'm specifically referring to the mind's ability to heal the body."

Clay thought about that. "Well, everyone knows about the power of suggestion: Give someone a placebo, a sugar pill, tell them it's a new experimental drug, and sometimes—" He shrugged.

Haines leaned forward. "What if—it was possible to take the ambiguity out of the equation?"

"What do you mean?" asked Clay slowly.

"What if, in a hypnotic reverie, the mind, carefully guided and channeled, could perform its own—healing?"

Clay stared at him. "I think I see where you're going—and I'm not sure I like it."

Haines pointed at his host's chest. "Those spots of yours: What if—we were to heal them?"

"Is that even possible?"

Haines slowly nodded. "I've seen it. In the Philippines and in Vienna. I've observed dozens of 'operations.' And—I've performed a few myself."

Agitated, Clay got up and went over to the mantel. "I don't know, it sounds awfully spooky—what's the downside?"

"There is none. If it works, you'll have a huge burden off your mind. If it doesn't—" he shrugged and smiled. "It's a little like taking chicken soup for a cold; it can't hurt you, and, who knows, it might even help."

Clay returned to his chair. For a long time they sat in silence, then suddenly he clapped his hands. "All right, let's do it."

"You mean, right now?"

"Right now."

Once again, Clay settled back in his chair and closed his eyes, as Haines guided him to the mountain meadow and then down the path into the glade. At the fork in the path, Clay, as before, chose to go to the right, and before long he was in the sunlit clearing.

"Don't lie down," Haines warned him. "This time, we're going on. Look beyond the hummock: You see the path that leads out of the clearing?"

"Yes," murmured Clay.

"Take it. Let's see where it leads." He waited for a five-count. "Is that another fork up ahead?"

"Mm-hmm."

"Which way should we go this time?"

"Left."

"Left it is," nodded Haines. Then after another five-count, he asked, "Do you hear a noise?"

"Yes."

"A soft roaring?"

"Um, yeah. What is that?"

"It's a waterfall. When you go around that next bend, you'll be able to see it. Let me know when you can."

After a few moments, Clay said softly, "Wow."

"Beautiful, isn't it," exclaimed Haines softly, as if he, too, were visualizing it.

"Yeah. Incredible."

"What do you like best about it?"

"Well, the way the spray flashes in the sun, as the water hits the rocks down there. Man, look at the rainbow!"

"Yes," agreed Haines, "it's—beautiful!" He waited a five-count. "But I'm afraid we've got to get going."

"Can't we stay a little longer? I wish I had my camera!"

Haines waited a five-count, then said, "Time to go. Do you see where the path actually goes behind the waterfall?"

"Yeah, but. . . ."

"What's the matter?"

"Well, where it goes out on those rocks—they look wet, kind of slick."

"I see what you mean," said Haines, as if he really could. "But look, over there to the left. Isn't that a way around the rocks?"

"Yeah!" said Clay, optimistic now.

"Think you can go that way?"

"No problem."

"Good, let's go. Tell me when you're ready to go behind the falls."

Clay, eyes closed, frowned slightly in concentration, then relaxed. "I'm here."

"Okay, go in. Now, do you see that metal door?"

"Yeah, what's it doing here?"

"A pretty good place to put it, don't you think? If you don't want everyone coming here."

"I suppose so. What's in there?"

"A fully equipped hospital."

"You're kidding."

"Open the door and see."

Clay's mouth opened. "Wow!"

"We need to go to the OR. It's down on the second floor. Take the elevator on your right."

"Okay. What floor?"

"Sub-level Two. Then turn right, and tell me when you're at the door that says 'Operating Room'."

In a moment, Clay, eyes shut, perfectly still, said, "Okay. Should I go in?"

"Yes, and lie down on the table."

Clay frowned. "Shouldn't I get undressed or something?"

Haines lightly hit his own forehead with the heel of his hand, for not remembering. "Of course. See that locker on your left? Put your clothes in there, and put on the blue johnnie you'll find hanging in it."

"I hate these things," said Clay. "They never fit, and they never cover you."

"Well," said Haines, chuckling softly, "the operating team are all old hands at this. By the way, you're going to have the best thoracic surgeon in the hospital. I'll be your anesthesiologist, so before we start, I need to ask you: Do you have any allergies I should know about?"

"No."

"Okay. You see that clear plastic breathing mask, by the oxygen tanks there?"

"Yes."

"Put it over your nose and mouth and lie down on the table, while I turn it on. Now breathe."

Clay wrinkled his nose.

"What's the matter?"

"Doesn't smell good."

Haines frowned, then smiled. "Oh, sorry, I had you on ether. I'm switching you over now to nitrous oxide—is that better?"

Clay smiled. "Much better."

"Right, from now on don't talk, because I won't be able to hear you with the mask on. Just nod or shake your head. Understood?" Nod. "Good, now breathe deeply."

Clay, otherwise motionless, breathed deeply, as instructed.

"You're going under," intoned Haines. "This is going to be a perfect operation, and when you come out of it, you're going to feel wonderful."

Clay smiled and nodded.

"Now, I'm turning up the anesthesia, so you'll be well under when the team arrives."

Clay nodded, almost imperceptibly. His breathing slowed and deepened.

Haines said softly, almost sepulchrally, as if speaking to Clay from a great distance, "They're coming now. There are four of them: the chief surgeon, his associate, his chief nurse, and her assistant. . . . He's aligning his cut, and now he's taking a small, spinning saw-wheel and opening your chest. . . . Now clamps. . . . Now they've put you on a heart-lung machine. . . . Everything's being done mechanically for you now. . . ."

Haines stretched for a moment in his chair, then bent back to his task. "Now the surgeon is checking the x-rays one last time. . . . Now he's lifting your right lung and holding it in his left hand. . . . Now, with his right, he is taking up a scalpel. . . . This is the most difficult part of the operation, because the two spots on your lung are so close to your heart. . . ."

Haines frowned, alarmed; his patient had stopped breathing. "Keep breathing," he said softly. "Just because it's difficult, doesn't mean you should hold your breath."

Clay's chest enlarged, and Haines relaxed. "That's better. . . . You just keep breathing and leave the operation to them. . . . The surgeon is cutting now, deftly removing the two spots. . . . He's grinning; he got all of it. . . . The team is congratulating him. . . . You're going to be all right. . . ."

Clay nodded ever so slightly, a tear running from the corner of each closed eye.

"They're sewing you up now. . . . And now the surgeon is so happy, he and his assistant are doing a high five." Haines chuckled. "He's a cocky one, but I like that in my surgeons. . . . And now they're giving you back into my hands and leaving the OR. . . . I'm turning down the nitrous oxide. . . . You're coming out of the anesthetic. . . . But don't try to get up yet. Just lie there, while I wheel you into the recovery room. . . . How do you feel?"

"A little woozy," Clay responded, his eyes shut, "and my chest hurts."

"That will pass fairly quickly. By the way, the operation was a complete success. They were able to remove the spots, without any damage to your heart."

"That's a relief."

"Here we are in the recovery room, and look: They've brought your clothes in. Can you get them on?"

"I–think so." Clay frowned at the imagined effort.

"Anything wrong?"

"My chest is still sore."

"I'm not surprised. Oh, and here's your watch and your wallet; I kept them for you during the operation. I mean, it's a first-class hospital, but you can never be too careful."

"Thanks, I appreciate it."

"While you were under, I got some directions: If we follow the green line in the hall, it goes to an elevator that goes straight up to the meadow."

"Let's do that," murmured Clay. "I'm kind of beat."

"I should think so, after all you've been through."

"Well, it was worth it."

"I'll say! Here, let me get that door for you. Now follow that line to the elevator. Want me to help you?"

"I think I can make it." He frowned.

"What's the matter?"

"Still a little woozy."

"Here, I'll get the elevator. Get in now. That's good. Next stop, the meadow."

Clay smiled.

"Okay," announced Haines, "here we are, right back where we started from. When I snap my fingers, you will wake up, feeling relaxed and refreshed, and remembering very little about the operation, almost as if it was a dream."

And with that, he snapped his fingers.

Clay opened his eyes and looked around the library. He yawned. "There's no place like home, is there, Toto."

"What?"

"Wizard of Oz."

"Oh. How do you feel?"

"Wonderful—I think."

"What do you remember?"

Clay shook his head and smiled. "My most distinct memory is of a perfectly gorgeous mountain waterfall! I'd really like to go back there. And bring my camera." He frowned. "Guess you can't do that, though."

"They're working on it," said Haines laughing. "What about the operation?"

"Well, the last clear memory I have is of you, administering the wrong anesthetic."

"Sorry about that," Haines grinned ruefully, and they both laughed. "After that?"

Clay looked over at the fireplace. "Well, it was really strange. I wonder if I might have had an out-of-body experience or something, because during the operation, I seemed to be hovering above them, looking down and watching them work on me." He shook his head. "Probably just a dream."

Then he raised his eyebrows and smiled. "But that surgeon was something else! I like it when my surgeon's so good, he's a little cocky."

He chuckled at the recollection, then yawned again. "I'm tired. And a little woozy. I think I'll turn in." At the entrance to the library, he turned. "And Trevor? Thanks."

18 | the ebenezer syndrome

THE CAMPFIRE WAS ALMOST EMBERS. But if he went to bed before he reached a decision, he would only toss and turn in his sleeping bag. So he pushed the unburned ends of the firewood to the center, stirred up the coals beneath them, and turned to the last chapter of the Trevor Haines story.

The "operation" was a week ago. The next day he had slept in, not coming down until shortly before lunch. At which, the conversation had been light, both men not speaking of what had taken place in the library the night before.

But at dinner that evening, Haines had apparently decided it was time to reveal his grand strategy for the use of their now sizable war chest. It was grand, all right: He envisioned a clinic and center for research into all aspects of hypnotherapy. There would be hypnosurgery, such as he had performed last night, and hypnotherapy for the reconciling of relationships with loved ones who had gone to the Beyond. There would be hypnoregression, to heal trauma buried deep in the subconscious or in the long-forgotten past. He already had a staff in mind—

men and women well-grounded and experienced in each of the disciplines. As for funding, the ten million in their war chest would be a good start, but of course much more would be needed to adequately endow it.

Clay was nonplussed. "Do you have a name for it?"

"I was thinking we could call it the Armstrong Research Clinic—the ARC, for short."

Clay had mixed emotions. "Well, I'm not immune to flattery, but—what sort of role do you envision me in? I mean, other than the obvious one: earning and raising the money that would be needed to keep it going."

Haines laughed. "Oh, you'd hardly be on the sidelines! To waste your organizational gifts would be worse than foolish; it would be criminal. You would be chief administrative officer."

"And you would be the director?"

"Only if you wanted me to be."

"Well, it doesn't make sense otherwise." He mulled over what had been proposed. "Where were you thinking of locating it?"

Haines hesitated. "Well—the perfect setting, the one most conducive to therapeutic healing would be—" he fell silent.

"Come on," Clay encouraged him, "out with it."

"Right here. At *Fallingwater East.*"

Clay blinked. Then he smiled, "Well, that would certainly advance the timetable!"

"By about a year," Haines nodded emphatically. "In fact. . . ." His voice trailed off.

Clay exhaled. "It's quite a concept," he conceded. "Rather breathtaking. I'll have to give it some thought."

Then he smiled. "But regardless of what I decide, I want you to extend your stay here—indefinitely."

Haines, an expression of surprise on his face, asked, "Are you sure?"

"Quite sure. You're the best thing that's happened to *FW* in a long time."

"I—I don't know what to say."

"Then don't say anything. Just get your clothes and whatever else you need, and move in."

Haines was speechless.

"And while you're gone," Clay added, "we'll run a phone line into your room and another for your computer."

His guest found his voice. "I'll need to go to the town-house—Mother's *pied à terre* in New York, where I've lived since she died. Then I'd like to run up to Boston for a few days to visit my sister."

"Sounds like a plan," said Clay. "When will you leave?"

"No reason not to leave today. And you can look for me to show up on your doorstep with all my sundries—" he calculated the number of days he would need—"on October tenth, a week from this coming Tuesday."

"Perfect. I'll know by then, if the ARC is a go."

Haines smiled. "You'll know something else, too: that you're cancer free."

Clay laughed. "You're awfully confident."

"Just be sure to get another set of x-rays before they do that biopsy."

Clay did just that. The biopsy was scheduled for Wednesday morning, the fourth, at the hospital. On Tuesday he prevailed upon Doc Finlay to request one more chest x-ray. He was about to drive down to the hospital the next day, when the phone rang.

It was Doc Finlay, sounding perplexed but upbeat. "You're not going to believe this! *I* don't believe it! But those spots on your lung? They're gone!"

"Gone?"

"Completely. Not even a trace. The radiologist thought it must be someone else's x-ray, but he double-checked; it's yours, all right."

"Then—I'm clear?"

"Yup, whatever it was, it's not there now."

"Is that possible?"

"Until now, I would have said no. If it *was* cancer, and it just about had to be, I've never heard of a complete remission. But— these x-rays say otherwise."

Clay had spent the remainder of yesterday in a state of shock, and then today he'd received a shock of a different kind: Dorothy Hanson had drowned after being tortured.

The fire was glowing coals. He'd promised himself he'd go to bed, when it was done. But it was, and he wasn't. Well, as long as he could see some red. . . .

In nine days he would turn 65, the once-traditional retirement age. Having nearly been retired from life, it seemed an appropriate time to take stock. What would have gone into his obituary in the *Wall Street Journal*? That he'd done a lot of deals? He couldn't even remember them. That he'd made a lot of money? Anybody could do that (though he took some pride in having set aside for each of his daughters more than he himself had inherited).

But what about those daughters of his? He practically had to bribe them to come see him. They didn't seem to care about him—but then, when had he ever taken the time to care about them? Or their mother, for that matter. Sheila had taken her life, because she had finally given up. What? Hope. That he would ever take the time to care.

Clay shuddered. He would like to blame that little insight on a spot of mustard or an underdone potato, but. . . .

I don't care much for that guy, he told the Ghost of Christmas Past.

To his surprise, the GCP was sympathetic: He explained that caring was something you learned as a child, from your parents' behavior towards you. A parent could care naturally for a child only as much as his parents had cared for him. Clay's parents had not cared that much—because *their* parents had not cared.

Bottom line: He was trapped inside who he was.

Thanks a lot, Clay snapped.

But the GCP wasn't finished: You *were* trapped—until now. Now that you have seen the truth, it remains to be seen if it will set you free.

Great, now comes the part where the Ghost of Christmas Future shows me what's going on the old tombstone. Will my daughters have to pay mourners to come to my funeral?

He braced himself for the fast-forward.

But the GCF must have overshot, for the tape stopped at the part where Scrooge wakes up. And realizes it's all been a dream.

So now, here was Clay, standing next to old Eb at the window, with that boy down there hollering up that they haven't missed Christmas, after all! There was still time to change what would go into that *WSJ* obit.

Clay Armstrong was not an emotional man. So it was disconcerting for him to find tears in his eyes. Must be the smoke from the fire—except that there was no fire anymore, and besides, he was always careful to position his chair upwind.

What did people of his age and circumstances do, when suddenly overcome by the Ebenezer Syndrome? If they already had a favorite charity, they endowed it beyond its wildest dreams. But what if they, like him, had always felt that charity began at home? What if the gifts they *had* given were mainly so they could think of themselves as givers, not takers?

The responsible thing, he supposed, was to set up a foundation and hire administrators to ensure that his hard-earned funds were dispensed wisely.

Ah, but here Ebenezer Armstrong was uniquely fortunate: He had the perfect vehicle through which to start giving back— this clinic that Haines had proposed.

So—how did he really feel about Trevor Haines? Until the hypnotherapy session and his "operation," he would have classified him as a lightweight—a clever and amusing dilettante, but certainly no one to get involved with in a major undertaking.

And now? Clay had just been given a reprieve from certain death. A prolonged and exceedingly painful death. Thanks to Haines. He did not know what Haines had done, but he did know there was nothing spontaneous about his remission.

So, while Clay Armstrong still had reservations about Trevor Haines (and he'd be kidding himself, if he pretended otherwise), he was going ahead. They would build the ARC.

He went to bed and slept soundly. In the morning, he made coffee, struck the tent, and packed up the Land Cruiser. Checking his watch, he calculated he would be home before noon. He'd done what he'd set out to do, when he came up here yesterday: made up his mind about going ahead with Haines, and come to grips with the death of Dorothy.

Except, he was not doing too well processing the reality of her death. A moment ago he had almost called her, to find out if she'd heard from Ed and Nigel how their deal had gone in New York.

As soon as he was on I-93 South and more or less running on autopilot, he did turn on the cell phone, and found that he had a voicemail message to call Chief Burke. Immediately.

"Chief? You wanted to talk to me?"

"Yes. You should have told me you were leaving town."

"It was only for one day."

"Doesn't matter; you're a principal suspect in a murder investigation."

"Sorry," he said, meaning it.

"Well, I thought you'd be interested to know that they've found the car that Dorothy Hanson had rented. In the woods, off the Mid-Cape. Apparently she'd been run off the road, between exits 9 and 10."

"Any clues?"

"They found her shoes. Apparently she'd kicked them off, trying to get away on foot." Pause. "Oh, and one other thing: She may have been run off the road. There were several scrapes with black paint on the rear end of her vehicle. We're having it analyzed. Just thought you'd want to know."

"Thanks, Chief," he said, not meaning it.

He did not tell him about the possibility that there might be a third person with some peripheral knowledge of Dorothy's mission. Or that he'd managed to ding the right front bumper of his Land Cruiser. His black Land Cruiser.

19 | mid-life crisis

IT HAD BEEN A GREAT PARTY, Ban Caulfield thought, one of their all-time best. A sumptuous buffet, with the weather staying warm enough for most of their forty guests to be outside on the deck—and a long and lingering sunset. It painted the scattered clouds with gradually deepening shades of red-purple, as the Irish folk group *Skellig Michael* alternated haunting, plaintive ballads with lively toe-tappers that reminded everyone of *Riverdance*.

The guests had departed, the clean-up was done, and the last load of dishes was in the dishwasher. Ban and Betsy Caulfield were out on the deck, enjoying the afterglow.

"In a way," Ban said in mellow reflection, "this is the best part."

"Everyone had a wonderful time," his wife replied. "As they left, they said so, but I think they really meant it."

"You throw a great party."

"It was your party, too."

Ban nodded. "More than once tonight, I thought: It doesn't get any better than this—even though I hate that cliché." He looked out at Provincetown's tiny lights on the northern horizon. "Ever thought how lucky we are to be here? To have the friends we have? Ten years—if we'd stayed in Roanoke, we'd have maybe three couples we felt this close to."

"More like two," she mused. "We didn't have any idea what we were getting into."

He smiled. "Our friends thought we were crazy. Me, leaving the paper, just when I'd become features editor."

"And me walking away from the Colonial Dames, after my aunts had worked so hard to get me in. And both of us leaving the club, when we'd *finally* made it to the top of the A ladder!" She shook her head. "Moving to Cape Cod to join a religious community—Aunt Till called it just plain crazy!"

"There were times I thought she was right," said Ban smiling. "But it's been worth it. Young Ban at Tufts, en route to med school, and Rachel," he chuckled at the thought of their 14-year-old, "bravely coping with each *crise du jour*—we've got a lot to be grateful for."

She gave him a wry smile. "Try to remember that, the next time you're asked to spend a morning weeding in the abbey's vegetable gardens, or organizing a bike ride for the middle schoolers."

They both laughed.

She shivered. "I'm going in."

"I think I'll stay out a little longer. Leave the dishes; I'll put them away when I come in."

Through the sliding glass door, he could see her curled up on her favorite end of the sofa with the latest Mary Higgins Clark. He realized again how fortunate he was to have her. Down-to-earth practical, full of common sense, she was the perfect foil for his romanticism. It was pretty obvious now, that their marriage had been made in heaven. She was not the sort of partner he might have wanted, but clearly the sort he needed, to keep him anchored in reality.

Then why—

He did not allow his mind to go there. Instead, he gazed at the faint yellowish smear on the northwest horizon. That would be Boston, 40 miles away and well below the line of sight. Sometimes in the night sky, you could see pinpricks of light coming towards it from the right—planes descending on final approach to Logan.

Ban was 44, a journalist turned historical novelist. He'd always wanted to be a writer. When he graduated from The University (in Virginia there was only one University, though graduates of Washington & Lee or VMI would take strong exception to that), he was fortunate enough to get a job on the Roanoke *Tribune*. Ten years later, he'd become features editor— pretty fast-track for 33.

And then he'd had the Accident.

Each year on Memorial Day weekend the Caulfield clan gathered at the Homestead. Many families did the same at the old resort, and while Ban did not look forward to it, he could not duck it. His great-grandfather had instituted the gathering and his grandfather had made it clear that they were expected to attend.

Moreover, they would go riding. All the Caulfield men rode. It was in their blood, their grandfather said. Caulfields had ridden with Jeb Stuart in the War to Repel the Northern Invader. A few of the South Carolina Caulfields, Tories to the core, had even ridden with the British against the rebels, and one had named his son after Lord Cornwallis's Commander of Cavalry, Banastre Tarleton.

The cavalry gene had skipped the third Caulfield to bear that name. But as much as Ban hated riding, his grandfather's call to horse was not optional. So he rode with the others, dreading the cavalry charge that traditionally ended their rides.

Sure enough, as his mount (almost) cleared a stone wall, he'd been thrown, striking his head on the way down. When he didn't revive, help was sent for, and he was rushed to the hospital.

As he came to, he heard the examining doctor tell Betsy it was a miracle that he was still alive. That, except for a severe concussion, he was otherwise unharmed.

To everyone's surprise including his own, Ban took the doctor's assessment seriously. In his heart, he knew his life had been spared for a purpose; now his head demanded an explanation.

It was two weeks before he was fit to drive again. The moment he was, he'd sought out Father Dowell, the Episcopal priest for whom he'd once served as an acolyte. He found him in Richmond, in a graduated-care facility for retired priests. Spinal stenosis had just about invalided him, and cataracts clouded his eyes. But the old cleric's inner vision was perfectly clear.

He remembered Ban and was not entirely surprised at his visit. "I pray for all my boys. Every day. So," he smiled, "I thought maybe one day you'd come."

Ban told him his reason for coming.

"Well," the old priest responded, "if God did extend your life, why do you suppose He did?"

"Father, I don't even know if God exists!" He didn't want to hurt the old man's feelings, but after coming all this way, there was no point being less than totally honest.

The priest nodded. "Do you think He does exist?"

"Sort of. I used to. My grandmother did. But there's—" Ban hesitated.

"So much evidence to the contrary?"

"Yeah," replied the younger man, relieved. "I mean, it's comforting to think there's someone up there who cares, and that there's an afterlife—all that stuff. Grandma believed it. And if it's true," he said smiling, "there's no doubt she's up there."

"You said you *used* to believe—when was that?"

"When I served at the altar with you." He paused, going back in his mind. "At Communion, when you said it was the transformed body and blood of Christ." He paused. "I knew that somehow it was true."

"It still is."

"But I was only 13, Father! I went away to prep school and The University—it never seemed real after that."

The old priest looked out the window. Ban was not sure he could see what was out there, but there was no question he was seeing something.

"Do you ever pray?" asked Father Dowell.

"Only when they announce we're turning back to the airport, because of engine trouble," Ban responded with a chuckle.

Father Dowell was serious. "But now you think maybe He may have spared your life—why would He do that?"

Ban frowned. "That's what I came to find out from you."

"If you came from Roanoke, it took you more than three hours to get here. You must have thought *some* about it."

The younger man nodded without answering.

"What occurred to you, Banastre?"

The latter was startled; no one had called him that since his mother died. "Well," he said, at length, "if it was God, He wants me to live—differently."

"How?"

"I don't know. More for Him. Less for me." He grimaced. "This sounds awful, but I don't even want to *say* that, because putting it in words—legitimatizes it. Gives it power."

Father Dowell tilted his head. "And you don't want to do that—why?"

Ban slammed his palm down on the arm of his chair. "Don't you know how to do anything but ask 'why'?"

"Sure," said Father Dowell with a smile, "lots of things. But why don't you want to answer it?"

"There you go again!"

Father Dowell was unperturbed. "My son, you've driven a long way. And you thought a long time before deciding to come. You want an answer. And before you leave, you'll have one—*if* you cooperate with the process."

"Which means?"

"Answering questions that begin with why."

With a sigh, Ban acquiesced. "Okay."

"Why don't you want to admit He might want you to live for Him?"

Ban was angry now, and he no longer cared about the old priest's feelings. "Because I've met some of those people, and you know what? They're wackos!"

"What people?"

"The ones who raise their hands and go around praising God!" He tapped the side of his head. "They're nuts!"

Father Dowell laughed. "Banastre, you're an Episcopalian! Of *course* they're going to seem crazy!" He paused and then murmured, "God's frozen people," and laughed some more.

"I don't see what's so funny!"

The old priest made an attempt at a more serious demeanor. "Would you like to meet some people who are trying to put God first, and who won't seem crazy? There's a choir coming to Roanoke in a few weeks. You should go hear them. I've met them, and I think you'll be impressed. And," he smiled, "a number of them are Episcopalians."

◆

Ban took Betsy to the concert, during which she kept whispering to him how good they were (she'd sung at Briarcliff). At the reception afterwards, he discovered that the singers were members of an ecumenical abbey on Cape Cod, that many had been to college, and that, as promised, there were even Episcopalians among them.

He found himself asking a great many questions that began with why. The more he heard, the more intrigued he became, until he decided that the *Tribune's* readers would appreciate a feature about this unusual abbey. And since he was the features editor. . . .

That was how he'd come—and he never left. During his initial visit, he and Betsy, who'd accompanied him, had been invited to join one of the small weekend retreats that the abbey hosted. They did, and in the course of it, determined to put God first in their lives.

Ban soon decided it was too much of a story to cover in a light Sunday feature. He took an unpaid sabbatical from the paper to do a proper book—and never went back. At the end of that summer he and Betsy felt God calling them to become members of the abbey. He never did finish that book, but he wrote an historical novel—a decidedly unflattering portrait of his namesake, destined to earn him the enduring enmity of the South Carolina Caulfields. *The Butcher of Cowpens* did well enough that the publisher wanted another, and thereafter he'd turned out about one a year.

He squinted at the tiny lights to the north, trying to distinguish which belonged to Wellfleet and which to Provincetown.

He was 44 now, and no longer as enchanted with abbey life as he had been. Betsy still was—in fact, more now than ever. She was in the touring choir, and had recently become involved with the effort of some of the abbey families to start home-schooling their children. With young Ban at college, it would affect only their daughter, Rachel.

Just before he left, his son had taken his own formal vow to become a member of the abbey. His mother had been so proud of him that day! After the vows service, she had squeezed her husband's arm and whispered that she had never dreamed she could feel so—fulfilled.

He'd hugged her then, and the next day he'd gone down to Hyannis, and using most of his last royalty check had bought her a new station wagon, a dark blue Saab 9-5. Just because he loved her.

But he also envied her. She was excited about what she was doing, looking forward to what each day held in store. And everything she did, she did well. And was thus in great demand. She was so busy, in fact, that he practically had to make an appointment to have a serious talk with her.

He'd tried once, to tell her how he felt. He waited until after ten, when the hum-level in the house finally subsided, and the phone would not ring. Where phones were concerned, the abbey observed Grand Silence, refraining from calling one another between ten at night and eight in the morning (except in emergencies).

That night, just as he was getting to the hard part—that he was 44 and all was not well—the phone rang. It was one of Betsy's friends, with a personal crisis that only Betsy could resolve. Half an hour later, the caller felt better, but Ban was no longer in the mood to share his own personal crisis. He didn't try again.

Each day he sat in his office, gazing out at the bay, writing novels about families opening the West and surviving the Civil War. Novels with strong romantic themes, in which the women always had time to listen to the men; in fact, there was nothing they would rather do.

Like the woman he would be meeting tomorrow.

But he did not let his mind go there.

20 | not by chance

BAN CAULFIELD CHECKED THE COMPUTER on his handlebars: he was averaging 20.4 miles per hour. Not bad for a Sunday afternoon in October, considering he wasn't pushing it. There was no one on the bike path ahead of him, or (he checked his mirror) behind him, either. The path, on an old railroad right-of-way that ran from Dennis nearly to Wellfleet, was a blessing for walkers and nature lovers of every stripe and variety. As it ran through dune and marsh, you could see fox and deer, and occasionally a huge turtle.

But Ban seldom used it. For a serious cyclist, it was infinitely more hazardous than the road. Even the Mid-Cape was preferable, except at the peak of the season, when it was often bumper to bumper. Those who were convinced they knew what was best for others, would have preferred that all cyclists be restricted to the bike path. But for anyone traveling faster than a leisurely pace, it was dangerous. Cape Cod had a leash law, which many dog owners routinely ignored when they were on the path. There were tots on training wheels, hot dogs on roller blades, and mini machos on dirt bikes who were convinced they were live-action figures in some video game.

But the bike path's greatest hazard was white-haired octogenarians determined not to go peaceably into that dark night. On bicycles they'd not ridden in half a century, they were so unsure of themselves that if you came up behind them and gently said, "Coming by on your left," they would invariably *turn* left, directly into your path. The safest thing was simply to blow past them without warning. It might terrify them, but at least left them upright—though Ban dreaded the day he'd see in his mirror someone he'd just passed, clutching his heart.

For Ban, cycling had become a positive addiction, much as running had for many younger, thinner fitness buffs. A runner once himself, he'd gotten his 10K down to 43 minutes, when his knees started to go. That was when he'd reluctantly switched to cycling. Then one day, gliding downhill in Nickerson State Park, it had clicked, and he'd never looked back. To compare running with cycling now, was like comparing cross-country skiing with downhill. The former might be invigorating, but the latter was sheer excitement.

The excitement, of course, was addictive. The faster he got, the faster he wanted to go. And since he was in good condition, improvement was solely dependent upon hours per week in the saddle. He'd gotten his time for ten miles (39 laps around the Orleans rotary) down to 26:22, but further improvement was unlikely; he was already riding 120 miles a week and would have to up that to 150, to go any faster. Still, 22.8 mph was not bad for a 44-year-old recreational cyclist—a far cry from Greg Lemond's legendary 34 mph charge down the Champs-Elysées to win the Tour de France by eight seconds in 1989. But not bad.

If he thought about it (and he was careful not to), he was spending an inordinate amount of time cycling—at a time when he could ill afford to: His current project was in serious jeopardy. His final deadline—as in done, or dead—was the end of Thanksgiving weekend, if it was going to make its already-announced May pub date. Today was October 8, and the working draft was still not finished. He had six more chapters to go—and then a complete re-write. It would be a miracle, if he got it done on time—and he did not feel particularly in line for one.

Worse, he sensed that the publisher might be looking for an excuse to terminate their relationship. The sales of his historical novels had plateaued some years ago, and the last two had fallen off the plateau. When that happened, he'd thought of changing publishers. But it wasn't the publisher's fault, he came to realize; the country's tastes were changing.

People wanted shorter books with shorter chapters, a writer friend told him. The average reader no longer had the attention span to get through anything longer than a *Time* magazine article, before turning out the light. Zip it up, another said; people's taste buds had become jaded. You had to give them a shot of Tabasco—you know, *Laissez les bons temps rouler.*

But Ban refused to change (he called it compromise). And so his sales dwindled, and the reviews cooled. One particularly nasty reviewer wondered if Banastre Caulfield were not the rakish *nom de plume* of an old-maid history teacher from Dubuque. That got on the Internet, which meant it got *everywhere,* until even his friends were embarrassed for him.

He checked ahead and in his mirror; the bike path was still deserted. Where was she?

Arriving at the semicircular rest area north of Eastham, where they'd first met, he dismounted and sat down to wait. On a Sunday afternoon two months before, he'd gotten a flat and pulled in here to change the inner tube—only to discover that the spare which he kept in his emergency repair kit under his seat, was not there. Then he remembered: He'd given it to Brother Bartholomew who'd flatted without a spare, and then forgotten to replace it when he got home. Great! Six miles from Eastport and two miles from the nearest phone.

He was contemplating riding home on the rim, when a woman on a celeste green Bianchi had passed by. "Got everything you need?" she cheerily hailed him. It was traditional road courtesy, to which the traditional reply was, "Thanks, I'm fine." It was almost Ban's reply, until he realized it was only male pride keeping him from telling the truth. "Um," he called after her, "you wouldn't have a spare tube, would you?"

She'd stopped and turned around and come back. "Yup. You got everything else?"

He nodded, grinning sheepishly. "I thought I had a tube, too, only I gave it to someone."

She got a tube out of her kit—which was better equipped than his, he noted—then stuck out her hand. "Saralinda Armstrong," she announced forthrightly, looking him in the eye and giving him a firm handshake, just as her mother had taught her.

"Ban Caulfield. This is the first time this has ever happened to me."

"The first time you've ever had a flat?" she asked, incredulous.

"No," he replied laughing, "the first time I haven't had the fixings."

When he'd changed the tube and re-inflated the tire, they rode the rest of the bike path together. And found that they agreed on just about everything.

The next Sunday he happened (by chance, he assured himself) to be on the same stretch of bike path at the same time. And sure enough, she had come along, and they had ridden together. All the way down to Dennis this time, and he bought her a Coke, before they returned.

The third Sunday, it was not by chance that he was there. And every Sunday since.

21 | the game

MONDAY MORNING, eight days after they had left for New York (and five days after the discovery of their colleague's body), Ed Forester guided the old green Camry wagon past Joe's Bar and Grill and up the bluffs road, trying to tune out his passenger.

"I can't wait to see the Old Man's face," Nigel Rawlings exclaimed, "when we tell him how we got the winning bid!"

Forester made no reply. He had undertaken to school Nigel in the finer points of high-stakes venture capitalism, but after nine days in New York with him, Ed's patience was frayed nearly to the breaking point.

Hiring Nigel had been Dorothy's idea. One morning, when both he and Clay were feeling a bit creaky, she'd pointed out that neither of them was getting any younger. They were, in fact—she'd leaned back and assessed them with a critical eye—both getting a bit long in the tooth. A&A had grown to the point where they really needed a junior partner—someone to stay up nights worrying, while they both took some serious anti-heart attack measures. Like sleeping.

They'd acknowledged she was right, but being loathe to tamper with what had become an unbeatable combination, they'd done nothing to implement it.

In the end, they didn't have to. A brash young (well, 32) Wall Street gunslinger named Nigel Rawlings had contacted them. He'd been observing their play for several years, he informed them, and the more he saw, the more he liked. Like them, he was not happy anywhere but at the high-stakes table, and like them, he seldom lost. But they had finesse that he lacked. They could teach him more in a year than he could learn in several years on his own.

So he had a proposal for them: He would work for them for one year, as their indentured servant, as it were. If he quit before the year was up, or if he gave them just cause to terminate their contract with him, they would owe him—nothing.

If, on the other hand, he pleased them and demonstrated that he would fit smoothly into their operation—as he was supremely confident that he would—then on November 1, one year from the day he officially joined them, they would pay him one million dollars. *Plus* 5 percent of the firm's gross every year thereafter.

It was outrageous! But—fair. And exactly suited to Clay's and Ed's temperaments. They signed the contract and dealt Nigel in at the high-stakes table. Now, in 22 more days, his year would be up, and they would pay him a million dollars. And in the following year his share of their profits would probably run three or four times that. No matter, he had proven well worth it.

And on the New York trip they were returning from, he'd shown just how good he really was. His preparation had been flawless, and he had stayed ice-cold, when the other side was sweating. Forester would tell Clay that Nigel was going to make a valuable addition to their operation.

But as a conversationalist, the kid was so two-dimensional that Forester began finding excuses to spend as little time alone with him as possible. All Nigel could talk about was how they had just scored or would soon score. And while the venture capital game was Forester's life, even *he* needed a break from it, from time to time. There *were* other things in life besides doing deals.

Which, he smiled grimly, had been Amanda's exact words, when she'd given him the ultimatum.

"I hate Cape Cod!" she'd declared, when he informed her that Clay was moving the firm there. "I went to summer camp there when I was fat, and was teased the whole time—'Manda, the Panda,' they called me. I swore I'd never go back!"

"Come on, honey," he'd cajoled, "you're not fat now, and you don't have to go to camp, and no one's going to call you—" and then he made the terrible mistake of starting to laugh.

She froze. "I'm not going! If you go, you're going alone!"

"Be reasonable," he'd pleaded. "The letterhead doesn't say Armstrong & Forester; it says Armstrong & Associates. If Clay wants to relocate to Cape Cod, that's where we're going."

"Not we, paleface. You. Choose."

"Mand, it's my life!"

That's when she'd said the words.

Later, when she'd calmed down, he'd tried to give her some idea of how important the work was to him. "It's a passion, really," he mused, seeking an analogy that would convey it. "It's like aerial combat. We're fighter pilots, with Clay the top gun and me his wingman, keeping the bad guys off of him."

"You make it sound like some kind of game," she said with dripping sarcasm.

"It *is* a game; the money's just a way of keeping score."

"Well, I'll grant you're good at it," she admitted. "We've got more money than we'll ever need. I just don't see why you can't do it in New York."

"Because I'm Clay's partner, and he wants to do it on Cape Cod!"

"And you can do it only with him?"

He nodded. "He's the best. I knew that, when he out-maneuvered me five years ago. I knew that, no matter how good I got, I would never be as good as him." He shrugged. "So I joined him. And now, *nobody* is as good as we are."

She still wasn't getting it.

He tried harder. "When I'm doing a deal with Clay, all my senses are sharpened. My awareness is heightened. It's like I'm on something! There's millions on the table, and we could lose it all—or double it!"

"A couple of risk junkies," she muttered.

"Sometimes at the end of the day we're both soaked with sweat, but the adrenalin is still pumping. So we play darts and drink beer, until we come down."

"You make it sound like sex," Amanda retorted with disgust. She suddenly tilted her head. "You and Clay, you're not—"

He laughed. "It's nothing like that. Actually, it's a lot *better* than that."

She sighed. "I almost wish it *was* that; then I'd be able to understand it."

She never did understand. When he moved to the Cape, he gave her an uncontested divorce and a more generous settlement than any lawyer would have asked for. He didn't care; it was only money.

He never looked back. Buying a townhouse in Eastport's Teal Pond Estates, Forester soon became involved with a Realtor who loved her work as much as he loved his. They never married; there was no reason to.

He *was* a risk junkie, he supposed, as he turned into *Fallingwater East*. The stakes were higher now than they'd ever been. So high, that other venture capitalists who didn't have the heart or stomach for the technical climbing they were now doing,

nonetheless had enough confidence in them to form a pool that
A&A could tap, any time they wanted to increase their position
tenfold.

And what they were doing really *was* like climbing sheer
rock faces and overhangs without a rope. There you were,
two thousand feet above the valley floor, hanging from your
fingers and the pitons you were driving, your life literally in
your hands. You took your time, planning each move with
infinite care, fighting down fear as it welled in your throat. In
extreme climbing, there were no second chances. One mistake,
and you would be plummeting earthward, screaming your last
scream.

But—if you conquered your fear and summited, the wild,
heart-pounding exhilaration was unlike anything you'd ever
known in your life!

They got out of the car, and Clay came to the front door to
meet them.

"Scratch one flat-top!" exulted Nigel. "Wait till you hear how
it went! I mean, we were *good!*"

"In a minute," Clay nodded, smiling. "Ed, I need to have a
word with you."

Forester followed him into his office, surprised when Clay
shut the door. "What is it?"

Clay told him of her drowning.

"I—I can't believe it! Dorothy!" His eyes brimmed. "Who's
going to show us the way to Oz?"

Two months before, Clay, in an uncharacteristically whim-
sical mood, had organized a surprise birthday party for her.
("Never mind which one!") They were to come as the sidekicks
of the Wizard of Oz Dorothy. Clay would be the Scarecrow, he,
the Tin Woodsman, and Nigel, the Cowardly Lion.

"Why do I have to be the Cowardly Lion?" Nigel had objected.

"Because you're the newie," Forester had explained.

Now, he was in shock.

"Ed, there's something else. Which I'd rather you hear from me, than later on."

He filled Ed in on the horrible details surrounding Dorothy's drowning.

"If I find whoever did it before the police do," he said quietly, "there won't need to be a trial."

Clay nodded. "My sentiments exactly."

Forester looked at him. "She was over there doing something for you, wasn't she?" Clay nodded. "That have anything to do with it?"

"Might have," admitted Clay, without elaborating.

◆

Brother Bartholomew was coming out of Lauds, when his pager vibrated. He glanced down: It was the Chief's number. Odd, he'd just spoken with him the day before, and other than the paint analysis there hadn't been any new developments, or any likelihood of them any time soon.

The paint was interesting, though. Dorothy's car had been run off the road by a black Mercedes. An *old* black Mercedes— at least, older than 1982, when Daimler-Benz changed the paint formula on all their models. His heart went out to Dan Burke, who must feel even more frustrated: What were they supposed to do now? Interview everyone in southern New England who owns an old black Mercedes? He had just prayed for his friend; the stress must be unbearable.

He found out how unbearable, when he returned the call. Peg answered: "We're at the hospital. Dan's had another episode, the worst yet, and he's scheduled for angioplasty in an hour."

"I'll be there, as fast as I can."

Bartholomew set a new Eastport-to-Hyannis land speed record (moderate traffic), arriving 23 minutes later—to find Peg and the EPD's Sergeant Whipple and Officer Allen gathered around the Chief's bed. All wore expressions of concern— except the Chief, who was beaming.

"Look at you!" Bartholomew scolded. "Everyone's miserable, and you're—delighted!"

"Hey," responded the Chief, "*you* called this party! If you don't like it, call it off!"

Peg explained that after her husband had called Doc Finlay, the latter had insisted that the Chief take a stress test. Which indicated that an angiogram was called for. Which indicated that angioplasty was called for. Immediately.

But "immediately" seemed to have a different connotation for the Chief, who put it off—until the paint analysis administered its own stress test. "And," his wife concluded, "if the balloon doesn't work, they'll have to do a by-pass and—"

"Spare him the grim stuff, Peg," said her husband. "He gets the picture!" He turned to Bartholomew. "Obviously, I'm going to be sidelined for awhile. I'm counting on you," he shifted his gaze to include all of them, "all three of you, to keep the momentum going."

What momentum? thought Bartholomew, but he said nothing.

"Armstrong still looks like the prime subject, unless we hear otherwise from Interpol." The Chief shook his head and smiled. "But now I'm going to sound like our monk here, with his blasted intuition! Honest to God, I don't think he did it."

He turned to Bartholomew. "Go out there tomorrow and talk to him. See what *you* think. Then report back to me."

"No," interjected Peg, "report back to *him!*" She pointed at Sergeant Whipple. "Nobody is going to report *anything* to Daniel F. X. Burke, until the doctor says so! And he promised me the recovery period would be at least a week!"

They raised their eyebrows at her sudden vehemence. And silently nodded assent.

Bartholomew stayed with Peg during the operation. "You're

the best friend he's got," she said, her voice shaking. "But if you care for him, you won't let him get so run down."

He nodded. "I'll do my best, Peg, but you know how hard-headed he can be."

"Yes, I do." And she started to cry.

He put an arm around her to comfort her, and as she wept on his shoulder, he was grateful that his long-ago feelings for her remained just that: long ago. Nonetheless, he was relieved when her elder son arrived.

"Mom, I came as soon as I heard. How is he?"

"He's fine—now," she managed.

And in an hour, the doctor emerged to inform them that he was indeed fine.

22 | final courage

THE NEXT MORNING, Brother Bartholomew parked the old red pick-up in one of the spaces under the carved black oval sign with gold trim that announced the location of Eastport Cyclery. And sat in the truck.

Of all the difficult things his call required of him, the worst was having to ask people for money or favors. His father, Buck Doane, had never done it; neither had his grandfather. Doanes didn't ask for help, his father had taught him. You never bought on credit, never put yourself in a position where you would have to rely on the kindness of strangers. It was a tough code, particularly for commercial fishermen whose work was seasonal and unpredictable. But the Doanes had lived by that code, and it had brought honor to them—as it had to Andrew Doane, until he had become Brother Bartholomew.

Then he had to learn that relinquishing the right to own, to choose, and to marry—how they referred to their vows of poverty, chastity, and obedience—carried a caveat. No longer belonging to themselves, they had to allow God to show His love for them through the generosity of others. He had gone to Columba about it, as he did with everything that troubled him.

"Would you, for the sake of your pride, deny someone the blessing," his mentor had challenged him, "that comes with being inspired by the Holy Spirit to do something spontaneously kind?"

The young monk had no answer.

"Would you deny them the double blessing that comes from giving to an individual or group who has given up everything in response to God's call?"

Bartholomew remained silent. Not because he didn't know the correct answer, but because he could not, in honesty, give it. Then or now.

But neither could he sit here in this truck all morning. Lord, he finally prayed, you know how much I loathe this. And I know you want me to do it. So, change my heart. And give me the right words.

With that, he got out of the truck and went into the bike shop. The owner, Tim Miller, was at his work stand, adjusting the cables on a just-out-of-the-box mountain bike.

"Brother Bart!" Tim declared with a smile, "How's that derailleur working?"

"Smooth as silk," Bartholomew said with a grin. "Hard to believe new pulley wheels could make such a difference. And thanks, too, for fixing Brother Ambrose's clunker. He's hasn't had any problems since."

"Hey," the owner said smiling, "when we fix 'em, they stay fixed." He wiped his hands on a shop rag. "What can I do for you?"

Bartholomew hesitated. There was nothing to do but plunge in. "Some of the other Brothers are going to start riding. Getting into shape. They've got a couple of old beater bikes, but they're rusted and, well, pretty hopeless." He hesitated. "I was wondering—"

"Bring them in," Tim offered, "and we'll have a look at them." Then he smiled. "I've also taken in a couple of old road bikes as trade-ins I'd be willing to let you have."

The Bartholomew grinned. "That's great! I'll stop by this afternoon."

"Keep praying for my niece," said Tim, as they shook hands.

"We will," Bartholomew called over his shoulder.

As he got back in his truck, he wondered: Why had he been so reluctant to ask?

As he put the old red pickup in gear and headed for East Bluffs, he noted it was running rough. He should take it in to Eastport Auto Service and have Rick Cantrell look at it. But Rick, who'd been keeping the abbey's aging fleet afloat for twenty years, would probably tell him it was time to let it go to the old pickups' graveyard, and he didn't want to hear that now.

He'd grown attached to this old truck, and it didn't take a whole lot of discernment to figure out why. His father, Buck Doane, a commercial fisherman who'd been lost at sea while his son was a corpsman in Viet Nam, had had a truck like this—red, too. Besides, the old truck just *fit*. That was not too hard to figure out, either, since it was mainly *his* seat that had broken in *its* seat.

He was not looking forward to the next thing on the morning's agenda. The Chief had asked him to call on Clayton Armstrong and form an assessment. All he knew about the man who'd built the Frank Lloyd Wright house over on East Bluffs was what the Chief had told him. But if he were Armstrong, he would mightily resent some monk intruding into the very private matter of his office manager's death.

Worse, Bartholomew hadn't a clue what he was looking for, as he turned in to the driveway of the weird-looking copy of *Fallingwater*. He grimaced at the equally weird-looking copy of Rodin's *Balzac* on the front lawn and tried to imagine the sort of person who would want such things, let alone put them in such harsh juxtaposition.

All at once, he chuckled. Clearly these were a few of his favorite things. And this Armstrong fellow did not care one whit about what people thought of his taste. Well, he shrugged, time to find out. He rang the bell.

When the houseman arrived, Bartholomew stated his business. The former disappeared and in a moment returned. "Mr. Armstrong is having breakfast on the terrace, if you would care to join him."

"Look, if he's busy," said Bartholomew, distinctly uncomfortable, "I can come back later."

"No," James assured him, "he would like to see you now."

He found Armstrong taking advantage of the unseasonably warm October morning, probably the last in which he would be able to have his breakfast outside. The Atlantic was calm, and so still that it came ashore in little wavelets that made an almost apologetic *plashing* sound.

"You don't look like a monk," said the master of the house, not unkindly.

"Well," Bartholomew looked down at his navy blue windbreaker and khaki pants, "this is what we wear most of the time. We only robe for services and special occasions."

"Would you like some melon, or a cup of coffee?"

"No, thanks, I won't take up much of your time. Chief Burke's in the hospital, Mr. Armstrong. He's asked me to assist in the investigation. In particular, he wanted me to show you this key again, to see if it triggered anything you might remember, or could tell us about it." Removing the key from its bag, he handed it to his seated host.

The latter took it and was examining it, when it slipped from his grasp and fell into his breakfast, specifically onto the stick of butter. "Clumsy of me," Armstrong muttered, inadvertently pressing it even deeper into the butter, as he sought to retrieve it. Wiping it off, he handed it back to the monk. "Sorry about that."

Bartholomew was aware of what had just transpired, but he chose not to make anything of it, instead asking, "What do you make of it?"

"Well, as I told the Chief, it looks like a safe deposit box key. But I've no idea where such a box might be. Do you think my—property—might be there?"

Bartholomew shrugged and said nothing, not taking his eyes off the mirror-calm sea.

"I've talked to the manager of RKL Investments up in Boston," Armstrong offered. "He said Dorothy left the bank the moment she took delivery."

"Yes, that's what he told the Chief."

Armstrong's eyes widened. "It seems our local constabulary is more proficient than I'd given them credit for."

"Well, you know," replied Bartholomew with a smile, "When the foeman bares his steel, your tax dollars go to work." His smile faded. "When she realized she was in danger, she might have stopped at a bank—either one where she already had a box, whose key she kept with her, or," he got up and walked over to the low stone retaining wall, to observe the wavelets far below, "one where she was so well known, she could obtain a box quickly enough that her pursuers wouldn't realize what she'd done."

Armstrong stared at him. "Do all monks think like you?"

"I hope not," Bartholomew chuckled. "It's a knack I seem to have picked up recently."

"Why do you say they didn't know what she'd done?"

Bartholomew hesitated; he'd not even told the Chief this. But if Armstrong was their man, the more pressure they could bring to bear on him, the better. "If they'd known, they wouldn't have tortured her."

He turned back to the sea and watched a lone gull gliding

along the bluffs at eye level. When he spoke, it was slowly—more to himself than to Armstrong. "She must have known she could not hold out. That even if they found out what they wanted, they'd never let her live."

A cloud passed over the sun, and the temperature on the terrace dropped. Shivering, Armstrong suggested they adjourn to the adjacent library. There, under the gaze of Mrs. Armstrong's portrait, Bartholomew put himself in the victim's place: "She's determined they're not going to win. It's night, and they're in a storm. If she can get over the side. . . ."

He glanced at Armstrong who was visibly unnerved, and hesitated. And then went on. "She throws herself overboard. And once she's in the water, she's able to evade them by ducking under the surface each time their light sweeps towards her."

Bartholomew's scalp tightened; this was a little *too* real. "What incredible courage! On the verge of drowning, everything in her wants to scream. But she keeps silent."

"Stop!" pleaded Armstrong, "I don't want to hear any more!"

"There's just one other thing," Bartholomew went on relentlessly. "She knows there'll be an autopsy when they find her. And the diamond and the key will mean something to someone." He looked at his host. "That someone can only be you, Mr. Armstrong."

"I think you should go," gasped Armstrong, shaking.

Bartholomew nodded and opened the door out onto the terrace, then turned back. "I'm sorry; I think she loved you very much."

23 | the twain meet

CLAYTON ARMSTRONG STOOD shaking, his eyes brimming, in the library of *Fallingwater East*, when a silhouette appeared at the door to the living room. It was Trevor Haines. Under his arm were some long, rolled-up papers. "I thought you might want to see a set of preliminary sketches for the clinic I had drawn up. I realize they're preliminary, but they can give us a reference point on which to build."

He went to the old nautical chart table, and unfurled them, weighing down the corners with a conch shell, a large leaded glass fish, a Steuben ashtray, and a copy of Peterson's *Field Guide to Eastern Birds*. "Now here's where the reception area will be, and these are counseling rooms—" He paused and looked up at his host, who had not moved. "Clay, what's the matter? What's happened?"

"Someone was just here, about Dorothy Hanson's death. It was—upsetting."

"I can see that," said Haines solicitously, as he came around the table to put a comforting arm around his friend. "Who was it?"

"Someone the Chief of Police had sent. A monk from the abbey."

"A *monk*? Where is he?" he demanded, coldly.

"He just went out on the terrace. He may still be out there, for all I know."

"We'll see," murmured Haines.

As he went out on the sunlit terrace, Brother Bartholomew shielded his eyes from the bright sunlight. He yawned, suddenly tired—so tired, all he wanted to do was go home and take a nap. Which he hardly ever did in the middle of the day.

Before walking the length of the terrace to the steps that would lead to the lawn and the front of the house where his truck was, he went over to the railing. He was fascinated by the stillness of the sea. Flat and dully shining, it looked like rink ice, waiting for the first skater.

That had been a heavy session in there with Armstrong, cruel on the surface of it. But the man clearly knew where the key fit, and had clearly attempted to make an impression of it in the butter. He'd had to get to the core of Armstrong's emotions, and was pretty sure he had. Whatever Armstrong might be hiding, Bartholomew was convinced he had nothing to do with the death of Dorothy Hanson. Which was what the Chief had sent him out here to ascertain. In which case, mission accomplished.

But had he gone too far? Did the end—getting Armstrong to spill what he was withholding—justify the means? It was a matter of life and death, *literally*, his head argued.

Then why did he feel so—crummy? Why did he feel like he needed—absolution?

A shadow fell across the railing next to him, and he turned to see who had come so silently up behind him. Squinting into the sun, he couldn't make him out, other than that it was someone he didn't know.

A thin man, well groomed, long blond hair, aquiline nose, and dark, very dark eyes.

"Who are you," the man demanded, "and what are you doing here?" His tone and bearing were such that if Bartholomew had not already met Armstrong, he would assume this was the master of the house.

"I'm Brother Bartholomew. I'm here at the request of Chief Burke. May I ask who you are?"

"No, I mean, what are you *really* here for?"

Bartholomew contemplated just turning and walking away. But whoever this person was, he was obviously here at Armstrong's bidding—and was, therefore, part of his reason for coming. "I came here to see Mr. Armstrong, and I was just leaving."

The other man softened. Somewhat. "Well, don't let me detain you."

But now Bartholomew was curious. Who was this arrogant, peremptory— "I'm sorry, I didn't get your name."

"Trevor Haines. I'm a business associate of Mr. Armstrong's." He did not hold out his hand.

Now Bartholomew was more than curious. He looked into the man's eyes. The whites were smoky and shot through with fine lines of red, but the pupils—he'd thought they were just dark. But they were like obsidian! He could not see into them. He felt his scalp tighten.

"Don't do that!" Haines commanded.

"Do what?"

"Look at me that way!"

Bartholomew felt something he had not felt in nearly thirty years. Not since Viet Nam. Fear. He felt like running. "I don't know what you're talking about."

Haines glared at him. "You said you'd come to talk to Mr. Armstrong. You've talked to him. Now leave."

There was nothing Bartholomew would rather do. But he was also tired of being ordered around. What he'd really like to do is pitch this guy over that railing, down on the rocks below.

Haines took a step backwards. "I said, leave. And I think it would be wise if you did not return."

Bartholomew shrugged. "I have no reason to. Although I did enjoy my talk with Mr. Armstrong. I wouldn't mind seeing him again."

"You stay away from him, do you hear me?" Haines shouted. "He's mine!"

"What?"

"You heard me!" exclaimed Haines through clenched teeth, struggling to get himself under control.

"Man, you are weird!" muttered Bartholomew, turning to go.

Weird, he repeated to himself, as he got into the pickup.

24 | the lines are drawn

TREVOR HAINES PULLED UP TO THE PAY PHONE outside the Eastport Cyclery and made his call. There was a cell phone installed in the Bentley, but he could not risk the possibility, however remote, of someone with a scanner happening on his call. Not this call.

"Just checking in," he said cheerily, when the call went through.

"What's the situation?"

"Everything's going tickety-boo, tickety—"

"I don't have time for this."

He assumed a more professional attitude. "Everything's proceeding according to plan. Armstrong called me yesterday to tell me he'd gotten the results back from the x-rays: The spots are gone. He also credits me for the healing, and he's decided to build the ARC. In a few more days, he'll be ready for Phase II. This weekend, his daughters are coming for his 65th birthday, and he's planning to tell them about the ARC. Then, a week from Friday, we sign papers, and the ARC becomes a reality."

"Sounds perfect."

"It is."

"Too perfect. Whenever you start off this glowing, I know something's not right. What is it you're not telling me?"

"There's nothing I'm not telling you!" Haines shot back. "Why do you always assume I'm holding something back?"

"Because, dear brother, you always are."

"Well, I'm not now!"

"But if you were . . . if there might be something which I would be unhappy about . . . what would it be?"

He thought for a moment, and then smiled. "That I have no lead on the whereabouts of the diamonds?"

"No. I already know that. Because if you did have, it would have been the first thing out of your mouth. I'm not happy about that, but that's not what's troubling me . . . what *is?*"

Haines winced. "Before I left, I mentioned *them* to Armstrong."

"You did *what?*"

"It's all right; he assumes they're a worldwide consortium, organized to manipulate the commodities market."

"How much did you have to drink?"

"Lena, it wasn't that bad! It was a mere quip—he's already forgotten it."

"I'd have thought you'd learned your lesson out in Sedona! Or down in New Orleans! You know, one more screwup, and—"

Haines shuddered. "Let's keep this positive."

"What you just told me—is still not what's troubling me."

"Well," said Haines, looking as if he were about to be sick, "I don't know if this is it, but there seems to be a monk on the case."

"*What?*"

He repeated it.

"How can that be? Monks don't get involved in police investigations!"

"Apparently this one was invited by the Chief of Police."

"Is he the sort of monk that could be trouble?"

"He's from the friary at Faith Abbey."

"Hmm—considering the abbey's proximity. . . . You're not calling on your cell phone, are you?"

"Of course not!" exclaimed Haines. "What do you take me for!"

"We won't go into that. Who is he?"

"Brother Bartholomew."

"What's your assessment?"

"He's a naïf, but a strong one. I caught him trying to read me."

Pause. "I would advise you, between now and next Friday, to exercise *extreme* caution. Do *not* let your ego slip its leash. And keep your tongue bridled, which means no alcohol."

"Don't worry; I want this as badly as you do."

"You have no idea how badly I want this! In fact, after what you've just told me, I think it's time I got involved."

"How? I don't want you coming down here and messing up what I've spent so much time and effort putting together."

"Don't worry; my involvement will have nothing to do with what you're doing; you won't even be aware of it. But those diamonds are my future, and I intend to have them."

◆

When he got back to the friary, Bartholomew sought out Anselm. "There's something I need to tell you. This morning, when I was out at the Armstrong place, like the Chief had asked, there was a man there who—" he frowned. "It was his eyes. I couldn't see into them." He closed his own, as if to shut out the memory of them. "I've only seen eyes like that once before. In 'Nam. A captured VC commander, who'd ordered an entire village executed, including old people and infants, for having given aid to a wounded Marine. I made a point of going to look at him, to see what kind of man could do such a thing."

Anselm said nothing, and his younger friend continued. "Now I've seen him again. Or someone just like him." He shuddered. "He gave me the creeps."

Anselm thought for a moment. "I think you ought to go see Columba. He's been asking for you, anyway."

Bartholomew started to leave, when the Senior Brother added, "I'm going to put you on my most-urgent prayer list, until this matter gets resolved."

For the past ten days, Columba had been in his bed, his spirit soaring, even as his strength ebbed. His Brothers had taken turns being with him, and his attitude of joyful expectation had been a source of inspiration and encouragement to them all, and to the whole abbey family.

Bartholomew entered the room that Columba shared with Anselm and Dominic. In the glow of the lamp on the night table, a Brother in the chair beside Columba's bed was reading Celtic poetry to the old monk. Seeing Bartholomew come in, he yielded the chair and exited.

Columba turned his head on the pillow and smiled at his young friend, fixing his blue eyes on Bartholomew's. "I see you've met him."

"Who?"

"The one I warned you about."

"Yes—I guess I have." Bartholomew shivered. "I told Anselm: He gives me the creeps!"

The old monk chuckled. "They always do." Then he turned serious. "You remember now, God allowed this to happen."

"Why?"

Columba sighed and took a deep breath. "You know up here," he tapped his forehead, "that God is stronger than the enemy. But the only way you are going to know it down here," he motioned toward his chest, "is to walk through a confrontation, staying as close to God as you can get."

Bartholomew looked at his dying mentor. "In that case, I think I just flunked."

Columba took his hand and gave it a weak squeeze. "You didn't. This was just the opening round. There'll be others. Maybe not with this one. And maybe not right away. But you'll go many rounds. God's training you to be His pugilist. To fight the good fight. And you can trust Him; He'll never over-match you. As long as you heed His instructions, and do *only* what He tells you, you'll be able to defeat any opponent you face, no matter how daunting."

The effort had exhausted him. Columba closed his eyes, and soon his breath was shallow but steady.

25 | the next big thing

SAMANTHA ARMSTRONG LOOKED at the clock on the dashboard, as she turned the Volvo wagon onto the bluffs road. "We're early," she announced. "Good! I want to have a little chat with my father."

"You really think you should?" asked the thin, nervous, dark-haired man in the passenger seat.

"Gottfried," she sighed, "we've been over this: The king of the venture capitalists is *not* going to capitalize on my fiancé's venture!"

"But he's promised to make the code available to the world, and that's all I want. It's why I'm leaving Big Red."

Samantha shook her head. "He'll promise you that, and he'll mean it. But then, just as things are finally coming together, he'll sell your business out from under you. To someone who wants to make the same egregious profits as our illustrious corporation. I'm telling you," she declared, braking for her father's driveway, "altruism is *not* the core of his nature."

She stopped at the front door, and James came out to see if he could help with the luggage. "Since you're the first, Ms. Samantha, you get your choice of rooms—except for the Cerulean Blue, which your father wants to save for Ms. Saralinda."

"Very well, James, give Mr. Franc the Emerald Green, and for me, the Burgundy Red." She laughed. "It sounds like I'm ordering wine." She turned to her companion. "You see? I told you Father was quirky."

"He seemed normal enough up in Cambridge."

"Of course! He was on your turf. But now you're on his."

She turned to the houseman. "James, inform my father I'll be out on the terrace. Oh, and could you mix us a batch of Breezers, please?" She glanced up at the sun. "It's late enough."

Grandfather Asa had picked up a summer concoction that had become a year-round family tradition: *Anjebo* rum, Bacardi lemonade mix, and the secret ingredient: fresh mint buds, all whirred with ice in a blender. Tangy, frosty, and smooth, they were served in fluted champagne glasses, with a large crystal pitcher standing by, for the inevitable refills. The correct name, according to her grandfather, was "Sea Breezes," but his three granddaughters had dubbed them "Breezers," and it stuck.

Pretending it was warm enough to be outside, Samantha took her favorite chair, pulled it over to the railing, and put her feet up—on the railing, exactly as she always had. Exactly as her father had asked her not to.

At 37, she was her father's eldest. She had spent most of her early years alternately striving for his approval and demonstrating her indifference to it. Magna cum laude at Yale, 6th in her class at Harvard Medical School, she was now assistant director of development at the Randolph Corporation, one of the pioneers in genetic research. She'd always been too focused on her work to have time for men—at least, that was her stock answer to well-meaning friends (and herself).

But now there *was* someone—a brilliant but eccentric German geneticist in her department. Gottfried was three years her junior, but he fully shared her passion for mapping human DNA, the last frontier. And gradually, under Samantha's careful tutelage, they were discovering that they shared other passions—for Bach and Mozart, whose music, with its infinite mathematical subtleties, was aural genius, joyfully exploding.

And *very* gradually, they were discovering each other.

Everything was fine, until her father, in Boston on business last year, had invited them to lunch. He'd asked Gottfried about his work, and as the young researcher enthusiastically described his quest, Samantha had seen a glint in her father's eye that she did not care for.

Gottfried Franc had spent the past seven years at the seemingly impossible task of cracking the Genome Code, the three-billion-character DNA that defined the human species. It was a Sisyphean task, the genetic equivalent to proving Fermat's Last Theorem. But this was an age for achieving the impossible. An English mathematician named Andrew Wiles, after ten years of solitary calculation at Princeton, had, in fact, obtained Fermat's proof. And now this young German—and a handful of others racing on identical quests—were on the verge of doing the same for DNA.

Once they'd done it, the whole gamut of genetic killers—cystic fibrosis, multiple sclerosis, muscular dystrophy, Lou Gehrig's Disease, et al.—would be suddenly curable. And henceforth, medical history would be referred to as before the Code and after it.

But Gottfried Franc was not merely mapping the Code; he had an intuitive sense of what to do with his data, once he'd assembled it. He was pretty sure he knew how to manipulate the genes, to achieve the cures—and Samantha's father sensed that he knew it.

Her father's expression made it clear: He had just come on the Next Big Thing.

And as usual, his timing was exquisite. Gottfried Franc was not happy in the windowless, mausoleum-like edifice with the big red R on its roof. Initially the Randolph Corporation had given him every assurance that the fruit of his labors would be made available to the world, once they had made a reasonable profit—enough to recoup their not inconsiderable investment, and give the stockholders fair return.

But now, as he approached the end of his quest, extreme security measures had been imposed. Guards at every entrance to the building checked the contents of all attaché cases coming in or going out; iris identification was required for admission to the labs; and no notebooks, laptops, or floppy disks were allowed off the premises. With Big Red holding the Genome Project ever closer to its vest (the ensuing patents would be priceless), Gottfried increasingly doubted their willingness to stand by their agreement.

Then Samantha's father had done a reprehensible thing: Three days later, without mentioning it to her, he had invited Gottfried to dinner and opened a whole new world to him. How would he like his own lab, his own staff, and a limitless annual budget? Mr. Armstrong was willing to gamble, not on what he would decipher, which rightly belonged to the Randolph Corporation, but on what this modern Columbus would discover afterward—what he would—or could—do with the Code, once it had been mapped.

When Samantha found out what her father had done—and that Gottfried had tentatively agreed to it, provided he could get out of his contract with the Randolph Corporation (for which A&A had retained a top law firm on his behalf)—she had gotten on the phone to him. He wanted the Armstrong Sisters to come for the weekend, to celebrate his 65th birthday? Well this one was bringing her fiancé, and she was coming early, to get a few things settled!

Now her father appeared on the terrace, smiling. "How are you, Sam?"

"I'm good, Father," she smiled back. "You don't look 65."

"I feel it, though," he sighed, sitting down. "Do you have to put your feet on the railing?"

"Oh, great," she said, removing them, "we're going to revert back to 1980. Just like we always do, when I come home."

He almost replied, then made a massive effort not to escalate with her. "I see you've brought Gottfried with you," he said calmly.

"Just like I said I would." She smiled as James appeared. "Ah, saved by the Breezers."

Taking one, she waited until James had departed, then turned to her father. "Let's see if we can get this done, before he comes down. He hasn't seen the nasty side of me yet, and I'm hoping to save that little surprise until later—maybe never. But you, dear Father, have an unusual propensity for bringing it out."

She put down her glass and glared at him. "Leave Gottfried alone. He doesn't know what an utterly ruthless, two-faced—"

Her father held up his hand. "I mean to keep my word to him, Sam, if that's what you're afraid of. But in the meantime, something's come up that changes everything—and I do mean everything."

In spite of herself, Samantha was curious. "All right, what?"

Her father smiled. "It'll have to wait until Saturday lunch, when you're all here."

"Well," she said, softening, "when he comes down, Dad, forget you're a businessman. For once, just be a father, if you can still remember how."

26 | night of the angel

GOTTFRIED FRANC LOOKED out his bedroom window at the interchange between father and daughter taking place on the terrace below. Samantha was clearly upset with her father and clearly speaking her mind. But the thing that struck Gottfried was: Her father allowed it. He loved her enough to tolerate her outrage. And she loved him enough to risk telling him *exactly* how she felt.

He envied her, more than she would ever know.

Raising his eyes to the horizon, Gottfried recalled the last night he had seen *his* father, ten years before. Ironically, that day had begun as the best of his life. At the Heidelberg Institute's graduation ceremonies, not only had he finished at the top of his class, he was the recipient of the coveted Kopfendorff Prize, awarded to the graduate who showed outstanding initiative and promise. It was not an annual award; nine years had passed since anyone had received the Kopfendorff.

Gottfried's father, Gustav Wilhelm Friedrich Baron von Franc, could not have been more pleased. The Baron was founder and director of Franc Pharmaceuticals, the global conglomerate that his only son would one day inherit. But the Baron was excited, not for that, but because his son seemed destined to eclipse all his accomplishments. And so the Baron chose to mark the occasion by hiring the largest banquet hall in Heidelberg and the most prestigious chamber ensemble, and arranged for a banquet that would be talked about for years, and invited all his friends to come. And they all came; no one regretted an invitation from the Baron.

At the banquet, the young guest of honor sat at the head of the table next to his father. There were many courses and many toasts, with many bottles of schnapps consumed. At the height of the evening, his father rose. He told the assembly that tonight was the night above all others in his life, and he was barely able to express the depth of his pride in his son, before being overtaken by his emotions. Not trusting himself to speak, he presented his son with the keys to a new Porsche Targa, which Gottfried would find waiting for him in the garage back at the Schloss.

There were more toasts to Gottfried's brilliance and future, some likening him to a young Siegfried, a new hero for a new Germany. Then the Baron and his cronies started singing the old drinking songs, so lustily it seemed as if a century had fallen away, and Heidelberg was once again back in its golden age. In truth, Gottfried thought, this night was for his father, not him. Which was fine, because he loved his father—albeit from a distance.

Much later, the gathering had dwindled to a dozen men standing around the piano while their wives waited to go home. The songs were marching songs now, of a more recent vintage. They had just started the Horst Wessel Song, when Herr Doktor/Professor Goltz, one of the Baron's oldest friends, leaned over to him and whispered drunkenly, "How *pleased* the Angel would have been!"

The Baron's smile vanished, and in a sudden fierce but controlled rage he requested that another colleague take the good doktor home, at once! The SS anthem continued unbroken; the camaraderie was instantly restored. But the moment stuck in Gottfried's mind.

He said nothing as he drove his happy, humming father home. The family's grand old Mercedes 770 Grosser sailed through the stormy night, its windshield wipers keeping tempo for the Baron's tune. In no time the twenty kilometers between Heidelberg and Mannheim had passed, and they were on their way up the winding drive to the Schloss, their ancestral home. As Gottfried negotiated the last switchback, lightning cracked and briefly illuminated the spires and smokestacks of Mannheim in the valley below. The headquarters of Franc Pharmaceuticals was down there, and this would be his daily commute—a pleasing thought, for the HQ had excellent research facilities, and earlier that evening his father had promised him a free hand to expand them in any direction he chose.

As he pulled up at the main entrance, a servant came out with an umbrella. He offered to put the car away, so that Gottfried could go in with his father, but the boy shook his head. He wanted to see the new Porsche.

As he guided the great black car into its berth in the garage, he could see the new Porsche down at the end. He got down from the Mercedes and went over to it—a piece of art, really, poised and ready in metallic silver, Germany's racing color. Standing still, it looked as if it were going 278K—its top speed, according to Stuttgart. Tomorrow he was going to take it out on the Autobahn and see if it was true.

Back in the main hall, he found his father still up, waiting for him. The Baron insisted they have one more cognac together, man to man, before retiring. He went over to the bar, poured them each a snifter, and switched on the Wagnerian overtures he kept cued up for such moments as this.

A fire crackled in the great hearth at the end of the hall. Other than occasional flashes of lightning, it provided the sole source of illumination and sent shadows leaping up to the shields and medieval armament that decorated the stone walls. Actually, there was one other source of light—a narrow beam from a spotlight in the rafters far above. It fell on a trophy case over the mantel, in which, against a purple velvet background, a medal gleamed—the Knight's Cross of the Iron Cross, the highest honor the Führer could bestow. It had been awarded to the Baron, who had served as chief of surgeons on the Eastern Front, and as that front had deteriorated, he had ultimately kept the entire hospital corps from collapsing.

Two ornate, throne-like wooden chairs flanked the hearth, and the 9th Baron and his scion each took one, cradling their globed snifters, and listening to the strains of *Tannhauser* echoing off the walls and hardwood floor. It was the perfect accompaniment to the storm raging beyond the tall leaded-glass windows, Gottfried thought—the perfect end to a perfect day.

And then he ruined it. "Father, who was the Angel?"

"No one," the Baron muttered, dismissing it with a wave of his hand. "A shadow from the past."

Any other son might have dropped it. But the trait which had won Gottfried the Kopfendorff was a rare linking of intuition and perseverance. "Tonight I'm interested in shadows," he said smiling, his eyes dancing above the rim of his snifter.

"Leave it alone, boy," growled the Baron, in a tone he had not used since Gottfried had outgrown Lederhosen.

Were it any other night, he might have. Clearly his father did not care to discuss it, and he usually acceded quickly to his father's wishes. But tonight he had heard many old, wise men—including his father—extolling his initiative and acumen. And because young Siegfried had consumed more than a few schnapps himself, and was now having a cognac, man to man with his father, he didn't leave it alone.

"Was Herr Doktor/Professor with you on the Eastern Front?"

The Baron got up, a scowl darkening his visage. "It's time we went to bed."

Finishing his cognac, he got up and started toward the bar, to leave the snifter before leaving the hall. But his son, no longer smiling, did not accompany him.

"Father, remember at dinner tonight, when you said that I could have anything I asked for? And I couldn't think of anything? Well, now I can: I want to know what Herr Goltz meant."

The Baron continued to the bar, as if he had not heard him. He put the glass down and was about to switch off the Wagner, when he turned and faced his son who was limned by the hearth fire behind him, the Knight's Cross gleaming behind him.

Perhaps because the Baron's own father had never honored him with such a banquet as he had given tonight—had, in fact, been ashamed of him for choosing medicine over a career in the officer corps, or possibly because he sought release from the shrouded wraiths that haunted his dreams—or simply because he'd had too many schnapps—Gustav Wilhelm Friedrich Baron von Franc decided to tell his son the truth.

He *had* served with distinction on the Eastern Front. He *had* rallied the *hospitalkorps* in its darkest hour. But the Cross was not for that. Hitler had indeed been pleased with his performance—so pleased, that he made the young chief surgeon his personal emissary to oversee the progress of his Final Solution. As such, he had visited each concentration camp and reported to the Führer personally back in Berlin. And the Reich's leader always made time to see him; only Speer had such access. Even at the end, in the bunker, he was shown straight in.

That was where—and for what—he had received the Cross. It was a soldier's medal, but the Führer had made an exception and awarded it to the civilian whom he said he valued more highly than any other, save Speer. It was the 8th Baron who had put it over the mantel, and who let it be known that it had been awarded for his son's service on the Eastern Front. And when his son succeeded him, the new Baron had made no effort to correct the legend.

Gottfried was dumbstruck. "What about Goltz?" he persisted.

"Goltz was at Auschwitz—the biggest of the camps, and in many ways the most efficient. Techniques were developed there that were subsequently used throughout the system."

The Baron did not want to go on. Neither did his son. But the driving strains of the Lohengrin Act III Prelude compelled them on.

Sensing the worst was yet to come, Gottfried demanded, "Who was the Angel?"

Slowly the words came out of the Baron's mouth, as if each were wrapped in barbed wire: "Mengele. The inmates called him the Death Angel. His staff, when they learned of it, nick-named him that."

And now it was Gottfried who could barely speak. "And you—were one of those? You worked with him?"

His father could not utter another word. But almost imper-ceptibly he nodded.

One more question remained to be asked, the most difficult of all. And with all his heart, Gottfried wished it had not occurred to him. But it had. "Father, was any of the research on which Franc Pharmaceuticals was founded, the result of Mengele's work?"

This time there was not even a nod. But neither did the Baron shake his head.

Gottfried left the Schloss before dawn. The Porsche's papers, with his name on the title, were in its glove compart-ment. On the way down to Stuttgart, he took the Autobahn and confirmed that it could do 278K. He sold it back to the factory for 165,000 Deutschmarks, only a few thousand less than his father had paid for it. Now with more than enough funds to get started in America, he flew to New York.

One of his professors at Heidelberg had recently transferred to Harvard Medical School. Gottfried called him, and the professor urged him to come up to Cambridge, where much of the cutting edge in genetics was occurring. Gottfried did, staying at first with the professor and his wife.

Thanks to the professor, word quickly spread that a German *wunderkind* was in town and looking for work. The Randolph Corporation made Gottfried an offer he could not refuse: They guaranteed to give him whatever he needed and go in whatever direction he chose. While Gottfried's command of English might have been hesitant, there was no hesitation in where he wanted to go.

His father had committed crimes against humanity that staggered the imagination. And had profited obscenely from doing incalculable harm to his fellow man. The Baron's son vowed to spend the rest of his life atoning for what his father had done. The greatest benefit he could possibly give mankind was to crack the Genome Code—and then destroy the genetic diseases that had plagued mankind for centuries. That would be his life's work.

When they'd asked him to name his salary, he thought for a moment, and then said 165,000 DM. *Kein Problem*, they assured him, though they were less ready to grant his next request: to make his findings universally available, as soon as they had recouped their investment in him. When they realized that they would lose him if they didn't agree, they did.

Gottfried's father had had little difficulty discovering his whereabouts. When he had called, Gottfried refused to speak to him. Then the Baron began sending letters.

Finally, Gottfried replied, in one brief paragraph:

When an Orthodox Jew marries a Gentile, as far as that Jew's family is concerned, he or she has ceased to exist. You did not marry a Jew; you just vivisected them and arranged for their more efficient liquidation. More than a million of them. So my response to you is theirs: You have ceased to exist.

After that, the calls and letters stopped.

But now, looking down at Samantha and her father, Gottfried found that, incredibly, he missed him.

LATE FRIDAY EVENING, Clay Armstrong's second daughter arrived, with her 12-year-old son G. Gordon in tow. The tradition he had established was that the weekend of his birthday lunch, his daughters should appear early for lunch Saturday, at the end of which he would give them each an envelope containing their annual tax-free gift of $10,000. "Breezers and Buckos," Serena Armstrong, 35, had dubbed it, and woe betide the daughter who failed to appear.

Then, even though they all lived within driving distance, they were expected to spend the afternoon together, enjoy a pick-up supper in the evening, and stay the night. They were free to leave after breakfast Sunday morning. His thinking was that even in this short time, the bond between them would be re-established annually. Though his daughters resented it mightily, he was right; they invariably left closer than when they had arrived.

Serena Armstrong, 35, lived in town and could easily have come over the next day for her father's 65th birthday luncheon.

But this year as a special birthday present, she had decided to inflict herself upon him a day early.

She had not always been a difficult child. For her first ten years she had tried desperately to be perfect. But there was no competing with the brilliant Samantha who was two years older, and so, at age 11 she decided to blow negative. Her parents tried discipline, counseling, prep schools—Deerfield ("Your sister was such a blessing here!"), Emma Willard ("No girl has *ever* done that here!"), and finally, after an anonymous gift of a new science lab, Vandercroft ("Your daughter has been such a—*challenge*—here!").

Serena was blessed (or cursed) with super-model features—large brown eyes, long blond hair, and cheekbones to die for. Moreover, so high was her metabolic rate—her roommates used to joke that they could warm their hands at her—that she could eat whatever she wanted and still see her hipbones. Which she checked often. For Serena's flaw was that, like her father, she was monumentally self-absorbed. The entire world revolved around her, and she collected a coterie of sycophantic friends who were willing to do the revolving, whenever the sun deigned to shine on them.

Bright enough to get into Yale and smart enough to stay in, she majored in English—and there discovered Dorothy Parker, the wryest wit at the Algonquin Roundtable. Once challenged to use the word *horticulture* in a sentence, DP had shrugged and said, "You can lead a horticulture, but you can't make her think." Her vicious/delicious ripostes had made her a legend, which ironically came to overshadow her genuine talent: DP created and ultimately defined what came to be known as the *New Yorker* short story.

But it was her poetry that Serena found most compelling. Her idol was, underneath, a hopeless romantic who tried to protect her too-vulnerable heart with layers of lacquered cynicism.

In her senior year Serena made a pilgrimage to Manhattan,

haunted DP's haunts, and returned to New Haven, determined to fashion her own life after DP's example. In Yale's renowned creative writing course, English 77, she discovered that while she did possess a modest talent, she could not deliver the goods under pressure, day after day. Reluctantly she gave up her dream of becoming a writer, but not of becoming DP. She started affecting a biting cynicism that soon had her friends begging her to stop—and then avoiding her, when she wouldn't.

The trouble was, she had so immersed herself in the role that she could not get out of it. She had always assumed she could shed her acid tongue any time she chose, like dropping an affected Oxford accent or a Southern drawl. But it would not *stay* dropped. Serena *was* quick and clever, and if ever blindsided by a social slight, real or perceived, suddenly the razor was back and flicking.

In the end, she gave up trying to be nice. For better or for worse, she would cast her lot with her feared and lonely heroine. She would become, in effect, "Dorothy Parker East"—a wry dig at the master of *Fallingwater East*, to whom she behaved so abhorrently that he would have gladly revoked her irrevocable trust, if he could.

That trust had enabled her to live away from home—as far away as San Francisco, where she immersed herself in the creative energy of that city. Four years later she had returned, with a love child named G. Gordon Armstrong, and several layers of lacquer over her too-vulnerable heart.

Arriving at *FW*, she announced to her shocked parents that they were moving in. It was a strain all around at first, but her mother loved G. Gordon, which made it easier. Then her father became interested in the boy's development.

Every new mother thinks her child is above average, and every grandparent agrees. Serena's father went a step further: He had his grandson tested, and the tests confirmed that G. Gordon was going to be a very special child.

At five, his grandfather taught him to play chess, and in two years G. Gordon was thinking three or four moves ahead, which was extraordinary. Moreover, he had the power of concentration to narrow his world down to 64 squares like a master. And—he seemed able to anticipate his opponent's strategy, as if he could see over the horizon.

His grandfather began to believe that perhaps the Armstrong gift had not been lost, after all. He began to take an interest in G. Gordon's schooling, which put Serena in a bit of a quandary: How much was too much? On balance, she decided she would rather have her father this way than disinterested. She'd been that route.

Then her mother had drowned. Things got very hard after that, because she blamed her father, as much as he blamed himself. Eventually he suggested that she and G. Gordon might do better in a place of their own, and he bought her a comfortable condo in the middle of Eastport.

Which they had left five minutes before pulling up in front of *FW*, in her fender-bent, rusted-out Jeep Cherokee. It was plug ugly, and the only reason she kept it was because she knew how much it bugged her father. When James came out to help, she said, "Is the Cerulean Blue taken?"

"Your father is saving it for Ms. Saralinda, Ma'am."

"Then it's not taken. I'll take it, and James, you can put a cot in the dressing room for my son."

James hesitated, then thought better of stepping into that maelstrom. "Very well, Ms. Serena."

"It's not 'Ms.,' James. If you have to give me a title, 'Miss' will do. I'm not ashamed of being unmarried. In fact, I'm grateful!"

28 | cerulean blue

AT 33, SARALINDA WAS THE YOUNGEST of the Armstrong sisters, and the least concerned with being on time. When her father once chided her, informing her that punctuality was the politeness of kings, she informed him that she could not conceive of a throne to which she would ever aspire.

Everyone was in the living room, enjoying their second Breezers and about to go in to lunch, when she blew in—literally. Wiping her forehead with the back of her hand, she explained that she'd encountered a heavy headwind on the bike path.

Beaming, her father poured her a drink and took it over to her, which gave him the opportunity for a *sotto voce* word with her. "You know, SL, if you lived here, you wouldn't need a tailwind to get to lunch on time. Or breakfast, or dinner."

"I know, Dad," she replied softly, putting a hand on his arm. "But I can't. Not now." Saralinda, known to her family as SL, was in the throes of a divorce. Her second, which was considerably more crushing than the first. She needed all the space apart she could get. Except at the moment, she had a bit more than she cared for: her son Jamie was up in Maine with her ex for the weekend.

"Well," said her father, "Just remember: I'll take you and Jamie any time, any way, under any circumstances; you know that."

"Yes, Dad," she smiled, relieved to hear James announce that lunch was ready.

As the others went into the dining room, Saralinda held back a moment. She looked up at the portrait of her mother over the mantel, struck once again by how much they really did look alike. They'd been alike in so many other ways, she thought, even though she was supposed to have been a boy. Samantha and Serena had inherited their father's common sense and strength of will. But Saralinda was like her mother, a free and gentle spirit.

Her favorite thing, when she was young, was to talk to the birds. She would mimic their calls, as best she could, and the birds, surprised, would reply. She would reply to their reply, and so it went, for as long as she was willing to play. Her favorites were the mockingbirds. Most of them were hams, and would give her a different call, each time she would reply to the previous one, trying to stump her. They would succeed with a *clucketty* chuckle, which was inimitable. Then they would celebrate their victory by running through their entire repertoire.

Also like her mother, SL was gifted artistically—too gifted, if such a thing were possible. Everything she turned her hand to, she could do not merely competently, but with surpassing grace. Her piano teacher urged her mother to take her ability seriously; so did her dance teacher. But her mother had refused to pressure SL in any direction. "When you're older, you'll know," she would tell her daughter, when SL would come to her, wondering what she was. "The day will come, when you'll know you were meant to be an artist or a dancer or whatever. Don't commit yourself, until you know for sure."

In college, it got worse. "The curse of the multi-talented," she called it. Yale had an outstanding art school, and SL took life drawing, line drawing, the Albers color course, and sculpture. In her spare time, there was a poetry group, in which she discovered an affinity for moments and the words with which to capture them. There was also a dance group, which she joined on a whim, and discovered that fluid motion came naturally to her, and that with her body she could express things she could never impart with words or lines or colors.

In her sophomore year she roomed with Flo Handley from Nyack, New York, who played the guitar. SL picked up the instrument, learned enough to accompany herself, then started singing old Joan Baez and Judy Collins ballads. By spring she was writing—and singing—her own material. The owner of a popular fern bar invited her to perform Saturday nights. She caught on, and soon there was talk of cutting a record, and gigs in Greenwich Village, and—

And finally she said goodbye to all that. The day came that her mother had foretold. It came on a Sunday morning, with her voice a little hoarse and her head a little mungey from too many Black and Tans. She looked at herself in the mirror and announced: You are an artist. You can dance and sing and play and write and compose. But you are first an artist. First and last and always.

What was more, she knew what her specialty would be: landscapes. She had just enough of her father's control, to appreciate a world with a frame around it, and just enough of her mother's freedom, to let that world happen the way *it* wanted to, rather than the way she might want it to.

SL did not think she was beautiful—too thin, too tall, eyes too wide, cheekbones too high. But men disagreed. She was never without male companionship, if she wanted it. The trouble was, the men she attracted were exactly like her. And the worst thing in the world was for a hopeless romantic to fall in love with another one. If one person in the relationship didn't have at least one foot on terra firma, the whole thing was likely to soar into the night sky like a rocket, but explode long before it reached the moon.

Having discovered this the hardest way possible, SL was kind—but not overly kind—to young swains dying of love for her. But then she got older, and she forgot. Her most recent disaster was her marriage to a Heathcliffe type, a landscape painter like herself, who spent the summers on Monhegan Island off the coast of Maine. The light there was simply incredible, Saralinda discovered, her first summer there. In Heathcliffe's sere and desolate, rockbound paintings, tiny wildflowers of cerulean blue began to appear, and everyone on the island knew he was falling in love with the new girl.

They married and had little Jamie and were happy for about a year. Then Heathcliffe began staying away longer and longer, and little red wildflowers began to appear in his work. When she discovered the two of them, she left with little Jamie and came home.

The divorce was handled long-distance, and without rancor. (It would never occur to SL to be resentful.) Her father, as he had for Serena, gave her a condo. But hers was up in Wellfleet; she had to be that far away for a while.

The light at Wellfleet Harbor was almost as good as at Eastport, and she threw herself into her work. Eventually she got good enough for the Anderson House Gallery, the toniest in Eastport, to make her one of their featured artists.

She also took up cycling—with a vengeance, and whenever Jamie was in school and she wasn't painting, she could be found whirling down the bike path or through the woods of Nickerson State Park. But her favorite thing was to take Jamie, who was six now, over to the pond early on a Saturday morning and teach him how to talk to the birds.

29 | christmas in october

THE BREEZERS WERE DOING THEIR WORK. The decibel level at the Armstrong dining table was rising steadily, as the Armstrong Sisters rediscovered how much they enjoyed one another's company—and their father's, too, which surprised them (though not as much as it surprised him).

To Gottfried the banter was bewildering. His head turned this way and that, as if following a doubles tennis match. During a momentary lull, he whispered to Samantha, "Is it always like this?"

"Only when we're all together," replied Samantha, smiling. "We're so glad to see each other, there's a kind of electrical excitement that builds between us. Like it used to, when Mother was alive, and we were kids." She put a hand on his arm. "But I can see how disconcerting it must be, Gosha."

Serena, sitting across from him, added, "It's Father's fault. He encouraged it; he said it would give us social confidence. But I suspect the real reason was because he was so good at it himself. I was thirteen before I bested him for the first time."

"Ah, yes, I remember it well," her father said to Gottfried with a smile. "Their mother had served codfish that evening, and when our daughters had turned up their noses at it, she informed them that the Nauset Indians—they were here first—regarded it as food to strengthen their minds. Whereupon, I observed that some minds could not bear much more strengthening."

"Whereupon," Serena interjected gleefully, "*I* observed: 'Oh, dear, what hath cod wrought?'"

Their laughter was punctuated by SL pointing to their guest. "Oh dear, look at poor Gottfried, trying so hard to be a good sport! The poor darling is wondering how on earth he's ever going to fit into this bizarre Gypsy entourage that masquerades as a functional family!" And they laughed until the tears came.

Later, after the roast beef, Yorkshire pudding, and Brussels sprouts, Clay Armstrong gently rang his wine glass with the edge of his fork and got to his feet, producing an envelope for each of them. "There's a check for each of you, and your sons, and your fiancés." As they smiled at his little quip, he turned to Gottfried and asked if he would excuse them, as they had some family business to discuss. When he had departed, Clay said to his daughters, "And here's something you *didn't* expect." He brought forth three more envelopes and passed them out. Mystified, they opened them, their eyes widening, as they took in the amount on the enclosed checks.

"That is your one-time, tax-free gift," he explained. "I'm giving it to you now, rather than letting it come out of my estate, because something rather extraordinary has happened to me, and is about to happen to *FW*."

Their father then told them about the sudden appearance of two spots on his lungs, which, given his history of heavy smoking, could mean only one thing.

They were shocked, speechless, their hearts going out to him. SL was the first to find words: "How long have you known?"

"A second set of x-rays confirmed the results a little over two weeks ago."

"Why didn't you tell us?" demanded Serena. "We may not always have gotten along, but hey, you're the only father we've got."

"I was having a hard enough time accepting it myself. I mean, I'd just lost a friend, ten months after spots showed up on his lungs. And since there was nothing you or anyone else could do, what was the point of telling you before now?"

They started objecting, and he raised his hands. "Hold on! There's a happy ending to this story!"

He told them about his classmate, who had originally come on behalf of the Class Gift Committee and—stayed. Without going into detail, he told them of his hypnotherapy sessions with Trevor Haines, the last of which resulted in the disappearance of the spots on his lungs. He told them of the research clinic that the two of them were about to launch, right there at *FW*.

They were dumbfounded.

Samantha had some misgivings, but she was still trying to process the cancer scare. Basically, what he did with *FW*, and his money, and his life—was his business.

Saralinda, who had almost lost her father and then regained him—all in the space of fifteen minutes—was in tears.

But Serena wasn't buying it. "Sorry, Father, but this guy sounds like Wally Wacko! But what *really* worries me is that you seem to be taking him seriously—you, the oracle of 'let's-stay-in reality'!" She looked at him carefully. "What's he *done* to you, anyway?"

"I guess you could say he's given me a fresh perspective on life. All my life I've been selfish—with my time and my focus, making money, lots of it, and losing contact with my wife, my children, everyone." He paused, but none of them contradicted him.

"Well," he went on exuberantly, "I feel a little like Ebenezer at the window: I haven't missed Christmas, after all! And now I want to make up for lost time. I'm taking care of you three first; those checks are just for openers. I'm setting up a $20 million trust fund for each of you. After that, whatever I have or can earn will go into the clinic."

Samantha and SL were so glad to have him back—and obviously changed—they were inclined to let him do whatever he wanted with his new lease on life.

But Serena did not share their enthusiasm. "Let me guess who's going to run this clinic: Could it by any chance be Trevor Haines?"

Her father frowned. "You have a problem with that?"

"Well, I think we'd like to meet this miracle-worker."

"I think you should. In fact, I've asked him to explain what we're going to be doing."

He rang for James, who appeared from the kitchen. "Would you inform Mr. Haines that the pleasure of his company is requested in the dining room?"

When Trevor Haines appeared, he was attired in a yellow cashmere sweater over an indigo blue linen dress shirt, with a navy-blue silk ascot, light gray wool slacks, and tasseled loafers.

After he was introduced, he said to the sisters, "Your father is a man of remarkable vision, and one of the *most* remarkable philanthropists it has ever been my privilege to work with. But he's entirely too modest. I've told him that unless the new entity bears the name "The Armstrong Research Clinic"—the ARC, and unless he agrees to function as its guiding light as well as its founder, I will not serve as its director."

He then proceeded to detail all the help that the ARC would offer, assuring them that he had already alerted the most highly qualified personnel in each of the disciplines he had outlined. Well before he'd finished, their eyes had glazed over, and when he finally asked for questions, there were none.

Their father thanked him for his thorough and helpful briefing, and asked if he might excuse them now.

When they were alone again, Samantha said, "You said you were going to phase out Armstrong & Associates. How abruptly?"

"We're signing the papers next Friday that will launch the ARC. A&A will disband as soon as possible thereafter, since the two entities cannot very well co-exist here."

Now it was Samantha who was concerned. "Not long ago, you gave Gottfried—certain assurances—on the strength of which he's about to make a decision that will profoundly affect the rest of his life—our life. If A&A is suddenly about to fold its tents. . . ."

"Point taken; I'll have to do some re-thinking there."

Serena stood up. "I'm sorry, but I don't like the way this guy who looks like he just stepped out of *Vanity Fair*—the *old Vanity Fair*—has insinuated himself into the fabric of your life!"

Her father scowled at her. "I don't think I like the sound of that," said her father.

"Well, I don't like the sound of the whole thing! Because it sounds like he's done a mind job on you! Big time! And frankly I wish you weren't signing the blasted thing into reality so quickly! Why can't it wait a couple of months? Why does it have to be next Friday?"

"Because, Serena, that's when he wants to do it!" her father retorted. "And since he's saved my life, I'm inclined to go along with him!"

"Well, I just wonder what he saved it for!" she shot back, leaving the room.

She went out on the terrace—and was surprised to find Trevor Haines there, at the railing, gazing out to sea.

Slipping up behind him, she startled him by whispering softly, "I know what you're doing. You're hardly the first so-called 'healer' to gain control over those he was pretending to help."

Stunned, Haines was about to reply, then abruptly shut his mouth. And just glared at her.

Unfazed, Serena continued, "I just wanted you to know that someone's on to your game."

He still didn't answer, but now he tilted his head back, and a slow, condescending smile spread across his face.

Wrong move. If she was angry before, she was in white fury now. "Because I am going to expose you! I'm going to have you investigated! I *know* you're a charlatan, and soon, *everyone's* going to know it!"

His smile was gone now, his black eyes blazing.

"Cat got your tongue?" she taunted. "Oh, I don't imagine the truth will out all at once. I expect it'll out in dribs and drabs—the death of a thousand cuts. Until you wish with all your heart that you had never set foot on this place!"

30 | watertight doors

AFTER SUNDAY CHURCH, Ban Caulfield changed quickly into his cycling gear, which now included a long-sleeved Lycra jersey and leg warmers. Though it was 58°, and the southwest breeze meant it would stay balmy, it *was* mid-October; as the shadows lengthened, it would get a lot chillier in a hurry. And he was definitely planning on staying out till sundown. For today, he'd announced to his household, he would attempt his longest ride of the season: the 53-mile round-trip to Provincetown.

They'd been suitably impressed, and he downplayed the effort. Just getting ready for the *Tour d'Espoir*, the abbey's annual bikeathon fundraiser. Most years, it took place in September, but this year, due to conflicts with the choir's recording date and the marching band's parade schedule, it had to be postponed to Veteran's Day.

Out in the garage, he stretched carefully, got down the red Trek 5000, topped off its tire pressure, and donned helmet and Oakleys. Then he said a prayer for protection—his only spontaneous prayer of the day.

Mounting up, he checked his watch. He would be on time. Just.

He had never mentioned Saralinda at home. In designing a modern warship, one of the chief concerns was watertight integrity. A ship of the line had to be able to take several hits below the waterline without sinking. The secret was to line the hull with a honeycomb layer of small, reinforced compartments. Under routine conditions these could be used for anything, but when General Quarters sounded, all the hull compartments were cleared and sealed. Each had a watertight door (oval-shaped because square corners were weaker), battened down all around with heavy steel toggle bolts. Such a compartment might have its outer bulkhead stove in by a mine or torpedo, but the sea would never get past its watertight door.

Some men believed that they could keep portions of their lives separated in mentally secure compartments, each perfectly isolated from the others. At least, that was the theory. In practice, few men who compartmentalized were able to sustain watertight integrity very long. Just as they were congratulating them-selves on having created a true unsinkable, some unseen, uncharted iceberg would rip their compartments from stem to stern, leaving them on the bridge, watching their magnificent creation settle slowly beneath the ink-black waves of the North Atlantic.

But that didn't keep them from trying. The illusion of a captain's paradise—of living one life in one's home port and another in one's romantic port of call—kept luring them on. They *could* have it both ways: The predictable security and stability of their family life. *And* the wild and unpredictable soaring and youthening—of something else. If they were clever enough—or powerful enough—they would be one of the very few who actually get away with it.

Ban Caulfield had never intended to become a compart-mentalizer. A good husband, good father, and good friend, he was also a good Christian, tithing to his church, giving to charity, and being scrupulously honest on his income tax. He was even a member of a religious community of people who felt called by God to live together and help one another put Him first.

But Ban was leading a double life. Not intentionally; it had just–happened. But once it had started to happen, he had let it continue. To see where it might go. Because he was a hopeless romantic. He knew that about himself and was comfortable with it; it was useful in his writing.

The present situation had come about at a particularly frag-ile moment in his life. He did not have to let it happen. He did have some close friends among the men of the abbey, including a few of the clergy. He could have gone to one of them. But it was hard to tell another man that he was falling apart.

Years before, right after he'd come to the abbey, Mother Michaela, leading a retreat for the abbey's men, warned them that affairs seldom begin with lust (though they usually wind up there). They begin with a severely bruised ego. And creative types are particularly vulnerable. They want so badly for one person to think they are Mr. Wonderful, that their yearning egos could lead them anywhere. And if the other person saw in them what they most valued at the core of their being, and if that person needed something in return. . . .

But Ban had long ago forgotten those wise words. And now, as the figure in the white windbreaker approached, all he could think was that the best part of his week–the part he'd been looking forward to since last Sunday–was about to happen again.

31 | just friends

THEY RODE IN SILENCE, Ban holding down the pace so they could talk easily if they wanted to. But Saralinda (he refused to call her SL) seemed content to ride without talking, and he respected that. With the bike path nearly deserted, they could ride side by side for miles, gliding though sandy hills, scrub pine woods, and open meadows.

Once, as they passed a copse of trees, a mockingbird greeted them, and Saralinda returned the greeting. The bird quickly sent her another, which she returned, but then they were out of range. Surprised at another side of her he had not known, Ban glanced at her beside him. But she was somewhere else, a sad place, he sensed. At times there was a wistful sadness about her, which nothing he could say seemed to dispel.

When they reached the end of the bike path, he asked her if she would like to stop for a Diet Dew (her no-cal caffeine of choice). She smiled and shook her head; if they were going to have any time in Provincetown, they needed to keep going. So they rode on, in single file now, as they were out on the Mid-Cape. To make it easier for her, he rode in front, although in truth she was, if anything, more fit than he. Pedaling easily, they shared the silence and the sun-drenched rolling scenery. When they came to the hills of Truro, on each ascent they just geared down and took their time. But what went up also came down, and the downhills were exhilarating. Being heavier than she, he could coast faster, and she refrained from teasing him about why.

In North Truro, they left the Mid-Cape, preferring the less-traveled 6A along the bay shore. Eventually they could see Provincetown and its Pilgrims' Tower, hazy in the distance. As they glided past the rows of ancient summer rental cottages, scarcely larger than cabanas, it felt to Ban like they were drifting back in time, to an earlier, less-complicated time, where happy endings were the rule, not the exception. Then came the new concrete condos where the opposite was true. And then they were in the old town itself.

As they entered the most colorful, people-crowded main street in New England, they dismounted and removed their cleats, joining the throng of street-strollers. They were walking along in sock feet, but no one noticed; in P'town, people let people do their own thing. Her hand found his, and they walked the length of the street that way.

Out on the wharf, they found a bistro where they could eat outside. They had Italian sausage sandwiches and tall glasses of iced tea frequently refilled, and absorbed the tranquil ebb-and-flow of their surroundings.

Sensing she had gone to her sad place again, he left her alone—but finally reached over and put his hand on hers. "Where are you?"

She didn't answer, and he had to look away, unable to bear the sadness in her eyes. He watched two Portuguese fishermen in the back of a commercial boat, sitting in the sun as they mended their nets. Then his eyes returned to hers; they couldn't help it.

But she was back from that place, and ready now. "Leo Zenetti wants to talk to me," she explained. "In New York. First thing Friday morning."

She had mentioned him before. He ran one of the most influential galleries on Madison Avenue. And Boston's Newbury Street. And Worth Avenue in Palm Beach. And M Street in Georgetown. Leo Zenetti was big time. There was none bigger.

"Saralinda, that's great! When did you find out?"

"Day before yesterday. Holly Anderson arranged the intro; she still does well with my oils, but my acrylics are too mod and abstract for 'the more traditional tastes' of her clientele—though they'll do just fine on Madison Avenue. I'd sent him a bunch of slides. Now he wants to meet me, and wants me to bring three of my pieces. Holly says it means a contract. He'll want an exclusive, of course."

"But this is terrific! It's what you've been working and hoping for, all your life."

"I know," she said with a smile, "so why am I so scared?"

He laughed and patted her hand. "You'll do fine!"

"That's what my father said, just before he let go the seat of the two-wheeler."

He grinned. "And now look at you! You're one of the best women cyclists I know!"

"*Women* cyclists?"

"Never mind. Are you going to drive down?"

She shook her head. "I want to get this over with. I'll go up to Boston, spend the night at the Airport Marriott, and take the first shuttle down in the morning." She stood up. "Come on, let's go to the point."

He got up and paid the bill; in twenty minutes, they were at Race Point, the northernmost tip of the National Seashore.

Putting their bikes in a rack where several others were parked, Ban secured them with a coiled wire lock he'd brought. At the edge of the sand, they left their helmets and cleats, too, and walked out on the crisp, cool beach. Where they stood and watched the gulls playing above the breakers, and tried to make out Plymouth in the hazy distance.

He put an arm around her. It was just a friendly gesture, he told himself. They were just friends. But then she leaned against him. Just a little. Just enough for him to know that she wanted his arm around her.

They walked down the beach, far down, listening to its music, wishing they could keep it playing, make it last. But they couldn't; no one ever could.

Just before they got back to the bikes, Ban said, "My father, down in Roanoke, is dying of emphysema. I've been talking about going down to see him. I think I'll go next weekend. Go down first thing Friday, change in New York, come back Sunday. In fact, that's a good idea you've got there: I'll spend Thursday night at the Marriott, leave the car there, and take the first shuttle. I should be in Roanoke before noon."

She said nothing, and he did not dare look at her.

But then, as he stepped onto the boardwalk, she slipped her arm through his. And gave it a squeeze.

32 | vespers

LATE THE FOLLOWING DAY, Monday, Brothers Bartholomew and Ambrose entered Norma's Café in the midst of an argument about bicycles. It carried them to a corner table, and continued, even as Isabel Doane came over with a jug of coffee in each hand. The one in her left had a brown handle; it held the good stuff for Ambrose. The other had a green handle—decaf for her son.

In their work habits—navy blue windbreakers, khaki pants, and boots—the two monks might have passed for civilians, were it not for a small blue cross embroidered on their light blue work shirts. They were arguing the pros and cons of handlebar shifters, when she arrived. Actually, the young one, Ambrose, who had opinions about everything including bicycles, was doing most of the talking. The older one was doing most of the listening—and occasionally, wearily, pointing out the flaws in his young friend's reasoning. Which only provoked the latter to further, louder discourse.

"Hello?" interrupted Isabel. "Don't they teach you any manners over there?"

"Oh, hi, Mrs. Doane," said Ambrose sheepishly. "Sorry, I guess I was too intent on making my point."

"It's all right, Brother Ambrose. I know *you* mean well."
"Sorry, Mother," sighed Brother Bartholomew.

"Well, I don't know why you come in here, if you don't even drink my coffee!"

"Mother," Bartholomew replied with a sigh, "I come in here, because it's the nicest place in town, to come and pause for a moment. It used to be the pause that refreshes, before I gave up the best coffee on earth. Now, it's just a pause. But if you don't want me to pause here, I'll go pause somewhere else."

At which point Isabel would have put her hands on her hips, were it not for the coffee jugs. "I don't know why you always get so—*testy* with me!"

Smiling, Bartholomew shook his head. "I don't know why, either. I think you know all my buttons, and you know the secret launch code. Each time I come in here, and you get on one of your rants, I tell myself: You don't have to go there. But then—I always do."

Whether it was the comment about hers being the best coffee on earth, or her place being the best pause—or simply because deep down she loved it when he came in and was only mad because he didn't come in more often—she chose to be mollified. Filling their mugs, she returned the jugs to their cradles, then signaled Suzie to take over, while she took a chair at their table. Leaning forward, her voice scarcely above a whisper, she asked, "How goes the investigation?"

Ambrose, who had thus far not been involved, leaned forward, too.

"Well," replied Bartholomew, keeping his own voice low, "with the Chief still on the sidelines, things are pretty much dead in the water. But even if the Chief were out and about, I don't think we'd be much further." He would have liked to tell her that the people who might have had motives, all had alibis. But that sort of thing, he shared only with the Chief and the investigating team.

Better to find out what *she* knew. Which she was, in fact, obviously dying to tell him, which was why she'd asked in the first place.

"All right, Mother," he said, winking at Ambrose, "tell me."

She frowned. "Young man, it's obvious I'm not the only one around here who knows secret launch codes!" Then, deciding it would be more enjoyable to share the town gossip than get angry, she relaxed. "Well, everyone thinks that Armstrong guy must have done it. That he must have been having a–*thing*–with his office manager, and that it went sour, and he hired somebody to off her."

Bartholomew breathed an inner sigh of relief; they didn't know about the diamonds–so far.

"But what do *you* think?" he asked.

"Well," said Isabel, leaning further forward, as did the others, until their heads almost touched, "there's got to be someone else involved–someone that no one's thought of yet. Someone in the background." She paused. "Find that person, and you've found your murderer."

Bartholomew stared at her. His intuition was telling him that she was right. He had nothing to go on, no tangible facts. But somehow he *knew* she was right–and he had a hunch who it was.

Ambrose caught his eye and tapped his watch, and Bartholomew's eyes widened, as he glanced at his own. "Sorry, Mother," he said, getting to his feet, "but we've got about eight minutes to make Vespers."

When he hurriedly fished out three dollars, his mother started to object–then didn't, perhaps realizing that her continuing refusal to let him pay might be keeping him from coming in more often.

The two Brothers made it to the friary with about thirty seconds to spare—just enough time, thought Bartholomew, as he struggled into the floor-length cream-colored garment and green surplice. The maneuver was always awkward. He had been getting into this robe for 18 years, and he still couldn't do it gracefully. He smiled, recalling the last visit of his Franciscan friend, Father Svet, the Bosnian mountain priest. Now *there* was a monk whose robe practically flowed onto him!

His Brothers were forming up in a column of twos. Grabbing his *Antiphonale Monasticum*, the thick black book with all the services, he found his place in line, just as the procession entered the great stone basilica.

Peace descended, as it always did. Well, not always: In the beginning, he had frequently resented these services, even though they had played a key role in his being drawn to the religious life. The Monastic Hours—Matins, Lauds, Terce, Sext, None, Vespers, and Compline—seemed almost designed to cross one's will.

No matter what one was doing, when it came time to go to one of these offices, one simply had to drop it. One day he'd spent an hour raking leaves and had to stop just before he could pick up the piles. There was a wind that afternoon—enough, that if he left the leaves until after the service, he would have to rake them up all over again. He had dutifully left, and let the wind do its worst, but while the others were chanting the Psalms in Latin, he had railed inwardly at God.

Why do You do this? Why do You deliberately waste my time, when You know how much I've got to get done?

Whose time?

That was the moment he first realized how far from surrendered his heart truly was. He had given his life to God. But that was the easy part; he would spend the rest of his life getting his heart surrendered.

Some orders did this in quiet contemplation. Some in

teaching and healing. In begging and giving. In carrying His light to the ends of the earth. And some, like the monks and nuns of Faith Abbey, sought to praise him in their work and worship.

To be content to let their lives be prayer—that was what Bartholomew had to learn (and was learning still). If his first call was to worship God, so be it. If God chose to have him worship Him at certain hours, singing His praises in Latin, so be it. And if that was to come before all other tasks, and occasionally even mean having to re-rake leaves, so be it.

Not my will but Thine be done, O Lord.

As Columba had promised, it *was* getting easier. He actually looked forward to these interludes of peaceful praise. There was a reassuring timelessness to them; no matter what was going on in the world, *this* was what was going on *here*. What God wanted. The way He wanted it. The way it had been done for centuries. And would be done long after Bartholomew was buried with his Brothers in the Abbey's corner of the local cemetery.

That thought carried serenity with it, and he smiled as he found his place in the *Antiphonale* and blended his voice with the others.

33 | will you ask?

ONE MEMBER OF THE ABBEY was not at peace during that Vespers service. Not in the least. Not with the eyes of the Transfigured Christ meeting his gaze, every time he raised his head. Ban Caulfield could not face his Savior, not now.

The compartmentalizing worked everywhere but here. Away from here, he could shut Saralinda so completely out of his mind that she did not even exist. He could be a husband, a father, a writer, and the head of an abbey household, totally devoted to what he was doing. No one would ever guess there was another side. And sometimes, he even forgot himself. So much so, in fact, that he could vehemently condemn public figures who got caught doing—exactly what he was doing.

Then, when he was with Saralinda, the rest of his life was forgotten. He lived in the now—a free spirit, without obligations or responsibilities. Free to follow his heart, wherever it might lead. If anyone were to ask him then, about his other side, he would not lie—but it would never occur to anyone that there might be another side.

He had been forthright with Saralinda, told her right off that he was married with two children, and a member of the abbey. And she had been equally forthright, about her two failed marriages and her son. But he had never gone into the depth of spiritual commitment that had brought him to the Cape and caused him to become a member of the abbey. And she had never asked. There were many things she hadn't asked.

What they talked about on their long rides together was his writing and her painting. And how much they felt the same way about so many things. They were true kindred spirits, separated only by a dozen years and some surface circumstances.

A fragile flower had grown up between them, and both of them had watered and nurtured it, shielding it from harsh reality. And now it was ready to bloom.

Only here, in the presence of all-seeing God, was the watertight integrity of Ban's compartments compromised. On this holy ground, under His steady gaze, the toggles on Ban's mental doors kept loosening. Under the seals, seawater was seeping in, the bilge pumps were straining, and the captain was beginning to wonder if his was a fool's paradise.

What in God's name was he thinking of? He had given his life to God, vowed before Him to love and honor the woman beside him, the wife He had given him, till death did them part. Was he actually considering betraying that trust, putting asunder what God had joined together?

Whoa, his other side exclaimed. Let's not get things out of proportion here! First of all, *nothing* inappropriate has happened! Ever. During all their rides. And there's nothing to say that it will. Saralinda's a nice girl. A friend. That's all.

But he knew that wasn't all.

After the service, his wife walked home with him. Which was something that didn't often happen; usually Betsy had to meet someone or take care of something.

"I need to talk to you," she said gravely, as they walked along the dirt road to their home. For an instant his heart froze, then he realized it couldn't possibly be that.

"It's about Mark and Tina," she went on, "specifically Mark."

"What about them?"

Mark Rogers, 24, and Tina Gray, 21, had been in a relationship for more than a year, and now in a little over a month they would be getting married. The abbey did things a little differently than the world. Their young people were encouraged to relate to one another as brothers and sisters and/or friends. "What?" surprised outsiders would ask. "They don't date?" No, and it removed a tremendous amount of peer and social pressure from them, enabling the abbey's young people to form life-long friendships based on honesty and trust.

When they reached 18, they were free to leave the abbey, in which case obviously they could do whatever they wanted. But those who felt God calling them to remain, entered the same covenant that their parents had, accepting the abbey's ways and the ultimate spiritual authority of the abbess, or whoever was elected to take her place. Slightly more than two-thirds of the young people stayed.

Among those who became members, some would feel God calling them into the sisterhood or brotherhood. A few might feel called to remain single. As for the rest, inevitably a young man would feel himself drawn toward a young woman, and vice versa. Since God was the most important thing in their lives, and each wanted Him to remain so, it was imperative to discern whether the drawing was from Him. Each (unbeknownst to the other) would write a note to the abbess about the situation. (Often their notes arrived on the same day.)

If the abbess felt the relationship was of God, she would meet with them, and with her approval, they would start a relationship. Its purpose: to discern if it was God's will that they marry. A relationship might last a year or even two, before they became formally engaged and a wedding date was set. The relationship was to be chaste until they were wed; God expected no less.

To outsiders, the whole thing sounded almost puritanical, a throwback to the days when a marriage had to be approved by the town's pastor, and both sets of parents. To the abbey's young people, though, it was another relief. Working through their problems as they arose (often with the help of older, married members who had been through similar struggles), the young couple went through their period of adjustment *before* the wedding, instead of after.

It might be old-fashioned, but it worked. In thirty years, there had been 24 marriages and three divorces. And among those who had grown up in the abbey and married in the past 15 years, no divorces.

All told, there were 37 households in the abbey—each, an extended family or mini-community. The make-up of these households shifted every year or two, and at present in the Caulfield household was another younger family and their children, plus two unmarried young men. One of these was Mark, a strong, quiet, sensitive fellow who worked uptown in a florist's shop.

"He's always been a little closed off," Betsy was saying, "but recently he's gone so far back in his cave that I'm worried. They're getting married on the 18th of next month, and he should be excited, scared—you know!"

Ban nodded; he, too, had been concerned about Mark. "I'll talk to him."

After supper, he asked Mark to come out on the porch. Getting him to talk about himself was like pulling a ten-penny nail out of an oak tree. But years ago he had been one of Ban's regular cycling partners. He'd trusted Ban then, and might again.

To Ban's surprise, Mark was ready to talk; in fact, the pressure had been so building in him, that he welcomed the opportunity.

It seemed that Tina, who loved Mark as much as he loved her, wanted to show him a little more affection than he was comfortable with. And wanted to now, not four weeks from now. "I just want to do what's right," Mark concluded. "But frankly, it's getting awfully hard to say no."

Ban nodded, not trusting himself to say anything.

"I've told her: We've got to wait," Mark went on. "The Bible, the abbey—everything's pretty clear about that. The trouble is, part of me doesn't *want* to wait. Part of me agrees that it's stupid, when we're going to be married the rest of our lives. And that part's getting more and more strong!"

Ban was getting more and more uncomfortable. But he had to say something. "Look, Mark, what you and Tina are feeling is perfectly natural. But we've got a supernatural God, and He will give you supernatural grace to help keep things cool. All you have to do is ask Him."

Mark left, relieved.

Ban left, feeling a total hypocrite. He could not remember ever so despising himself. That night, before he fell into a troubled sleep, he heard a voice in his heart that he'd not heard in a long, long time.

And what of you, my son? Will you ask?

34 | game over

THE FOLLOWING DAY turned out to be the worst in Nigel Rawlings's life. When Clay Armstrong, the most senior partner of Armstrong & Associates, called its junior-partner-in-the-making into his office, Nigel assumed he was going to tell him how pleased he was with the results of the deal he and Ed had put together on their recent trip to New York (on which Nigel had done most of the work). When the market had opened that morning, the stock on their side of the merger was double where it had closed Friday. He had netted A&A roughly four million dollars.

Instead, Clay Armstrong had notified Nigel that, as of Friday morning, A&A would officially cease to exist. At first Nigel had thought he must be kidding; CA had a pretty weird sense of humor at times. As he gradually realized the old man actually *was* going to fold the company—twelve days before his golden payday!—he went numb.

For nearly a year Nigel had worked for nothing, learning everything they could teach him. Granted, what they'd taught him was priceless. But come on, they owed him a million dollars! That was their deal! He'd worked harder than he ever had in his life. But he'd also played hard. Since he was so sure of his eventual windfall, he had lived as if it was already in the bank.

The Nigel Rawlingses had expensive tastes. They were renting a house on the ocean in Chatham (until they could afford to build)—a big house, suitable for entertaining, that was setting him back just over $100,000 a year. He had also bought a pre-owned Hinkley Block Island '40 for $73,000. And was leasing a BMW convertible for his wife, and the newest, hottest Jaguar for himself. In addition, he had acquired a bottle-green 1953 MG TD that he was having meticulously restored.

But his greatest expense was unquestionably his wife, Rocky. When they met, she'd been one of that year's hot models in New York, while he was one of the hot gunslingers on the Street. She still had runway tastes, still had to have this year's clothes by this year's designer. And it took frequent outings to New York, to be certain she was still on the cutting edge.

In fairness, she'd warned him, when he'd flown down to be with her on a shoot in Puerto Vallarta, that she would be an extremely expensive merger acquisition. *Ningún problema*, he'd replied cavalierly, as he ordered another rum-dumb. Like seventy or eighty thousand a month? *Ningún Problema.*

Except that now it was *gran problema*.

The quieter life of Cape Cod had not been to Rocky's liking. Easily bored, she went out of her mind, after spending one leisurely Saturday on his boat (his favorite weekend activity). But she was also bored at home, bored in Chatham, and bored in Eastport.

The one time she was not bored was when she was traveling— with Nigel when he could get away, or with her traveling buds when he couldn't. And always first class. In March, when they'd flown down to Costa Rica (this year's getaway), he'd suggested that they go down tourist class as an economy measure. She thought he was kidding. He'd quoted one of his father's aphorisms, that the back of the plane got to the airport at the same time as the front. Her response: "Fine! You ride back there!"

It had been the vacation from hell.

Nigel had gone into his apprenticeship with a half-million-dollar nest egg, anticipating that it would carry them comfortably through his year of indenture. In six months it was gone. Their six-figure emergency CD's had bought them two more. The cash surrender value of his life insurance had covered another. Loans against his account at Smith Barney had paid for another, as long as the market held firm.

But he now was leveraged to the eyeballs, and the market had been far from firm. To say he was experiencing a cash flow problem was the understatement of the new millennium. Their beautiful cars had gone back, and Nigel was reduced to driving the MG to work, except when Rocky needed it. Then he would ride his bike to work, like Ed Forester. Moreover, his parents were so disgusted with his extravagant lifestyle that they refused to extend him a cent.

At least, Rocky was still with him. Barely. She was willing to wait twelve more days, until they were back in the good stuff. For good, because her husband was still one of the hot hands in the game. But for now, being poor was *really* boring, and she was not speaking to him.

Nigel was so desperate that last Saturday he had gone to see his grandmother in her posh graduated care facility in Essex, Connecticut. The family thought she had Alzheimer's, but whenever it came to money, the Alzheimer's went into remission. When Nigel had finally got around to asking her for a loan, she'd peered at her huge watch with its huge numbers and announced: "Twenty-three minutes."

"What?"

"That's how long it's taken you to come to the point of your visit."

"Gran! I just wanted to see you!"

"Oh, horse-hockey!" she exclaimed. She enjoyed scandalizing her well-bred offspring and their well-bred children. Then she'd asked him what he'd had for lunch yesterday. A peanut-butter sandwich. And dinner? Another peanut-butter sandwich.

"Well," she cackled, "sounds like you're trying to 'live off the smell of a greased rag,' as we used to say, when I was a girl." Gran liked to think of herself as a gritty survivor of the Great Depression, though that couldn't have been further from the case.

"Then you'll help me?"

"You bet!"

"Oh, Gran," cried Nigel, "thank you!"

"I'm going to help you by *not* giving you a dime! It'll be the making of you—best thing I could ever do for you!"

He was devastated. It took a lot less than 23 minutes to wind up his visit. As he left, Gran's benediction was another Depression-era expression: "Shirtsleeves to shirtsleeves in three generations!"

That, too, had been far from her situation—though it might soon be his.

Now, as CA concluded, Nigel lost it. "You can't do that! This is breach of contract!"

"I don't think so," replied Armstrong, taken aback. "Take a good look at paragraph 8: We were taking a gamble on you; we all knew that. But you were also taking a gamble on us. And you just lost."

Enraged (and terrified), Nigel then spewed verbal excrement all over the senior partner of Armstrong & Associates, venting all of his hurt and frustration of the past three weeks.

When he got done, Armstrong said quietly, "That outburst

just cost you a million dollars. You'd worked hard, Nigel, and had done a good job. I was prepared to give you the million anyway, as a parting gesture. But since your parting gesture seems to be of an obscene nature—and may indeed be your true nature—we'll just let the contract stand."

◆

Ed Forester's reaction was more constrained. But deeper. He, too, had trouble believing what his partner of nearly thirty years was telling him. "Clay, you can't do this! You can't just— quit! We've been doing this for so long—and doing it so well! Nobody's as good as we are! You know that!"

"I do know that," he said compassionately. "And you've been the best partner anyone could ever ask for. I never had to worry. I always knew you were there. Always knew what you were thinking. And knew that you knew what I was thinking. Most of the time, we didn't even have to talk."

He paused, and then told him about the spots on his lungs— that now weren't there. "So, Ed, try to understand: I think my life's been extended so that I can start giving back, instead of just taking," he concluded. "Trevor Haines is in the business of helping people, and now I'm going to be in the business of helping him help them."

Forester didn't know what to say. When it was clear that nothing could change Clay's mind, he brightened. "Well, at least let A&A go out with a bang! The Genome Project will be the greatest coup we've ever pulled off! They'll be citing it at Harvard Business School a hundred years from now!"

Clay just shook his head. "It's over, Ed. All of it. This Friday."

"But you can't just—pull out of the game!" Forester pleaded, his voice breaking.

His partner looked at him. "If it's a question of money, Ed—"

"It's not the money! You know I was never in it for the money! It was you and me—and the game!"

"Well, the game's over for me," sighed Clay, sad but smiling.

Forester turned away, so his partner would not see the tears in his eyes. "Well," he murmured, "I'm happy for you," and he quickly left the office and *FW*.

Later that afternoon, Forester returned, to try to make a better ending of it. He saw Clay in the library and was about to go in to him, when he realized he was not alone. There were plans spread out on the chart table, and bending over them on the stool next to his was Trevor Haines. He watched the two of them together, planning their future in animated conversation, and turned and left.

That night he called his new lady friend, whom he had met at a Realtor's convention that his former, long-time lady friend, also in real estate, had made the mistake of taking him to. The new one understood him much better than the old one ever had. And she *cared*. She could see in him the thing he valued the most at the core of his being. And she appreciated it; in fact, she thought he was—wonderful.

As it happened, she, too, was just getting over a relationship, one that for years had been very good, but had just recently gone very bad.

They talked for three hours that night, as Ed Forester poured out his feelings.

35 | only a dream

TUESDAY WAS TURNING OUT to be everyone's worst day. In the morning, Ed and Nigel had learned of the imminent demise of A&A. In the afternoon, the Armstrong Sisters, in an emergency session convened by Samantha, concluded that while they were all now in agreement with Serena's assessment of Trevor . Haines, none of them had any idea how to stop their father from making a terrible mistake, come Friday.

Only Serena, who always suspected the worst of everyone (and was seldom disappointed), had anything concrete to offer. Yesterday, after making inquiries, she'd hired a top-flight investigative firm in Boston, to do a thorough background check on Mr. Haines. She was particularly interested in learning if he'd ever been involved in anything that was, as Grandfather Asa might have put it, "not quite the clean potato." And she needed their findings ASAP. Before Friday. For that kind of speed, they'd informed her, their regular fee would have to be doubled.

"I told them to go ahead," she reported to her sisters. "What's a few thousand more, when our father's life is at risk?" They applauded her initiative.

But the one who was hit hardest that Tuesday was Gottfried Franc. Down on the beach he stared unseeing out at the pounding Atlantic. He, too, had just learned that there would be no more Armstrong & Associates. Which meant there would be no Genome Project under his leadership, no lab and staff under his command. It had all been—only a dream.

And now, it was a nightmare. Because he had not told Samantha, much less her father, of what had transpired at the Randolph Corporation on the morning of Friday the 13th, shortly before they'd left for the Cape. Increasingly concerned over Big Red's heightened security, and his sense that they were backing away from their original commitment, Gottfried had gone to the office of Susan Foster, the Randolph Corporation's Chief Operating Officer, who had hired him in the first place.

His hole card, which would give him the backbone to force them to honor their word, was Clayton Armstrong's absolute assurance that if he left Randolph and came with A&A, he would have everything he wanted. The human DNA code would be made available to the world as soon as they recouped their costs. It was basically the same deal he'd originally had with Big Red; the difference was, it was Samantha's father.

That was a big difference. Mr. Armstrong (he could not bring himself to call his fiancée's father by his first name) had been so considerate and understanding, that Gottfried had found himself thinking of him more as a father figure than a financier. It was a perspective that Mr. Armstrong seemed to encourage. Friday evening after dinner, he and Gottfried had gone out on the terrace to enjoy the full moon's rise out of the Atlantic. His host, in a mellow, reflective mood, had confided that he had only two regrets in life: not having put his marriage and family first, and not having had a son.

"Of course," he'd mused, "when a man says that, what he wants is a son just like himself, who will share his interests and want to do what he did, only maybe a little better."

Gottfried had not known what to say, but Mr. Armstrong was not really looking for a response. "The trouble is, sons seldom turn out like their fathers. If I'd had a son, he would probably have turned out like his mother—creative, artistic, gentle—traits which, at *this* point in my life, I might appreciate and encourage in a son. But which, twenty or thirty years ago, I would have in all likelihood despised, or at best considered inconsequential—at a time in *his* life when his father's approval would have been crucial."

Gottfried had been nonplussed. And saddened. For his own father *had* approved of him, despite the fact that he was not at all like the Baron. If only his father had not been—who he was. But nothing could change that now. Or change his determination to make atonement. And now here was a father who wanted a son—and a son who wanted a father. . . .

Earlier that Friday, in Susan Foster's office, he had demanded she account for the new security measures. Not caring for his peremptory tone, she had gotten a bit peremptory herself. "Gottfried, do you know how close the National Institute of Health is to cracking the Genome Code? Our source there tells us that they'll have it in less than six months! And we've just paid a fortune to find out that Henderson-Bartlett is even closer! HB's going to have it by the end of the year! You think we're going to risk losing our lead, just because you want to play in Mr. Rogers' neighborhood? It's grown-up time now, Gottfried! Time to come outside and play with the big boys!"

He was stunned. In all his time at Randolph, no one had ever spoken to him that way. Hurt gave way to anger. "You wouldn't even *be* in the race, if it wasn't for me! *I'm* the one who figured out how to speed up the computer tracking and cataloguing of the code. *And* what we're going to do with it, once we have it, and how we're going to achieve the cures—most of which is still up here." He tapped his right temple.

"That does it!" she'd exclaimed. "We're going to see Mr. Randolph! Right now!" And she practically marched him down the hall like a truant schoolboy, to the office of the founder and CEO, Joseph Randolph.

Gottfried had met Mr. Randolph only once, a year after joining the corporation. The old man had white handlebar moustaches, which reminded him of the Tenniel drawing of Lewis Carroll's Walrus, and had stopped in Gottfried's lab a few moments, as he escorted some Japanese investors on a tour of the plant. He'd been impressed by the intelligence and perspicacity of the CEO's summary and questions. Gottfried would have preferred not to be meeting him again under these circumstances, but Ms. Foster had a head of steam up and was not about to simmer down.

After she'd heatedly conveyed the gist of their conversation, old Randolph looked at Gottfried. "Do you really believe that, given the incalculable value of your work, such precautions are exaggerated?"

It *was* a reasonable question. "I suppose not."

"Did you know that we caught one of Henderson-Bartlett's agents snooping around here three weeks ago?"

Gottfried was shocked. "No, I didn't know that."

"Under the circumstances, with HB having spent more than a hundred million to beat us if they can, and willing to stoop to anything to do so, if you were me, would you not want to protect your investment?"

"Well, of course."

"Then I don't see what the problem is."

There was no problem, Gottfried realized. He felt a little foolish and was about to apologize and go back downstairs, when he remembered the main reason he'd gone to Ms. Foster in the first place.

He forced himself to raise the issue. And received the CEO's personal assurance that they would indeed give the code to the world, as soon as the ensuing patents had run their seven-year exclusive. "If we don't wait that long," the CEO explained, "we will, in effect, be giving our competitors *for free*, what we've spent nearly half a billion dollars to develop."

Put that way, the Randolph Corporation's position seemed eminently reasonable, thought Gottfried. Except for one thing: "Mr. Randolph, forgive me, but we both know that on the world market those patents would return your investment in two years, not seven. I am not averse to you holding the code a third year; that should generate enough profit to satisfy any investor and would make the corporation the unrivaled leader in the whole field of genetics. But to hold the code the full seven years? Well, that's—obscene."

Now it was Joseph Randolph's turn to get firm. "Young man, that is a noble sentiment, nobly expressed. But you seem to have forgotten that most of our profits go directly back into funding research such as your own. You, Mr. Franc, are hardly the only gifted scientist we are supporting here. There are at least a dozen men and women as bright as you, who are still years away from their breakthroughs. Indeed, the fruit of your work is going to fund revolutionary advances across the entire medical spectrum. The Randolph Corporation has done—and will continue to do—more for the advancement of medical research than any other organization on the planet."

As a closer, it must have brought the recent stockholders meeting to their feet in thunderous applause, thought Gottfried. It also happened to be true.

He would have caved at that point, had Ms. Foster kept her mouth shut. But she had to get her two cents in. "And don't forget," she smiled condescendingly, "we *own* what's in there," and she reached out and tapped his right temple, "just as surely as if it was written on the blackboard in your laboratory."

Gottfried stiffened, and then smiled back at her. "In kindergarten I used to enjoy being given the job of cleaning the blackboards. I would wash them so clean that no one could ever guess what had been written there."

Silence.

Then she said, "If that's some kind of threat, Gottfried, you'd better know that to protect our intellectual property, we'd have you so tied up in lawsuits that not only would you never work in research again, you wouldn't even be able to get a job driving a Boston taxi!"

Without replying, he'd turned and walked out, intending never to go back. But now his ace in the hole—his dream—had just been torn into tiny pieces—and held up to the wind, which had blown it far out to sea.

"Gottfried?" It was Samantha, calling to him from the south terrace far above. "What are you doing down there?"

He looked up at her, and then turned back to the ocean.

Making her way down the long, rickety flight of stairs as quickly as she could, she ran over to him. "Darling, what is it? What's happened?"

He just shook his head, his eyes filling.

"Tell me, Gosha! I have a right to know."

And so he told her.

And now Serena was not the only Armstrong Sister who hated Trevor Haines for what he had done to their father.

36 | a single slip

JUST BEFORE SUNSET THE FOLLOWING afternoon (Wednesday),
Trevor Haines's blue Bentley pulled into the gravel driveway of
FW–or rather bulled into it, scattering white stones onto the
grass. Instead of continuing on to the garage, where it now
occupied the fourth bay, it came to a grinding halt at the front
door. Out of it jumped Haines, who took the front steps two at
a time and slammed into the house.

He found Clay Armstrong in the library, perched on a stool
at the chart table, going over the floor plan for the ARC. "I'm
glad you're here," his host greeted him affably. "I can't figure out
what's going to go next to the Solarium. We had something in
there, then crossed it out, and I can't make out—"

"Your daughter's having me investigated!" Haines shouted.

"Oh, really?" replied Clay, still cheerful. "Which one?"

"Serena!"

"Well, good for her!" he said with a chuckle. "Should have
thought of it myself. You know, Trevor, considering the size of

what we're undertaking here, it's only responsible of us to do background checks on each other—although somehow I get the impression you already have." He tapped the plans in front of him and smiled. "Now come over here and explain to me what's next to the Solarium."

But Haines, still furious, did not move. "I want it stopped! Now!"

"What's the problem? We both know they're not going to find anything." He paused, his smile fading. "Are they?"

All at once, Haines relaxed and smiled. "No, of course not." He came over and sat on the empty stool. "Sorry for the way I stormed in here. I guess I thought—you didn't trust me, Clay."

Clay put an arm around Haines's shoulder. "Never mind, it's forgotten." He pointed to the floor plan. "Now tell me again: What's going in here, next to the Solarium?"

Haines laughed and said, "You know, I could really use a Breezer, just now."

"No sooner said, than done," said Clay, reaching under the table for the button that would summon James. When the latter appeared, he gave him the order, and in a few moments, James returned with a tray on which were two fluted glasses filled with the light silver-green liquid, and a frosty crystal pitcher of refills. Passing the tray to each of them, he left it on a side table and was about to return to the kitchen, when his master had a request: "Tomorrow evening, James, I'd like a proper banquet for Mr. Haines and myself. I realize it's awfully short notice, but it's for a special occasion." He turned to his friend and smiled. "A sort of pre-signing celebration."

"Very well, sir," said James, "is there any dish in particular that you would care for?"

Clay shook his head and smiled. "No, I leave that to your discretion, which will be excellent, as always."

"Very good, sir," said the houseman, exiting stage right.

Taking a sip, Clay set his Breezer aside, and bent over the plans. But Haines drank his quickly, and in a moment went over to the pitcher for a refill.

Instead of returning to join Clay at the plans, he paced restlessly around the room, pausing at the baby grand, which Sheila used to play. On the top of it were several 8 x 10 black-and-white portraits in silver frames, including a formal one by Bachrach of Sheila as a bride. That one was surrounded by an array of 4 x 5's, also silver-framed, of the Armstrong sisters, as they were growing up. The most recent additions were in color, of the two grandsons at play. And to the right was one in a wood frame, an 8 x 10 color photo of a handsome middle-aged woman in a gray Ultrasuede suit, with a champagne blouse and a burgundy scarf.

Haines looked at it more closely. "Dorothy Hanson, isn't it?"

"Why, yes," said Clay from his stool.

"Tragic what happened to her," Haines went on, appreciating the photo, "but that outfit certainly became her."

Clay looked carefully at him. "When?"

"Oh," said Haines casually, "when you introduced me to her."

His host said nothing.

"Or maybe it was one of those other times, in your office."

"She never wore that here."

"Well," replied Haines, a little hurriedly, "then I must have seen the picture on the piano here." He gestured to the room. "I often stroll in here, when I'm thinking."

Clay stared at him. "Alan Jones brought that picture over this afternoon. He'd taken it of Dorothy on the last night of their trip, right after she'd bought that outfit. He thought I would appreciate having it."

"Well, then," said Haines with his most ingratiating, self-deprecatory smile, "I couldn't have seen it, could I? I'm always mixing things up."

Clay said nothing.

"Well," said Haines cheerily, "let's see what we've put next to the Solarium," and he sat down next to his host.

But Clay, lost in thought, soon excused himself, "to take care of some business" he'd forgotten.

When he returned, he said, "Look, something's come up. I've got to make a quick trip up to New Hampshire. But I'll be back Friday morning—in plenty of time for our appointment at Gilbert, Chandler & Cooper's."

And, without waiting for a response, he turned and left.

37 | last call

HAINES SHIVERED AS HE STEPPED up to the payphone on the sidewalk outside Eastport Cyclery. Squinting in the dusk to make out the numbers, he punched in a call. He listened a moment, then said: "Wednesday, the 18th, 6:10. On Saturday, I informed—"

"I'm here. What happened Saturday?"

"I told his daughters about the ARC."

"How did they take it?"

"Samantha and Saralinda seemed all right with it, but Serena wasn't. Afterwards, she accused me of trying to con her father. And now she's got a firm running a background check on me!"

"We knew that was a possibility; on a project of this size, it's not unusual."

"But it's turned up Sedona!"

"Will you relax? I cleaned up that mess for you, remember? There's nothing to link you to it directly. But—how did you learn they'd—"

"I still have friends out there," Haines snapped. "One of them called me."

"On your cell phone?"

"Well, I—"

"You gave someone out there your number? We agreed that you were not to have any further contact with anyone out there!"

"Look," Haines replied, attempting damage control, "the call lasted no more than a—"

"When are you going to learn? The day they strap you to the table?"

"Lena! The deal's going through Friday morning," declared Haines, desperate to get on a more positive footing. "It will be signed in the lawyers' office at 10:00."

"How did Armstrong's associates take it?"

"Not well. From a couple of things he said at breakfast this morning, I gather the younger one went ballistic. But it was the older one who took it the hardest."

"I know."

Haines's eyes widened, and he stared at the receiver in his hand. "You *know*? How?"

"Never mind; it doesn't involve you."

"You're not—"

"I said: *never mind!*"

"Because if you think—"

"What I think is, you'd better finish what you have to tell me! And let's just cut to the bad stuff, shall we? The stuff you always save for last, hoping I won't ask."

Haines shuddered, and forced himself to go on. "They've also found out that I'm not on the Class Gift Committee."

"How do you know?"

"Because someone from the Yale Office of Development called me this morning. They'd received a query about my involvement and were trying to ascertain how someone might have gotten that impression."

"Does Armstrong know?"

"No," Haines said emphatically. "And he won't find out before Friday."

"How can you be so sure?"

"Because he's gone out of town and won't be back until just before the signing."

"And he can't be reached?"

"I think he's gone to his campsite, and when he does that, he turns off his phone."

"I thought he was staying put until Friday."

"So did I. It happened just an hour ago. All of a sudden, he just left."

"What precipitated it?"

Haines bit his lip. "Nothing. We were going over the plans, and he went to his work office, and when he came back, he said he was going up to New Hampshire, but would meet me at the lawyers' on Friday morning."

"Why did he go?"

"I don't know!" said Haines defensively. "Sometimes, he just goes up there to think. He's probably doing that now."

"You think he's getting cold feet?"

"Not a chance! Not after the healing."

"Then why am I beginning to smell–"

The best defense was an attack. "You don't smell anything! There's nothing *to* smell!"

"Trevor–"

"I'm sick of this!" His voice was no longer subdued, and he no longer cared who heard or saw him. "I'm sick of always being–"

"Trevor! What–have–you–done?"

"I haven't done anything!" he shouted. Then glancing around the empty street, he lowered his voice, though not its intensity. "I *hate* it when you get so accusative!"

"You'd better tell me what it is. You know what happened the last time."

"All right!" He tried to lighten up. "It's really nothing, anyway. I was a little rattled about the background check, and when he shrugged it off as 'just good business,' I got a little more rattled."

"Why?"

"I thought he might be losing confidence in me."

"Did you have anything to drink?"

"I did have one, but—"

"How many?"

"All right, two, but listen—"

"No, dear brother, you listen! You were not to touch alcohol until after those papers were signed!"

"I told you, I was nervous!"

"What happened? And remember, I always know when you're lying."

"I was commiserating with him about the loss of his office manager whose photo happened to be on the piano, and I commented on how much the outfit in the picture became her, and—"

"What outfit?"

"The gray Ultrasuede."

"The one she was wearing when—"

"Yes. Only she'd bought it over in Belgium on the trip."

"So you couldn't have seen it on her, unless—"

"Exactly. I made light of it, tossed it off and said I must have been mistaken. But it was right after that, that he left."

There was a pause. Then: "Do you have any idea what you've done?"

Haines did not reply.

"You've just implicated yourself—and possibly me."

"I tell you, I can handle Armstrong!" He was shouting again. "He's just gotten the x-ray results. The spots on his lung are gone! He thinks I'm practically Jesus Christ!"

"In all these years, you've never pulled a stunt like this one! We're going to have to pull the plug."

"No!" cried Haines, practically hysterical. "I know I can redeem this!" Then he clutched at a straw. "You don't want to lose your diamonds!"

"That's the one thing that keeps me from wrapping it up right now."

"I know I can fix this! Just give me 36 hours!"

"I'll think about it."

38 | some enchanted evening

AT 5:18 THE FOLLOWING AFTERNOON (Thursday), Banastre Caulfield registered at the reception desk of the Airport Marriot. Had Ms. Armstrong checked in? Yes. He reached for the house phone, and then stopped. Take a shower first. Get changed. Get *here.*

Back home on the refrigerator, next to the wall phone, he had left his flight numbers and departure times, and phone numbers. He was covered. As he'd left, his wife had cautioned him to drive safely. He had not. Coming up Route 3, he had gotten stopped for speeding, his first ticket in four years–$260 for going 21 miles over the 55 limit.

Get all the way here.

In his room, he unpacked his carry-on and hang-bag, laid out the black turtleneck, the navy blazer, the charcoal gray slacks–dark clothes to minimize the thickness at his waist. To make him look–and feel–younger. Firing up his laptop and plugging in the portable external speakers, he put a Nana

Mouskouri CD in its player, turning up the volume enough to hear it in the bathroom. Soon the quicksilver voice which could make any song sound good, made some old songs sound *very* good—"A Day in the Life of a Fool" and "Autumn Leaves" and "The Windmills of Your Mind."

In the shower, he let the hot, steaming water beat on him, washing away the speeding ticket and the other events of the afternoon. The day. The week. He took a long time in the shower (it wasn't *his* septic system, after all), letting it *all* wash away . . . the drooping sales, the hurtful reviews, all the weeks, the years. . . .

When he finally stepped out of the shower, the watertight doors in the bowels of his ship had swung shut—closed, battened, and tightly sealed. He was no longer 44 and unsure of himself. A writer whose best work was behind him and who was now consigned to imitating it. A lonely husband and self-absorbed father and lip-service member of a covenanted Christian community. He wasn't even married. He was just Ban Caulfield now, about 30–32. Just ole' Ban. Here. Now.

As he donned fresh underwear, he noticed the silver cross he'd worn on its silver chain ever since his conversion. He never took it off, even when he went swimming. But he took it off now, placing it on top of his shaving kit, so he'd be sure to remember it in the morning.

He dressed carefully, listening to Nana Mouskouri sing "Historia de un Amor," and then, as he put on his blazer and turned sideways to check his reflection in the full-length mirror (instinctively flattening his stomach), she sang "Malagüeña Salerosa." He had to smile; the driving Flamenco ballad made him feel like a matador, dressing for the *Corrida*. Would the bulls be brave? Would the matador?

He went to the phone and called her.

"I'm glad you came early," she said softly. "We can watch the sun go down from the penthouse bar."

"I'll be waiting for you."

A few minutes later, he was at the bar with a pint of Bass Ale, half listening to the piano player doing a David Lanz medley. He was floating now, drifting down the medley in a hazy reverie of what was. And might have been. And is. And might yet become.

He embraced the moment, became a sad, wistful non-hero in a sad, wistful French movie. A protagonist who *knew* without knowing, everything that was about to happen. In a way, it had already happened—and if it did happen again, it might not happen as well.

He also knew that what seemed like happiness would in time turn to sadness. Yet—was it not better to live it and be hurt by it, than not to live it—and always wonder?

He shook his head; too much Sartre. He was playing the game again—the one romantics played, when they were into game playing. There was a kind of wry, sad knowing to it all, tinged with fate and melancholy. And the certain knowledge that whatever was good was fleeting and would not last, as in *Jules et Jim*. So, he reasoned with himself, you might as well give it all up, and go back to the familiar. Except, what if—*something*—enabled you to hold on to the moment. Not long. But long enough—to always remember. Would that not make it—worth living out?

There was an arc to this élan—an acceptance of rain beating on a window and streaming away what was beyond the pane, or the tide coming in to erase the marvelous drawings that Picasso had made with a long pointed stick.

He'd been here before, on the upper edge of the arc. And if he could stop now, he would. Because it might not *ever* get any better.

"Hello," she said softly. "Been waiting long?"

He turned, and his mouth dropped open. Was this what happened when a dream became real? When the best dream you've ever had turned out to be—not a dream at all?

For the briefest of moments, the matador was scared. He was there, in the middle of the *Plaza de Toros*, facing a magnificent bull, big as a cathedral, and not the least bit slowed or head-lowered by the pic. A bull that might just, for a fleeting moment, not follow the cape, but hook left, into him, lifting him up, the horn reaching up through his intestines, his liver, his stomach. . . .

He shuddered. C'mon, Ban, you're not in Pamplona; you're here. And now she's here, too. Look at her.

The light was behind her, limning her features. Her dark hair was up in a French twist. She was wearing black—long, shimmering black, whose sole ornament was a gold chain around her neck, from which hung an antique cross in beaten gold.

"Your mouth's open," she said, her eyes dancing.

"Uhm—you clean up good," he stammered. It was the standard response of outdoors people, whenever they met indoors, dressed for an occasion. Trite, but it was all he could muster. He went back to staring.

"You clean up pretty good yourself," she said gently, and they both laughed. And suddenly felt a little shy with each other.

"Well," he said, matter-of-factly, "the sun should be setting over there behind the skyline in about eighteen minutes." Then he laughed. "Listen to me; I sound like a tour-leader."

She smiled and took his arm. "Why don't we take that table by the window."

They did. He had another Bass; she, a glass of cabernet. Without speaking, they watched the sun go down, and the lights of the Boston waterfront come on. She reached out and took his hand.

At dinner, Saralinda ordered oysters and roast duckling. Ban couldn't make up his mind and finally picked something so the waiter wouldn't have to wait. He was in a dream, following a script he had not written, that was better than any he had.

His eyes kept returning to hers—so deep, calm, and alive. Until finally she said, "You've got to stop looking at me that way; you're making me self-conscious."

He stopped. Seeking a topic of conversation, his eye fell on the cross she was wearing. "That looks hand-crafted," he said, admiring it, "and very old."

"It is. My grandfather, my mother's father, gave it to me, when my grandmother died. It was at least a hundred years old, when he'd gotten it for her on their honeymoon. In Mexico, right after he came back from the war."

"Why Mexico?"

"That's what I asked him, when he gave it to me. And then he told me the story of why Mexico." She looked out at the twilight and back at him. "You want to hear it?"

"Sure."

"Okay, but you're the first person I've ever told it to."

In college, her grandfather's roommate was from Brownsville, Texas. He'd been brought up by a Mexican governess—and so grew up loving Mexico. In 1940, the summer of their junior year, the two young men went down there in an old Model A, looking for adventure. "They found it. They went to bullfights in Mexico City, and got drunk on cheap wine, and even met a matador—a total Hemingway experience."

"For Whom the Bell Tolls had just come out," Ban offered, "making Hemingway the spokesman for a whole generation of romantic idealists."

She smiled. "Two of whom were soon picking their way over potholes and wash-outs in the dirt road that led to the coast, where they met a Ranchero singer called *La Llorona*—" She stopped and frowned. "Why are you smiling?"

"Because, my dear, on top of all your other gifts, you have the gift of telling."

She hesitated, not sure how to take that. "You want me to go on?"

"Of course! I'm back in Mexico City with your grandfather and his Texas friend and Ernest Hemingway and this singer—"

"No," she said, shaking her head, "the bullfights were in Mexico City. The singer was in Acapulco. And not Acapulco today; Acapulco in 1940. Primitive. But even then, there was a waterfront cantina at the base of the cliffs, where you could drink tequila and lime juice over ice with salt, long before anybody every thought of calling it a Marguerita."

Her meal forgotten, she took a sip of wine and gazed out at the gathering dusk. "There was this young boy who would dive off the high cliff 130 feet into the gorge. When you looked up from the cantina's terrace which was right at the water's edge, you could see him far up there—my grandfather said he couldn't have been more than fourteen—standing up there, shivering. Waiting."

"For what?"

"For the sun to set. By the shadow that suddenly covered the cantina far below, the boy could tell the moment when *los clientes,* looking out to sea, saw the fiery top edge of the sun disappear. That was his cue. As soon as the wave below him had washed completely out of the gorge, leaving it almost bare, he would launch—"

"*Out* of the gorge?"

"Yes, because he was so far up, and it took so long for him to come down, that by the time he hit the water, the next incoming wave would have filled the gorge."

Ban gazed at her; this woman could create a spell. Which enveloped her, as well, for she seemed to be hearing her grandfather tell it.

"Because the boy was so far up on the side of the cliff, he was still in the sun. All at once he launched off his narrow perch, like an eagle taking flight. Lifting off, his back arched, his arms extended like wings, he would soar, a golden eagle in the last rays of the sun. Then he would fold his wings and plummet earthward like a diving bird of prey—down, down into the deep shadows of the gorge, finally plunging into the cresting wave.

"And *los clientes*—wide-eyed, staring at the plume of water that rose up from the slight form entering it, realized that they had just seen something so beautiful—and brave—they would remember it the rest of their lives."

Ban stared at her, transfixed. "And then?"

39 | la llorona

THIS WAS NOT THE SCRIPT he'd had in mind, Ban thought, but Saralinda's story was—too good to mess up.

She smiled. "Nowadays there are many cliff divers in Acapulco, and they keep on diving. But in 1940, there was only the one boy. And he did it only once a night. People watching would give the cantina's proprietor, his uncle, a tip for him. Usually a dollar. In fact, anything less indicated what the watcher *didn't* get out of it. Then they'd go in to supper."

She took a bite of duckling, feeling guilty at having let it get cold. But both of them wanted her to go on.

"It was not a big cantina, and it was also a weekday; there weren't more than a dozen patrons in the dining room. My grandfather and his friend had enchiladas and tortillas and frijoles, with more tequila to wash it down."

She paused to take another bite and would have taken a third, but Ban prompted, "Then what?"

"Then, this girl with a guitar came in. She had raven-black hair and gold hoop earrings and a white *campesino* blouse and red *campesino* skirt."

She stopped, annoyed at his expression. "I know it's a cliché. Try to remember we're talking *1940*. Before literary snobs like you even knew what a cliché was!"

"Ouch!" he exclaimed. And added, "Sorry; I deserved that. And please, don't stop. I'm really into this old movie; next reel, please."

"My grandfather said that she lived each ballad she sang, and was so striking that she'd sung four, before he realized that she was blind."

"*What?*"

"Completely blind. My grandfather was shocked. All he could think of was those poor nightingales who'd had their eyes put out with needles, so they would sing the more plaintively. He was spellbound, unable to move or even think. All he could do was listen."

Ban shook his head. "Me, too."

"As she sang one old but timeless ballad after another, he said that time and space just–fell away. He was in another world, his heart accepting totally whatever her heart was saying, wherever it was going. He couldn't understand Spanish, but it didn't matter; his heart knew exactly what her heart was telling his."

She paused. The next part must have been hard for her grandfather, because it was hard for her.

"And then–she sang the saddest song he'd ever heard– that he could never hear again, without seeing her."

Ban asked, "Did it have a name?"

"*La Llorona*–the story of the ghost of a forlorn mother searching the streets of Mexico City for her lost children." She looked at him. "The singer had also lost a child. That was why she could sing with such heart-rending pathos–and why they called her that."

"What happens next?" he managed, now totally in Acapulco with the young American who had lost his heart to the blind singer, who had lost her sight to—

But Saralinda smiled and shook her head. "Ah, that's another story, for another time." She looked at him. "But you've asked the right question: What happens next?"

"I pay the bill," he said, smiling to make light of it. He paid it, and they left the restaurant.

When the down elevator arrived, they got in, and she pushed 7. He pushed 5. End of story.

Except—when they got to 7, she said, "Is this—good night?"

"Well," he said, trying to remain nonchalant but betrayed by the huskiness in his voice, "a gentleman would see a lady to her door."

"I never thought of you as less than a gentleman."

"I never thought of you as less than a lady."

They got off and went to her door. Where she looked up at him. "Would a lady invite a gentleman in?"

"Would a gentleman accept the invitation?"

"Why don't we see: I have a small bottle of Bailey's, which I put in a large bucket of ice, before leaving."

He smiled broadly. "Sure'n how could ye know that Bailey's was my Achilles heel?"

She opened the door, and he followed her in. Lifting the little bottle out of the mostly melted ice, she opened it, and poured its creamy brown contents into two hotel tumblers. Handing him one, she raised the other in a toast. "To the loveliest evening I've had in two years—at least."

He raised his glass. "To an evening I—will never forget."

They drank and put the glasses down.

She turned to him, and he put his arms around her and brought her close. And murmured, "If we stop. Right now. We haven't done anything we can't tell our children about."

She smiled. "Bridges of Madison County."

"Yes. An honest movie that—"

He was about to say something insightful, but she put a finger to his lips. And looked into his eyes.

Returning her gaze, he started to tremble.

At which, she smiled. "My cliff-diver. Shivering with cold. So scared. And brave."

He launched out into the setting sun, and then, folding his wings, plummeted down into the depths of her eyes and kissed her.

Time stopped. When he came up for air, the wave was washing out of the gorge.

The most beautiful creature on earth was looking up at him, and—he dived again.

Slipping her hands inside his blazer, she reached up, and separating her hands, as if she, too, were diving, she lifted the jacket off his shoulders and let it fall to the floor.

Now he was hurrying—to undo the top clasp of her dress in back. But the chain that held the cross had somehow gotten caught in it. He tried to dislodge it—gently, so as not to break the spell. But it would not come free. He became—quietly—more insistent.

She started to reach up herself; her fingers knew the secret. Then she stopped—to let this scene play out the way it would.

His impatience was building, verging on anger. Taking the cross in his hand, he was about to give it a quick yank, which would have freed it, when he looked down at the object in his hand. A century and a half fell away, and he saw the goldsmith who had fashioned it. Who had etched and gently hammered it, trying to put into the precious yellow metal all his love for the One who had loved him—that much.

Tears came to Ban's eyes. His mouth opened, but no words would come out. He could not take his eyes off the cross.

Far below, in the bowels of his ship, the captain could feel through his feet, the multiple explosions of watertight doors being blown off their hinges.

He looked down at her. "I can't."

"I know."

He bent and picked up the jacket.

"Will you go to Roanoke?"

"No. I'm going home. Now. Because," he looked at her—so beautiful, so exactly what he'd always dreamed of, and so much more—"if I don't, in another hour or two, I'd be back here, at your door, knocking."

She just looked at him. In her eyes there were tears, too.

40 | last supper

THE LONG, PLAIN OAK TABLE in the low-ceilinged dining room of *FW* could seat 24 guests (in straight-backed, Frank-Lloyd-Wright-designed discomfort). And occasionally it did, the last occasion being Samantha's summer coming-out party, twenty years before.

This evening (Thursday), there was only one guest, seated at the head of the table, his back to the swinging door to the pantry leading to the kitchen. Trevor Haines was dining alone.

But dining in solitary splendor. For even though his host had gone out of town abruptly, the man who had stayed for so many dinners felt certain that Clay Armstrong would have wanted him to proceed with their celebration banquet. He had, therefore, given James the menu for that evening. There would be eight courses: Oysters Rockefeller, followed by escargots. An endive salad. A filet of trout amandine. Then quail. Then lamb chops with sautéed baby carrots, onions, and potatoes. Followed by crêpes in cherry brandy sauce. And finally,

English Stilton cheese with water biscuits and red currant jelly.

Out of consideration, he had given the menu to James early in the morning, realizing it would take him most of the day to prepare it. It did. James had to make four trips into town, to procure the necessary ingredients. And while James worked in the kitchen, Haines had been busy, too, down in the basement, going through *FW's* extensive wine cellar, selecting the ideal accompaniment to each course. He gave the list to James, suggesting that he might want to procure a better port than the one in the cellar, perhaps a bottle of Graham's (which had occasioned a fifth trip into town).

It had been well worth the effort, decided Haines, patting his lips with the linen napkin and contemplating the last of the crêpes, and the last of the Château Margaux '76 which he'd chosen to complement it. At the moment he did not have room for the Stilton, but that was the advantage of dining leisurely in the European manner: If you took your time, there was always room for a little more.

On the audio system, Derek Bell was playing the Irish harp, while outside the horizontal window, a waning quarter moon hung over the calm Atlantic. It was a perfect evening—and James was a superb chef; whatever else he changed, he would definitely keep him on. It was, in all, a perfect world.

The only cloud on the horizon had been that little slip over the photograph of Dorothy Hanson. That was stupid, and his host, ever astute, had clearly been troubled by it. Yet there had been no serious damage done—nothing that Trevor Haines, at the top of his form, could not smooth and rectify upon Armstrong's return.

He allowed himself to dwell, just a little, on what his situation would soon be like. Once he had led Armstrong through Phases II and III, he would be ready for IV and V—after which, his control over his host would be absolute. Others would come to his clinic for help, and his reputation would grow and expand. He would train other disciples, open other clinics, extend his domain. . . .

Power, thought Haines, with a languid smile, really was the ultimate narcotic. As anyone who had ever tasted it, knew. You could never let it go. And never get enough.

It was also true about power's tendency to corrupt, and absolute power corrupting absolutely. There were those who considered him depraved, and ample evidence for their case could be found among the wreckage of the lives he'd left behind in Sedona and New Orleans.

But this time, there would be no mistakes.

He traced the outline of the wine star formed on the white linen tablecloth, as the candlelight from the silver candelabra refracted through the remaining contents of the cut-crystal goblet. Taking another sip, the last, he noted an odd edge to its taste, of which he had been hitherto unaware. Rolling the wine to different corners of his mouth for a palate check, he decided that, yes, there was a faint brackishness that should not be present in a '76 Margaux.

Had he been in a restaurant fine enough to offer such a wine, he would have beckoned the sommelier to his table and asked him to taste it. And without his having to say a word, the dismayed chief steward would have returned the bottle to the kitchen, and suggested a replacement, compliments of the house. Alas, in this case it was *his* cellar—or soon would be.

Well, he was ready now for the Stilton. You see, a little patience and—as he reached under the table for the button that would summon James, he noticed something: In the bottom of the now-empty wine glass was a residue of tiny white crystals.

What were *they* doing there? His eyes widened in horror, as he realized what they signified. And at that instant a searing pain cut across his stomach, as if someone had slashed him with a cavalry saber.

Lurching up from the table, sending plates, silverware,

glasses, and candelabra crashing to the floor, he plunged through the swinging pantry door. Beyond was the kitchen, and beyond it was the garage and his car. . . .

But in the kitchen, blocking his path and leveling the muzzle of a 9mm Beretta automatic at his stomach, was—his would-be assassin.

Haines glared at the latter and sneered with incredulity. "Did you honestly believe that—*you*—could stop—*me?*"

Blam, blam! The Beretta jumped twice. At point-blank range there was no missing. Both bullets hit Haines in the stomach. But as that portion of his anatomy was already convulsing from the poison, and as all the fine wines that had collected there had fairly anesthetized him, they had little impact.

Haines laughed. "You think *poison* can kill me? You think *bullets* can stop me? Don't you *know* you're dealing with someone who is more than mortal? *Fool!*"

The Beretta fired again, and Haines staggered to his left and burst out the side door onto the long terrace. At its end was a flight of stairs down to the front lawn. All he had to do was get across the lawn to the front gate, and. . . . He made his way down the terrace in a grotesque, shambling gait.

Behind him, the Beretta sounded again and again—as fast as his assailant could pull the trigger. Bullets were flying everywhere, ricocheting off the slate tiles, off the railing and stucco walls, smashing through windows.

Not one hit its intended target. And at length the gun fell silent.

Haines reached the stairs and stumbled, half falling down them. And then he was on the lawn. He had won! He turned and screamed his contempt at his pursuer. "You see? You sad, pathetic little creature? I'm invinc—"

But modern automatics carried fifteen rounds in their clips, not nine, like the old Colt .45's. His assailant had not emptied the weapon, but had merely conserved the remaining rounds, until a hit was a certainty. That moment was now. Two more shots rang out, striking Haines in the left shoulder and upper left thigh.

"Practice makes perfect!" he cried, shrieking with laughter, as he scuttled crablike across the moonlit lawn.

But the slide action of the Beretta was still forward; there was one round left in its chamber. Frantically Haines's pursuer ran after him, for the final shot. A *coup de grâce* to the base of the skull—but the lawn was uneven, and the last round discharged prematurely. Nevertheless, it did strike Haines. But only in the hand. He turned and screamed his derision. "Look!" he held up his hand, punctured in the palm by the bullet. "Stigmata! What an honor!"

But as he turned to resume his nearly victorious flight, he had forgotten the fountain. Tripping over its rim, he pitched forward and on the way down struck his head on the great bronze stomach of Honoré de Balzac.

For a moment the blow rendered him senseless—just long enough for his pursuer to reach him, and with both hands thrust his head underwater and hold it there, till the stream of tiny bubbles from the corner of his mouth ceased.

On East Bluffs, someone might fire one or two shots without it being reported. But not fifteen. Police sirens now wailed in the night, growing louder. Every on-duty vehicle in the Eastport Police Department was racing to the scene.

The assassin vanished, leaving behind a strange tableau: the fountain of *Fallingwater East* bathed in silver moonlight, with the broken body of Trevor Haines lying at the feet of the lumpen *littérateur*.

41 | calling all cars

As the headlights of Chief Burke's old white Oldsmobile Bravada swept the driveway and front lawn of Fallingwater East shortly before midnight, they revealed the presence of practically the entire rolling stock of the EPD.

"What the—" the Chief momentarily lowered his voice. "Sorry, Blessed Mother," then raised it again, as he got out of his vehicle. "Lieutenant Bascomb," he demanded of the senior officer present, "what is everyone and their dog doing here?"

"Chief!" replied the senior officer present with a smile. "What are *you* doing here? Aren't you under doctor's orders to be home, recovering?"

"It was only angioplasty, Leo, for—crying out loud!" He brought himself under control. "What have we got here? And do we really need *all* these people?"

Leo pointed to the fountain where a small crowd had gathered, including Doc Finlay and the duty EMT team with the town's rescue truck. "Deceased white male, late middle age, multiple gunshot wounds to the thigh, abdomen, and—"

But the Chief was already crossing the lawn. "Sergeant Whipple?" called Leo behind him to the next senior officer. "I want all unauthorized personnel off the premises. Put Officer Carey at the front gate and keep everyone out. This is a crime scene! And send Officers Buchman, Vankevich, and Perkins back to the station; we're not fighting a *war* out here!"

At the fountain, the Chief greeted the slight, graying form of Eastport's oldest General Practitioner. "Well, Doc, here we go again. How many gunshot wounds?"

"Six. But that's not what killed him."

"What do you mean?"

"Well, when I got here, his head was underwater. I mean, unless he's amphibian, that's how it ended." Doc Finlay frowned. "He also had a fresh, severe contusion on his forehead, which means he could have been rendered unconscious."

"And drowned—accidentally?"

The GP nodded. "It's possible. But not likely."

"Why not?"

"Well, all those bullets, for one thing. According to Officer Allen who's been through the house, the first shots were fired in the kitchen. At least, that's where the blood trail begins."

"Show me."

"Here she comes now," said Doc Finlay, pointing to the young officer approaching across the lawn. "She can show you better than I can."

"Well, *somebody* show me!" Then, to Trish: "Officer Allen, you want to tell me what you think happened? Let's make that: show and tell." And he nodded for the doctor to accompany them.

With a powerful Maglite, the young officer led the way to the steps up to the terrace and started up them, pausing halfway. "See the smear of blood here along the railing, Chief?" She continued up to the terrace. "And now, look at that broken window, and those bullet scars on the tiles." She highlighted each with the flashlight's beam. "Bullets were going all over the place out here, and he was probably running for his life."

She turned to the side of the house. "Look at that blood spatter; at least, that one hit him. But not this one," and she illuminated a small crease in the stucco, close by the spatter. "I'm pretty sure that's a ricochet. Whoever was doing the shooting was a lousy shot."

She led them into the kitchen. "As nearly as I can tell, the first shots were fired here. He was having dinner in there," she nodded toward the swinging door between the pantry and the dining room, "when something spooked him so badly, he jumped up, knocking everything to the floor, and came out here. At least," she pointed to a dark blotch on the floor, "that's the first blood I've found."

The Chief nodded. "Good work, Trish," he murmured, then went through the swinging door into the dining room. Surveying the shattered crystal and porcelain on the floor, he came back to the kitchen. "So—it started here, and ended out there?" He nodded in the direction of the front lawn.

"We'll have a better idea in the daylight," Trish confirmed, "but it seems so."

"Hmm," mused Doc Finlay, "he was one tough hombre." The Chief looked at him quizzically. "I mean, he gets hit here, then three or four more times down the terrace and the stairs—and he still has the strength to make it to the fountain. I wouldn't be surprised if he tripped there and hit his head as he fell. And that was the only way whoever was after him was able to kill him: Hold his head under, to finish what all the bullets hadn't."

Trish shuddered, and the Chief said, "That's pretty gruesome, Doc. You sure?"

"Well, I can't be *sure* without an autopsy—but we'll get one, ASAP; in fact, I'll have them take the body down to Hyannis right now." He started for the door, and then turned. "I *am* sure about one thing: Whoever did it, hated the guy about as much as it's possible to hate someone."

As Doc Finlay went out, Sergeant Whipple came in. "Oh, *here* you are, Chief; I've been looking all over for you."

"I've been here all the time, Otis," he replied with a smile. "Who was on the premises when it happened?"

"That's what I was coming to tell you: There's a housekeeper/ cook named James Fiske. He was here; in fact, he'd prepared the victim's dinner. By the way, the deceased's name is," he consulted his notes, "Trevor Haines."

"Never heard of him."

"He's apparently been a guest of the owner. Since last August."

The Chief surveyed the kitchen—the used pots and pans in the sink, a small tray of cheese and crackers and jelly ready to go in. "This James—was he also serving the meal?"

"Right. Until a noise from his quarters in the basement caused him to go down there. Someone had apparently thrown a rock through his little basement window. He was down there, when he heard the candelabra hitting the floor, and was on his way back up, when he heard the shots."

"And?"

"And he was pretty scared. In fact, he still is."

The Chief rubbed his chin. "He could have thrown that rock himself—what do you think, Otis? Did the butler do it?"

The sergeant thought for a moment. "Well, if I had to commit now, on the strength of five minutes with him, I'd say no. Unless the old geezer is the greatest actor I've ever seen."

The Chief nodded. "Anyone else around?"

"One of Armstrong's daughters, and her twelve-year-old son. They were up in her room, watching television."

"What?"

"What 'what'?"

"What were they watching!"

"Oh. *ER*. In fact, that's what *I* was watching, when I got the call."

The Chief suddenly yawned. "I was asleep. The two upstairs—when they heard the shots, what did they do?"

"They were plenty scared. But the mother—she's a piece of work—went over to the window, and saw something going on at the fountain. Then she heard the sirens, and whoever was at the fountain ran away."

"Man or woman?"

"She couldn't tell. It all happened pretty fast."

"What did you mean by 'piece of work'? You think she was giving you the straight skinny?"

Otis hesitated. "Hard to say—she gives 'attitude' a whole new meaning."

"Oh she does, does she? Bring her down here. I'll be in the, um," he tried to remember where he'd talked to Armstrong, "in her father's office."

In a few moments, Serena Armstrong entered. "I was informed that the chief of the local constabulary wished to have a word with me?"

"Thank you, Ms.—"

"Armstrong, like my father. And don't do that."

"What?"

"That 'Ms.' stuff! I don't have a problem with being identified as unmarried. Marriage is a sucker's game." She smiled. "I enjoy the occasional wallow in the politically incorrect."

The Chief raised his eyebrows. "Well, um, Miss Armstrong, how well did you know the deceased?"

"Well enough to detest him," she said with a candor that would have made Dorothy Parker proud.

"Why?"

"Where to begin? Shall I start with the oleaginous way he oozed himself into the fabric of our lives? Or would you like to hear about how he preys—correction, preyed—on the innermost medical fears of the upwardly vulnerable?"

"Whoa!" exclaimed the Chief, "Don't—"

But she would not be whoa-ed. "Or how enraged he got, when I threatened to expose him for the con artist he really was? We already know he came here under false pretenses, telling my father he was from his Yale class's gift committee. And I'm sure there's a lot more." She nodded in the direction of the front lawn. "Whoever dispatched that creep deserves a medal: They've done the world a great service!"

The Chief exhaled. "It's you who deserve the medal." He chuckled, in spite of himself. "You've just given me enough motive for ten murderers! Too bad I didn't have my tape recorder on," he said, fishing in his pocket and bringing out a small micro-cassette recorder.

"Turn it on, Chief," said Serena. She took out a cigarette, inserted it into a lacquered cigarette holder, and lit it. Inhaling deeply, she let the smoke drift out her nostrils, as if she were in a Dashiell Hammett novel.

With her cigarette holder, she pointed at the recorder. "Is that thing picking me up?" The Chief nodded. "Good. You'd asked me about Trevor Haines. How do I detest him? Let me count the ways, starting with the oleaginous way he had oozed himself into the fabric of our lives. . . ."

And word by word, she repeated her previous description, leaving nothing out.

42 | *dos incommunicados*

THE FOLLOWING MORNING, a sun-drenched Friday, a little after eight, Brother Bartholomew appeared at the door to Chief Burke's office.

"I just heard! Why didn't you call last night?"

"There was no reason for both of us to lose a night's sleep," his friend said with a weary smile. "I didn't get to bed until after three and got up before six."

"Dan, what are you thinking of!"

"You sound just like Peg! At least there are no ifs, ands, or buts about this one: drowned, after taking six bullets. *And*," he nodded toward the telephone, "Dr. Morton in the pathologist's office just called: On top of all that, apparently whoever did it had first tried to do it with poison."

"Shades of Rasputin," murmured Bartholomew.

"Who?"

The monk told him about that other monk, and then looked at him again, his concern growing. "Dan, are you supposed to be here?"

The Chief was about to reply, but then—closed his eyes and let his head sink into his hands.

Bartholomew glanced out into the main office. Seeing Leo, he called, "Lieutenant Bascomb? Your boss is in trouble."

Leo hurried in and agreed. "We've got to get you home, Chief. I'll have Arnie Buchman drive you."

Too weak to object, the Chief nodded. Then he requested that Bartholomew be the one to take him. In the latter's red pickup, he mustered what remained of his strength and briefed his friend on the case.

"I want you to work with Otis and Trish. Like last time. They're running the investigation. Reporting to me." He raised his eyes and smiled. "You know what they say about a good team: If it ain't broke. . . ."

His eyes fell shut. And then opened, as he summoned his last reserves. "The victim's a guy named Haines, apparently a close friend of Armstrong's. At least, he'd been staying with him for a couple of months."

Bartholomew turned and stared at him.

"What is it?" asked the Chief irritably.

"I met him! That time I went out to interview Armstrong. Creepy guy; really weird." He paused. "Dan, was he there two weeks ago?"

"You mean, when Dorothy Hanson—? Good point." With difficulty the Chief pulled out his Daytimer. "My mind is like sludge in a cold crankcase." He flipped some pages. "The only time Haines was *not* there was from," he turned another page, "September 28 to—October 10!"

Bartholomew hit the steering wheel. "And she picked up the diamonds on the 2nd and was washed ashore on the 4th!"

"Bingo!" cried the Chief. "*Finally* this thing is beginning to make sense!" He grinned at Bartholomew, but his friend was not smiling. "What's the matter?"

"This is spooky: My mother called this shot."

"Huh?"

"Monday. I was in Norma's with Brother Ambrose. After she'd caught me up on the town buzz, she said something odd." He slowed while a white builder's truck with *Haig's Homes* on the side, made a left turn.

"C'mon, what did she say?"

Bartholomew smiled at the recollection. "It wasn't too hard for her to see we were up the creek. And she said—" he closed his eyes to get the exact words, "that it would be someone we hadn't thought of yet. Someone in the background."

"Well," said the Chief, "I guess we know where you get your intuition."

Bartholomew shrugged. "Anyway, it looks like she might be right." He frowned. "We need to talk to Armstrong, see if he might've mentioned the diamonds to Haines and forgotten it."

"Yeah, well, good luck!" the Chief scowled. "Armstrong's disappeared." He told his friend that according to his partner, Ed Forester, Armstrong left Wednesday to go up to his property in New Hampshire. He'd planned to be back early this morning. But when Forester went in to work, he found a message from Armstrong on his answering machine: He'd decided to stay up there till Monday. He asked Forester to tell Haines, and also to call Chandler, Gilbert & Cooper, where he had scheduled a meeting this morning."

Bartholomew rubbed his eyes. "Did Forester say what time the call had come in?"

The Chief nodded. "Guess."

"Last night?"

"You mean, around the time we got the first report of someone firing off a gun on East Bluffs?" The Chief smiled wryly. "How does 10:32 strike you?"

"Like an extraordinary coincidence, or—"

"—or someone going to a lot of trouble to establish an alibi. The trouble is, *Señor Armstrong está incomunicado.* He's apparently turned off his cell phone."

Bartholomew grimaced. "We have to wait till Monday?"

"Not necessarily. I've explained the situation to the State Police up there. They know where his place is, and they're going to have a little look for him."

All at once, the Chief groaned and slumped lower in his seat.

"Almost there," his worried friend encouraged him.

"Good," he whispered, "'cause I'm almost dead."

He made a last effort to complete the briefing. "So: We've got a housekeeper, male, who's unlikely, and a smart-mouthed heir, female, who's too likely. And she's got two sisters—not present, not accounted for. One's up in Cambridge; the other's gone to New York for the day. And then there's Forester and some younger guy named Rawlings who works with them. And that's it, so far."

Briefing completed, the Chief either passed out or fell asleep, Bartholomew was not sure which. He had to half-carry his friend into the house, where he turned him over to a scared and angry Peg Burke who promised God and Bartholomew that her husband was going to bed for two days, and would not be communicating with anyone—repeat, *anyone*—before Monday.

Leaving their home, Bartholomew headed for the Armstrong place, to check in with Otis. Only two patrol cars were present now—Otis's, and one at the front gate, to keep out the curious and the media. Bartholomew found Otis in the kitchen, patiently taking the housekeeper, James, hour by hour through the events of the previous day.

"Sergeant Whipple?" Bartholomew interrupted. "May I see you for a moment?"

Otis excused himself, and he and Bartholomew stepped out on the terrace. The monk told the sergeant of the Chief's condition and of his briefing. "So, if there's anything I can do to help—"

The tall, thin, balding officer smiled and shook his head. "There really isn't a whole lot, right now." He checked his notes.

"There is one thing: The youngest daughter, Saralinda, is due back from New York this afternoon. She lives up in Wellfleet with a seven-year-old son. The Chief had wanted to conduct all the initial interviews himself. But if he's in no shape, it would be a big help, Brother Bart, if you could talk to her."

"Let's wait and see how the Chief is on Monday."

Just then, Bartholomew's pager went off: He looked down and saw it was the friary's number. "Think they'd mind if I made a local call?"

"Help yourself," said Otis, "you're on police business." And with that, he returned to the kitchen.

Bartholomew found a phone in the library and called the Friary.

"Oh, good, it's you," said Ambrose, who had placed the call. "Anselm wants you home right away. Columba's died."

43 | death of a monk

THE FRIARY WAS SUBDUED, filled with a sense of loss and mourning. Columba, the oldest Brother, had been lingering on this side of the veil for several days. Which had enabled each of them to spend some time with him, remembering happy times, reading old Celtic tales to him, praying with him, or just being there. But it was still strange to realize he was gone.

Seeing Bartholomew arrive, Ambrose came up to him. "I'm sorry," he said. "I know you were close."

Bartholomew nodded without speaking, because he was not sure he could speak.

"Anselm wants to see you. He's out in the garden."

The older monk nodded again and went to find the Senior Brother.

Anselm was strolling down the path by the roses, his hands clasped behind him, when Bartholomew found him.

"How are you doing?" Anselm asked.

"I don't know yet. He's—always been there."

Anselm nodded. "That's the way I felt. Still do," he sighed. "God really loved him. I was with him at the end, and I've never seen a gentler passage. He was there, and then he wasn't."

Bartholomew swallowed hard.

"Actually," Anselm went on, "he started leaving us three days ago. He just got happier and happier."

Bartholomew nodded. "When I was with him, night before last, he seemed to be seeing something I couldn't see. And he just—beamed." He smiled. "He always was a bit fey."

"Yes," Anselm chuckled, "our Irish monk from Sandusky. But you're right; he was as close to a Celtic mystic, as we're likely to see."

"And last night, when I looked in on him, he whispered, 'Can you hear them?' I couldn't. But I knew he could." Bartholomew stopped bothering to hold back the tears.

"They have much to sing about," Anselm agreed, his own eyes full. "He fulfilled his mission."

Bartholomew looked up at him. "He told you about the glow?"

"Once," responded Anselm. "When I was young and needed to hear it."

The two men fell silent, and Bartholomew recalled the time many years before, when he was new to the religious life and struggling with his call. Late one afternoon, he'd gone to Columba, who was preparing the ground for the planting of their eight-tree "orchard."

The old monk had leaned on his hoe and listened to the young novice pour out his heart. "My mother is disappointed in me. She doesn't say it, but I can feel it. When she tells me what a wonderful doctor my cousin has become. Or how well my other cousin is doing in the State Department. Or how respected my father had been, among all the men who knew him. Or how her prize pupil, a guy in my class, had gone on to become a Rhodes Scholar at Oxford and won a Fullbright and had just been given tenure at Harvard. And then she looks at me, the gardener, the handyman with a Dartmouth degree, who's thrown away his education—and his life."

Columba had gazed out at the bay, where the setting sun was firing the sky with shades of crimson. He waited a long time without speaking. Then he said, "Did you know, my son, that there is a glow around your soul?" Bartholomew had just stared at him. "How large a glow depends on how obedient you've been to the will of your Heavenly Father, and how much other souls have been blessed by your presence on earth. When your soul returns to heaven, the size of the glow around it will indicate how well you've fulfilled your mission on earth."

He had watched the sun completely disappear, before deciding to tell the young monk the rest. "I have seen your glow, Bartholomew. At the rate it is growing, when you die it will be greater than the combined glows of all those you've mentioned."

Shaking his head now at the recollection, Bartholomew wept.

"Go and be with him," said Anselm, indicating the apple orchard, its trees now full-grown and laden with fruit. Bartholomew, eyes streaming, went to the little slatted bench that Columba had made eighteen years ago, with the help of the always questioning young novice.

He couldn't pray; he couldn't even think. He just sat there. And after a while, he sensed Columba there, too, in spirit.

◆

The next morning, he sought out Anselm again. The latter was in the stable, looking at a cut that Countess had somehow gotten on her hindquarters. He invited Bartholomew to join him on the stable bench.

"I didn't sleep much last night."

The older monk nodded. "Columba?"

"Yes. I don't know why it's hitting me so hard. I mean, I loved him; we all did. But—I can hardly breathe!"

Anselm looked at him a long time, without speaking. Then he said, "It's your father."

Bartholomew stared at him.

"Losing your father was the worst thing that ever happened to you—and now it's happening all over again."

The younger monk struggled for air.

"Columba was God's gift to you. So that you could complete working out your father/son relationship."

Slowly Bartholomew nodded. "I'm not sure I understand it, but—the vise in my chest is loosening."

Anselm smiled. "Give it time. It'll become clearer. And come back and talk to me about it."

Bartholomew's eyes filled. Tears came easily now—unbidden, but not embarrassing. "Thanks, I will."

He got up to leave, then smiled. "Look, as long as you've got your black bag out, maybe you can help me with something else that's been bothering me: Why am I having such a hard time getting along with my mother? I mean, it seems like every time I go into Norma's, we get into it. Especially if I forget to pray for grace and forbearance."

Anselm chuckled. "Could be the same root."

Bartholomew nodded. "I'd figured out *her* anger. She resented the fact that when my father died, instead of my being there for her, I disappeared, too—into a friary. But I can't figure out *mine*—I mean, beyond twinges of subconscious guilt for having left my widowed mother to go into the friary."

"How old is she?"

Bartholomew had to think for a moment. "Seventy-three."

"Answer this quickly: How old do you think of her as?"

"Mid-forties."

"Why?"

"I suppose because—that's how old she was, when I went to 'Nam."

"And your family was still intact."

"Then—"

Anselm laughed and patted Countess's flank. "It could be that simple: Subconsciously you resent her for getting older. Because it means that she's heading towards death. Your other parent is getting ready to abandon you."

Bartholomew stared at him. "You think?"

"I don't know." He smiled. "But you might try thanking God for *both* your parents."

The funeral that afternoon was attended by the entire abbey family. It was a simple service, exactly as Columba would have wanted. Before the altar rested the casket, of old heavy pine. It had been made in the Brothers' workshop, smoothed and stained by many hands. Inlaid in its cover was a Celtic cross, carved by Brother Dominic. It was a sunny day; shafts of light slanted down through the high clerestory windows of the basilica.

The Mass, which Columba had requested, was Rheinberger's Mass in G. The Gradual was similarly stirring: Sheutky's "Send Forth thy Spirit." And during the service, the Brothers chanted the 23rd Psalm in English, followed by two Psalms of farewell in Latin. As the ancient phrasing rose and fell away, it seemed to wreathe the great stone columns like incense smoke, wafting up to the distant rafters and lingering there.

As the congregation came forward to receive Holy Communion, the choir sang Russian anthems by Kedrov, Rachmaninoff, and Glinka. As Columba once put it, the Russians elevated you into the presence of God and sustained you there—as if God Himself had raised you up in His palm to His eye level.

The Communion hymns, sung by the congregation while the choir was receiving, were "Come, Risen Lord," in the old hymnal, and "I Will Raise Him Up" in the new one. And of course, the hymn of St. Patrick: "I bind unto myself this day, the strong name of the Trinity."

For the recessional, a solitary piper (one of the abbey's three) played "Lord Lovat's Lament." Behind her came eight

Brothers (one of whom was Bartholomew) carrying the casket on their shoulders, down the long center aisle, through one shaft of sunlight after another, as the abbey family followed behind in solemn procession. Listening to the piper's mournful tune, Bartholomew wept again. No matter, everyone was.

At Eastport's cemetery, as they approached the abbey's corner, the lone piper awaited them on a knoll, playing a Celtic slow march. The abbey family collected under the trees around the gravesite. A gentle breeze shifted the limbs above them, altering the pattern of sunlight.

It was so peaceful, thought Bartholomew, who stood a little back and up the side of an adjacent hill. All at once he felt great love for this family that God had gathered. Some were sad, some were praying. All were quiet, even the little ones.

All were aware that they were family.

And that was Columba's farewell gift to them, he thought: This peace, and the quiet joy of his passing, served to re-focus and re-order things. Sometimes, in the abbey family's commitment to the pursuit of excellence and its Benedictine work ethic, achievement tended to eclipse contemplation. God used saints like Columba and events like this to restore the balance.

The children filed by, each dropping a flower down onto the lowered casket. Then the Brothers and the rest of the family took turns with four shovels, filling in the grave. When it was finished, one of the children, who had a helium-filled balloon, let it go, and all watched it sail higher and higher, until it disappeared.

Goodbye, Columba, thought Bartholomew. Your glow will be so large—and the tears came again.

44 | i've got a little list

BY MONDAY MORNING, after two days of enforced bed rest, Chief Dan Burke was like a caged tiger—recently captured and not yet accepting the narrow parameters of his confinement. Friday he'd gone straight to bed and slept six hours. After getting up for supper and feeling like he'd been in a train wreck, he'd slept twelve hours more. Saturday he took a nap in the morning, had lunch, took another nap, helped Notre Dame's football team in their game with West Virginia, until he was confident they didn't need him anymore, and napped again.

By Sunday, after another twelve-hour night, he was up and raring to go. But his wife informed him that the only place he was going was to their church, St. Joan of Arc over in Orleans. He agreed, thinking that after Mass he could wheedle her into letting him go for a quick visit to the station. But when the Mass was ended, so was Dan Burke. He went straight home to bed, rousing himself only to help the New England Patriots, until he decided they didn't deserve his help.

By Monday he felt like his old self. Peg let him go out in the morning, making him promise to come home for lunch and not make any afternoon plans. He agreed—but his mental fingers were crossed. He still intended to do all the initial interviews himself. It was not lack of confidence in his investigative team. It was just that he had supreme confidence in his own ability to detect the slightest aberration or nuance, to hear what should have been there, but wasn't.

At the top of his list was Samantha Armstrong. Her sister Serena had called her with the news of Haines's murder, adding that, thanks to her honesty, she seemed to be at the top of the suspect list. Samantha had come down at once.

The Chief met the eldest Armstrong sister in *FW's* library— and liked her from the get-go. She was a no-nonsense, let's-get-the-job-done person—sort of like himself. From her, he was able to get an overall picture of Haines's relationship with her father, and learned of the plans for the proposed creation—the *imminent* creation—of the Armstrong Research Clinic. Which would have entailed phasing out Armstrong & Associates and would have soon absorbed all of her father's time and most of his money.

The Chief rubbed the back of his neck and told himself that he was not really tired. Not when he finally had motive—*gobs* of motive. And more suspects than he could shake a stick at. There were Armstrong's three daughters and two partners—and Armstrong himself, for that matter. Samantha had said that her father and Haines were close, but what if Armstrong had somehow learned of Haines's involvement (if any) with Dorothy Hanson's death?

"So, Ms. Armstrong, where were you last Thursday evening?"

"Up in Cambridge, in my apartment."

"Anyone see you there?"

"My fiancé. He was staying with me that night."

"Did anyone see the two of you there?"

"I don't think so; maybe the guy across the hall heard us."

"What were you doing around—10:30?"

"Watching *ER*."

"This fiancé—does he have a name?"

"Gottfried Franc."

The name sounded familiar, and the Chief riffled through his Daytimer, till he found it. "Works for the Randolph Corporation, like you do." She nodded. "And was down here with you, weekend before last."

"Yes."

"Any connection between him and Haines?"

"No," she said quickly. Too quickly. So quickly that somewhere below decks in the Chief's engine-room, an alarm bell went off. Actually, it was more like the silvery tone of a triangle in a primary school percussion band. It rang only once. But once was enough.

"Ms. Armstrong, unless your father has fallen off the face of the earth, someday I'm going to talk to him. If I find any discrepancy in what you've told me—anything, about which you've been, shall we say, less than forthcoming—I promise you: It will go *very* badly for you."

He meant it, and Samantha knew it. Pursing her lips, she said, "Chief, I think I'd like to amend my statement: My father had approached my fiancé with a proposition to establish and endow a full-scale research lab for him. Mr. Franc is on the verge of completing his mapping of human DNA, and with my father's help, he could be in charge of where his future research would go. A week ago, that offer was taken off the table. The sudden formation of the ARC would necessarily entail the immediate phasing-out of A&A, my father's venture capital firm."

The Chief made a note and looked up. "Would it be fair then, to say that Trevor Haines's scheme, if implemented, would destroy what might be your fiancé's one opportunity to take control of his destiny?"

"That's putting it a little melodramatically, but—yes. And now I wish I hadn't amended my statement."

The Chief smiled. "Don't regret it," he reassured her. "I was going to find out about this eventually. Hearing it from you up front, only makes you a less likely suspect." He paused. "Of course, I can't say the same for Mr. Franc." His little list seemed to be growing. "By the way, where is Mr. Franc now?"

Samantha looked distraught. "I—don't know. I haven't heard from him, since I left."

"And you've called him?"

"Tried to. No answer." She was ready to cry.

"Well," said Chief with a smile, "I'm sure he'll turn up." He tapped his chin with his pen. "But I'll need to have a little chat with him, when he does."

◆

Borrowing Armstrong's work office, the Chief talked to Nigel Rawlings. Who had come in to work on the slender hope that the sudden demise of the ARC's future director might scuttle the ARC itself, before it slid down the ways.

With a little probing, the Chief discovered that it was for the sake of fitness that Nigel had ridden in to work on the yellow Canondale out in the garage, and why it was so imperative that A&A remain in existence nine more days. Were it to vanish into the ether before that, Nigel would not only be out a cool million, he'd be out on the street with no prospects. Hmm, thought the Chief, bring on the motive bucket.

So where was Nigel on Thursday evening at gunshot time? Home watching television. What? *ER.* (What else?) Could his wife corroborate this? She could, if she'd been home; watching *ER* was about the only thing they did together anymore. She was not home? Nope, moved out last week. She was staying with a model friend in New York, who had (Nigel shuddered) loaned her a credit card.

Ed Forester was taciturn when the Chief met with him, and it took patient probing to discern that Forester had detested the deceased almost as much as Serena. Trevor Haines had single-handedly shot down the greatest venture capital team of the modern era.

Professing a lack of understanding, the Chief persuaded Forester to walk him through their most recent deal. Listening to him, the Chief had the eerie feeling he was debriefing a fighter ace who had just been victorious in aerial combat. And now this adrenalin junkie, hooked on the rush, had just been grounded.

Where was he Thursday night? Home. Alone? Yes, unfortunately; he had a new lady friend, with whom he was looking forward to spending the evening, but she'd had to go out of town on business. So what did he do? Watched television. Oh, great: the *ER* alibi again.

What was he watching from, say, ten to eleven? "48 Hours." Really? Yes, but it wasn't any good, so he'd switched to *ER*.

Abruptly the Chief yawned and closed his eyes. Suddenly blindsided by fatigue, it was all he could do to get out of the house and into his vehicle. It was only five minutes to his home, but he nearly had to stop and take a nap, to avoid falling asleep at the wheel.

His last thought, after he was safely in bed: What if they *all* did it? Like on *The Orient Express*?

45 | by the book

BROTHER BARTHOLOMEW RUBBED the back of his neck, as he switched on the old pickup's headlights.

Seeing him, Brother Ambrose asked, "Want me to drive?"

"I'm all right," declared the older monk. He didn't mind Ambrose usually, and sometimes even enjoyed having him around. But tonight, for some reason, he was bugging the day-lights out of him. Why, he wondered. Probably because ever since they'd gone into Norma's a week ago, Ambrose had been after him to let him get involved in the new case. And the more he pushed, the more Bartholomew resented it.

"When we get there," he informed the younger monk, "I want you to wait in the truck."

"Well, what am I along for, then?" asked Ambrose petulantly.

"Propriety."

"Huh?"

"Ambrose," he turned to him, "use your head! A monk doesn't go calling on a single woman alone. Especially at night."

"Oh, yeah; I see what you mean."

They were on their way up to Wellfleet, responding to the Chief's last request, before he'd packed it in that afternoon. He wanted Bartholomew to interview Saralinda Armstrong. Right away. With a report due in the Chief's office first thing in the morning.

But Saralinda had not been available earlier in the afternoon. Calling ahead, Bartholomew had ascertained that her son had a soccer match, after which she and three of the other soccer moms were taking their boys out for hamburgers and miniature golf. She would not be home until eight.

He had a bit of trouble finding her place, a little cottage on an unmarked back road through the sand, which looked like every other unmarked back road through the sand. He finally found it, and leaving Ambrose fuming in the truck, he knocked on the door.

When Saralinda opened it, she looked surprised. "You don't look like a monk," she said with a smile.

Bartholomew glanced down at his windbreaker and work-boots. "I suppose not."

She invited him into the cottage's little living room, which had one canvas on an easel and several others waiting their turn. There was enough light to get a good look at her, and now it was he who was surprised. She reminded him of Laurel–tall, lithe, willowy. He shook his head, as if to shake such thoughts out of it.

"Would you like some coffee?"

"Um–if you have decaf."

"We do," she said, going to the kitchenette.

In a moment, she returned with two mugs, and tilted her head, surveying him. "You–look familiar to me, but I can't tell where I've seen you."

He stopped short of saying that she, too, looked familiar. But she did.

"I've got it! You ride, don't you!"

"You mean, on a bike?"

"Yes! I've seen you on the bike path. You've got an old Peugeot, don't you?"

Bartholomew smiled. "Old, maybe, but it still has a few good years in it." Then he laughed. "And you've got a Bianchi."

"Right over there," she nodded at the pale green bike by the back door. "I didn't know monks rode bicycles."

"We also swim and run. Though we don't do triathlons. And we gave up bungee-jumping two years ago." They laughed.

She had a beautiful smile, Bartholomew thought—and realized he'd better get down to business. "Chief Burke asked me to come up and talk to you about—" he caught sight of her young son beyond her, doing his homework at the dining room table, "—what happened at your father's place last Thursday night. How well did you know Trevor Haines?"

"I'd met him only that once."

"When was that?"

"When he explained his clinic to us, at lunch last Saturday— I mean, a week ago last Saturday."

Bartholomew took a sip of coffee, wishing it were real. "What'd you think of him?"

"He made me uncomfortable."

"Why?"

"He was too polished. Too smooth. His ascot—or *foulard*, or whatever you call it—was showing just the right amount, and his wavy blond hair stayed so perfectly in place that I'm sure he used hair spray."

They both instinctively wrinkled their noses. And laughed. "And when he spoke," she went on, "he always had the perfect phrase." She looked at him. "People don't talk in perfect phrases."

"Bottom line?"

"I got the impression that he had a real crush on himself—and," she hesitated, "well, I hoped he didn't have one on my father."

Bartholomew finished the decaf. "What did you think of his proposal?"

"The ARC? It sounded pretty kooky to me. But a lot of my art friends are into alternative therapy, so I try to stay open-minded about it. And I guess he really helped my father, so—" she shrugged.

"How did you feel about your future earnings going into the clinic?"

She smiled. "Look around you." She gestured to the little cottage's interior. "I could afford better than this, but we don't need it." She lowered her voice and nodded towards her son. "*He* may need it some day, but my father's provided for him. He can go all the way to Oxford, if he wants to."

Or maybe he'll want to be a gardener, Bartholomew thought. "So it didn't bother you?"

"The only thing that bothered me was that I didn't want to see my father being taken advantage of. And Haines was doing that, for sure." She looked at him quizzically and then smiled. "You're trying to figure out if that's enough motivation for me to have killed him."

Bartholomew chuckled. "You do that often?"

"What?"

"Read people's minds."

"Only when I have to," she said, peering at him over the rim of her coffee mug. "How about you?"

"Only when I have to." They both laughed.

"I like you, Brother Barnabas."

"It's Bartholomew," he replied, "and I've got to be going."

"Sure you don't want a refill?"

He held up his hand. "I'd better not; I've got to drive." They laughed.

Then he remembered the other thing the Chief was sure to ask in the morning. "Um, just for the record, where were you last Thursday evening?"

She hesitated. "Up in Boston. At the Airport Marriott. I was taking the first shuttle to LaGuardia."

"What time did you check in?"

"A little after 4:00. You can check that with the reception desk, Brother Cadfael," she teased.

"Can they verify your whereabouts at 10:30?"

She didn't answer.

"Can anyone?"

She stopped smiling. "How important is this?"

"Do you want your name off the suspect list?"

She hesitated a long time. Then said simply, "Ban Caulfield."

◆

On the way home, Bartholomew refused to answer any of Ambrose's questions. In fact, he feigned sleep, letting the younger monk do the driving.

As soon as they reached the friary, he went in search of Anselm. Whom he found in the Senior Brothers' room, asleep in his bed. Dominic was sleeping in the bunk above. Neither of them had taken the empty bed that had been Columba's.

"Anselm," Bartholomew whispered, gently shaking his shoulder, "wake up."

The old monk opened one eye and squinted at Bartholomew, silhouetted in the faint light from the hall. "The thing that makes Grand Silence grand," the old monk whispered, "is the silence."

"My sentiments exactly," whispered the younger monk. "Except, I've got a potato that's so hot, it's burning my fingers, and it really can't wait till morning."

Anselm nodded. "I'll meet you in the kitchen in a minute."

Bartholomew went down, and a moment later, a sleepy Anselm, an old bathrobe over his pajamas, joined him.

"Well?"

Without using names, Bartholomew outlined the situation. "The woman in question was not about to reveal the name of the person who was with her at the time of the murder. It was only when I pointed out that by not doing so, she would become a prime suspect herself, that she did." He paused, and then, taking care not to reveal even the gender of the person in question, he said, "It was a member of the abbey."

Wide awake now, Anselm asked, "Does this—person know that you know?"

"No."

"Do they know that they are about to become involved in a murder investigation?"

"No. I mean, I don't think so."

Anselm thought for a moment. "Mother Michaela will have to be told," he mused. "But it would be better if it came from the person involved."

Bartholomew said nothing.

Anselm stood up. "We're going to do this by the book. Since you know who it is, and since we *are* a covenanted community—and *are* our brothers' keepers—"

"Or sisters'," interjected Bartholomew.

"You're going to have to go to the person, and tell them what's happened."

"Oh, dear Jesus!" Bartholomew groaned.

"Then you'll have done what the Word of God commands us to do."

Bartholomew looked pleadingly at the older monk. "Is there any other way?"

Anselm shook his head and sighed. "He never promised us a rose garden."

46 | importuning

IN HIS DREAM, A SMALL BLACK DOG had gotten hold of the leg of his khaki pants with its teeth and was tugging on it. "Ban," the dog said, "Ban." How did the dog know his name? How could it talk through a mouth full of khaki?

"Ban, wake up." It was his wife.

"Mmmf?" She might leave him alone, if she saw how asleep he was.

"There's someone knocking."

"Mmmh." Betsy could hear things in the night that no one else could. London could have used her ears during the Blitz, to augment their early warning system. She could also smell escaping gas which even the DEA's sniffer-dogs would miss. Still, he had to get up, if only to stop her from nudging him.

But this time, he could hear it, too. There really *was* someone down there. Knocking. At—he squinted at the digital alarm—11:47. This would fall into the category of importuning.

He got up, pulled on shirt and pants, and went downstairs, turning on the light, so that whoever was at the front door would stop importuning before they woke up the rest of the house.

To his surprise, it was Brother Bartholomew, whom he knew and liked, but who, other than on the bike path, he seldom saw. He looked like he had something on his mind. "Come in," said Ban softly. "What's up?"

Bartholomew looked around. "Can we go somewhere private?"

"Sure, come out on the porch." He led the way into the sun porch and closed the sliding door behind them.

Pointing to a cushioned, wrought-iron easy chair, he took the other one for himself. "Okay, shoot."

Brother Bartholomew hesitated, then finally asked, "You know about the murder over on East Bluffs?"

"Everyone does. Pretty wild."

"Did you know I'm helping with the investigation?"

"No. But you did last year, so it's not surprising." He smiled. "Any leads?"

Bartholomew did not return his smile. "A number of people had reason to want him dead, and right now we're checking on their whereabouts at the time of the murder. In other words, around 10:30 last Thursday night."

Ban went cold. He suddenly knew where this was heading. He wanted to throw up.

He looked at Bartholomew, who met his gaze. "Someone has given your name as one who could corroborate that they were not at the scene of the crime."

The breath went out of Ban. He just nodded. "Did they—say anything else?"

"Huh-uh. Just your name."

Ban closed his eyes, wishing with all his heart—and mind and soul and being—that this was a dream. A horrendous, cautionary dream, from which he would awaken, drenched in cold sweat and profoundly grateful to God that it *was* a dream!

Any moment now, a little black dog would start pulling on his pants leg, and he would wake. He would wake up, and it would still be last week. Oh, God, let it be soon!

He squeezed his eyes shut, but when he opened them, Brother Bartholomew was still there.

And so was the worst nightmare of his entire life.

"Thank you," he sighed, getting up and opening the sliding door.

"Sorry," said Brother Bartholomew as he left, though he looked not so much sorry, as immensely relieved.

Ban went back out on the porch, turned off the light, and stared out at the night. There were no stars, nor could he see the waters of the bay. There was only darkness. I've sold my birthright for a mess of pottage, he thought. And I didn't even eat the pottage.

He went back upstairs and looked in the bedroom. "What was it?" mumbled his wife, half-asleep.

"Nothing," he assured her. "Just someone who had to tell me something. I'll be in, in a little while," he added, knowing that she would now fall asleep.

In the sitting room off their bedroom, he donned socks and shoes, then went downstairs and got his leather jacket. He went out into the cold October night and walked down to the common. Above him loomed the dark shadow of the new basilica. He thought about going in, but it struck him as cold and forbidding in the middle of the night, with no lighting.

He knew that someday, after enough prayer from the heart had gone up in there, it would feel warm and intimate, even in complete darkness. He knew it, because that was the way Canterbury Cathedral had felt, the night he'd been fortunate enough to be among the group from the abbey who had been invited on a candlelit tour of that vast space. In total darkness it had felt not enormous or imposing but—cozy.

Tonight, however, he preferred their old chapel, which they

no longer used for worship, but which still had the little icon of
Jesus, over by the old pipe organ. Kneeling in front of it, he
looked into the eyes of the icon. And felt Jesus' eyes searching
his. And looking into the depths of his soul.

Tears came to his eyes, as he recalled how pleased he had
once been to have God search his heart. And know all that was
there. How clean he used to feel after such times, as if God had
reached down with a big Brillo pad and scoured him out inside,
till he shone.

But over the years he had allowed his heart to crust over
and harden. He still talked the talk—still prayed, still thought of
himself as a devout Christian. But it had been a *long* time since
he had, as they say, walked the walk.

And now what?

A cold, hard thought came to him: There is nothing left for
you here. You have betrayed your call, brought shame on your
family and your abbey. All you can do now is leave.

But I don't want to leave, thought Ban, in misery. "I don't
want to leave," he whispered to the icon.

The icon gazed back at him, calm, impassive. And then, for
some reason, he thought of Psalm 51. In the dark, he fumbled
for the old red prayer book. By the faint light of the votive
candle, he could barely make out the words—that a sin-beset
king had written three millennia earlier: *Have mercy upon me, O
God, after thy great goodness; according to the multitude of thy
mercies, do away mine offenses. Wash me thoroughly from my
wickedness, and cleanse me from my sin. . . .* He could read no
more, for the tears.

After an hour, with a deep sigh he got up and went out. He
knew what he must do.

47 | prime suspect

THE INTERCOM ON Chief Dan Burke's desk came to life. "Chief? It's Clayton Armstrong on the phone. He's back, and he wants to see you."

"I want to see him! Where is he?"

"At his home."

"Tell him to stay put; I'm coming over."

"Where have you been?" he demanded, as soon as he and Armstrong were alone in the library.

"Up in New Hampshire. Look, Chief," said Armstrong defensively, "the first I heard about Trevor Haines was when a State Police helicopter loud-hailed me yesterday to report to their nearest barracks. I did, and that's when I learned what had happened. I came straight home."

The Chief got up and walked to the window. "Tell me about your relationship with Haines. From the beginning."

Half an hour later, Armstrong was still relating the events, when the Chief raised his hand for him to stop. "Let me summarize the chronology I'm interested in: Haines comes in mid-August, initially for the week-end, claiming to represent the alumni fund, to hit you up for a gift. You invite him to stay on. He stays a week; you invite him to stay another. And a couple more. Then you invite him to move in." He frowns. "How, um—'close' were you?"

"Not close in that way," Armstrong said. "He was just—amusing. Interesting. Colorful, at a time when my world was descending shades of gray. And then," he hesitated. "He—may have healed me of lung cancer."

"*What?*"

Armstrong told him the story, and to the Chief, it was beginning to sound like *The X-Files.* All things considered, he preferred *ER.*

Aware that this part of his story was not registering, Armstrong skipped over it. The Chief let him.

"Anyway, that's when we got serious about founding the research clinic."

"Okay, let me see if I've got these dates right," said the Chief, turning on his micro-cassette recorder and consulting his Daytimer. "On September 24th, Alan Jones and Dorothy Hanson fly to Antwerp, to buy ten million dollars worth of diamonds for you. Four days later, Haines leaves to go to New York to pick up personal belongings to move in here—indefinitely. After that, he goes up to Boston to see his sister. On October 2nd Dorothy Hanson picks up the diamonds in Boston and starts down here with them. Somewhere along the way, she is waylaid, kidnapped, and tortured and manages to escape but drowns."

The Chief came back to check the little recorder, to make sure there was adequate tape left, then returned to the window. And his chronology: "We find her body two days later. Next day, I come out here, and you tell me that no one but you and Alan Jones—and the Antwerp diamond broker and the manager of

RKL–knows exactly what Dorothy Hanson had gone to Belgium for. And on the–" he checked his calendar, "the 10th, eight days after her kidnapping, Haines returns."

The Chief turned from the window and faced him. "Mr. Armstrong, I'm going to ask you again: Before Haines left, did you give him any indication that you had someone over in Europe picking up diamonds for you?"

Armstrong stared out at the Atlantic for a long time. "Yes. Though I'd forgotten it, when you asked me before."

"Okay," said the Chief, "We'll leave that for now. Let's move up to–" he glanced down at his notes, "Saturday, the 14th. Your birthday. That's when you and Haines told your daughters about the ARC, and how it was all going to happen at Chandler, Gilbert & Cooper's on Friday morning. Your daughters freak, but they can't do anything."

"I'd tuned them out; I was still totally sold on the clinic."

The Chief looked up from his notes. "Then, all of a sudden on Wednesday afternoon, something happens, and you take off for New Hampshire, leaving Haines here. The next evening, he has this," he sought the right word, "*banquet* for one, and gets killed–at almost the exact moment you call, purportedly from New Hampshire, to say that you've changed your mind and won't be coming back until today, and to ask Mr. Forester to alert Haines and GC&C."

Armstrong was frowning. "What do you mean, 'purportedly'? I *was* up there, camping out in my woods."

"Anyone see you?"

Armstrong was losing patience. "Who's going to see me back in the boonies!"

"Mr. Armstrong," said the Chief, letting his own temper show, "I'd advise you not to take that attitude." He held up his thumb and forefinger with a tiny slit of light between them. "I'm this far away from reading you your rights! So you'd–" he caught himself–"jolly well better hope someone up there saw you!"

Belatedly appreciating the gravity of his situation, Armstrong softened. "Well, there was the manager of the general store in Fairlee, Vermont. They open at 7:00. I was there about 7:03, to pick up the *Wall Street Journal*."

The Chief shook his head. "Not good enough. You need someone Thursday evening."

Armstrong shook his head. "I told you: I was camping. I wanted to be alone. So, I was."

The Chief rubbed the bridge of his nose and yawned. This was taking more out of him than he thought. "All right, let's go back to last Wednesday afternoon: What made you suddenly want to go up to New Hampshire, 'to be alone'?"

Armstrong sighed. "I guess it was my daughters' reaction to the ARC. Here, I wanted to do a good thing, to benefit mankind, and—"

"Hold it! I've talked to two of them; they were reacting to Haines, not to your desire to benefit mankind." He paused. "How did *you* feel about Haines Wednesday afternoon? Were you still as gung-ho?"

The Chief searched Armstrong's face carefully, and the latter seemed to know that if he lied, it would show. "I—admit I was having second thoughts."

"Why?"

No answer.

"It had nothing to do with your daughters' reaction, like you indicated a moment ago, did it?"

No answer.

"Mr. Armstrong," said the Chief, barely containing his temper, "if you're refusing to answer on the grounds you might incriminate yourself, I'm afraid you already have!"

"I just wanted to get away and think things over."

"No!" exclaimed the Chief, shaking his head. "You know what I think? I think somehow you finally put two and two together about Haines and Dorothy Hanson—like I did yesterday."

He put his face very close to Armstrong's and spoke very softly. "The question is: If he *was* responsible for her death, would you kill him for that?"

Armstrong paled, but said nothing.

The Chief would have gone further, but he was suddenly overcome with fatigue. He yawned. "I've had it." He turned off his tape recorder. "I'm going to have to think on this," he said, starting to leave. "Oh, and Mr. Armstrong? Don't leave town."

◆

Brother Bartholomew raked the last of the leaves into a pile and straightened his back. Still forty minutes to Sext. Plenty of time to get the garden cart and pick up these piles. . . . His pager vibrated, and he glanced down. It was the Chief.

"Listen," said his exhausted friend, when he went in the friary and called him, "I'm bushed, and going home to bed. But I've got to talk to you first. Meet me at Norma's in ten minutes?"

"Well, I'm kind of in the middle of—okay, I'll see you there."

Leaving the leaves to scatter to the four winds, he went to the old pickup and to Norma's. When he arrived, his friend was sitting at the table in the corner, nursing a mug of coffee. Bartholomew came up and said quietly, "You don't want to sit here."

"What do you mean?" said the Chief, keeping his voice down, "I don't want to be overheard."

"That's why this is the wrong table. Trust me: The acoustics in here are peculiar. This table can be heard by anyone standing back there by the grill. We want to be at that table in front of the window."

"Bart," the Chief sighed, "I'm dead tired—"

"My mother clued me in on this: This is the one table you *don't* want to sit at!"

"Okay, okay!" grumbled the Chief, picking up his mug and moving to the window table.

"So?" asked Bartholomew.

"So—what?"

"So, why are we here?"

The Chief propped up his head with his hand. "I want you to talk to Armstrong. I've just spent most of the morning with him, and he's managed to put himself back at the top of my list. I just want you to check him out first, before I arrest him."

Bartholomew was taken aback. "What's made you so sure?"

"Turns out, he *did* tell Haines about Dorothy Hanson's mission—and I think he realized that Haines had something to do with what happened to her. In which case, Haines had completely conned him. Which was why he cleared out and headed—purportedly—for New Hampshire. I think he stayed home and did him, then called to establish an alibi, and then beat it up there, making a point to pick up a paper at the general store, first thing in the morning." The Chief yawned. "So you go see what you think, while I crash."

At that moment, Isabel came over with the green-handled decaf jug for her son. Seeing it, he said, "You know, I've had it with decaf. Give me a cup of your best."

To his astonishment, his mother said, "No."

"What do you mean 'no'? For over a year you've been ragging on me, because I won't drink your coffee! Now, I want to, and you won't let me!"

"That's right!" she said, ratcheting up with him. "You've had the intestinal fortitude to get off caffeine and stay off this long? Well, I'm not going to be party to putting you back on it!"

The patrons of Norma's Café fell silent, absorbed in the unfolding drama.

"Mother," Bartholomew said quietly, "has anyone ever suggested that you are—perverse?"

"All right, mister! That does it! I'm not going to be part of *your* caffeine delivery system! Go somewhere else! And don't *ever* come back in here again!"

The Chief spoke up. "Whoa, whoa, both of you! *This is stupid!*" He looked around at the other customers. "All of you: Go back to your own business!"

They did. After all, he *was* the Chief of Police.

"And you two," he glared at his two friends. "Just. Simmer. Down." They did.

"Isabel," said the Chief more calmly, "sit down." He threw another glance around Norma's, and everyone turned studiously away.

Isabel sat down. After all, he *was* the Chief of Police. And no one had spoken to her that way since her husband, Buck, had died.

"Now, I'm sick of this squabbling between you," declared the Chief under his breath. "You two really care for each other, but it's not quite the way you want it," he was looking at Isabel, "so you chew on each other." He stabbed his finger on the table. "It stops." Stab. "Now." Stab. "Here." Stab.

He turned to Bartholomew. "And if God wants you off caffeine, then you'd—jolly well better stay off!"

Bartholomew nodded meekly.

"And now you can apologize to your mother! There aren't many men lucky enough to have a mother like her!"

"I'm sorry, Mother," said Bartholomew, meaning it.

"I'm sorry, too," Isabel said, meaning it.

Only then did Bartholomew remember Anselm's words. He thought of explaining it to her, then thought better of it. Instead, he said in a low voice, "Mother, forgive me. I've been a jerk. Dan's right: You're the best there ever was! And I will *never* forget that again."

48 | truth and consequences

WHEN BARTHOLOMEW GOT BACK IN THE PICKUP, he noticed that his hands were shaking. And realized that he really loved his mother. And that he'd had an awfully strange way of showing it. Well, that would change.

He put the truck in gear and drove out to *FW*, wondering if this trip was even necessary, given the incriminating—and convincing—scenario the Chief had put together. Still, Dan had asked him to check it out.

Turning into the driveway, he saw that for the first time since the murder, there were no police vehicles on the premises. He was shown into the library, where Clay Armstrong seemed glad to see him. Which surprised Bartholomew, since Armstrong had just been through a rather intense interrogation that morning.

"Are you the good cop?" Armstrong asked with a smile. "First the Chief, and now—"

Bartholomew shook his head. "I'm *no* kind of cop. I'm just trying to help by bringing a different perspective."

"Well, that's what *I* need right now, too: a different perspective."

When Bartholomew looked puzzled, his host frowned. "You *do* believe in the supernatural, don't you?"

"Of course," said the monk smiling. "I'd be in the wrong profession, if I didn't."

Armstrong seemed pleased. "Good. Can you stay for lunch? Because I've got some questions—I mean, if you have the time, that is."

Bartholomew considered for a moment. "Let me call home and let people know where I am."

"You can use that phone," said his host, delighted, "while I tell James."

In a few minutes, James had set up two trays in the library, with chicken salad, toasted pita bread, and iced tea.

Hardly had they sat down when Armstrong said, "Talk to me about supernatural healing. Because Haines, no matter what else he did, may have healed me of lung cancer."

Bartholomew thought carefully, before replying. "I'm going to give you my explanation. Not the abbey's. Not Christendom's. Just mine."

Armstrong nodded.

"There's always been good and evil. Man's known that intuitively, and science is just now beginning to consider the possibility of a fifth dimension: a moral dimension. The thing to remember is: There's no such thing as 'neutral' supernatural power; it's either of God, or—"

Armstrong, his mouth full, waved to interrupt. "Don't tell me there's a devil," he managed. "Please, don't insult my intelligence."

The monk smiled sadly. "I wish there weren't. C.S. Lewis said that the devil's cleverest trick was to convince modern man he didn't exist."

Armstrong shook his head. "If I bought that, I'd have to buy—"

"The whole package? Well, for the sake of hypothesis, suspend your disbelief for a moment. You asked about supernatural healing. When it comes from God, His ways are mysterious. Sometimes He answers prayers for healing with miraculous results. Sometimes the healing is not the physical one we asked for, but an inner, unseen one." He smiled. "And sometimes the healing takes place in those *around* the one being prayed for."

Armstrong was growing impatient. "What was it—or wasn't it—with Haines?"

"The enemy can also heal. In fact, he can imitate much of what God does. For his own purposes." Bartholomew paused. "Sometimes you have to judge the tree by its fruit. A good tree can't bear bad fruit, and vice versa." He looked at Armstrong. "What was the fruit of your healing?"

His host thought for a moment. "The ARC. Which Haines would control. Which nearly took over my house. And my business. And my future. And my mind. And alienated my family."

He got up and started pacing. "But look: I'm awfully glad I'm healed! Where does—God fit into that?"

Bartholomew shrugged. "He may have allowed it, because of the good it's *going* to do. God is—God. He can even take something the enemy intended for evil and turn it to good."

"What do you mean?"

"Well, look at what you want to do now: help others. I think God could use this new desire to great effect—if you'd let Him help you."

Armstrong said nothing. He was looking up at the portrait of his wife.

Bartholomew followed his gaze. "I'm told," he said gently, "that she died of clinical depression."

Armstrong nodded.

The monk took a deep breath. "Well—if there was ever a field of medical science that needed research assistance, it's that one." He paused. "Why don't you found a center for clinical depression?"

Armstrong did not respond. His gaze remained fixed on his wife's face.

Bartholomew looked at his watch. "I've got to be going."

"I'll walk out with you."

As they descended the front steps, Bartholomew looked at his host with an apologetic expression. "I just remembered the reason I came out here: The Chief thinks you found out that Haines had something to do with Dorothy Hanson's death. He thinks you were so angry at being totally conned that you killed him. Is that true?"

Armstrong looked at him and then out at the statue gleaming in the sun. "All but the last part," he finally said.

"Any idea who did kill him?"

"No, and I don't even want to think about it."

Bartholomew nodded. "I wouldn't, either." Then he brightened. "You know, that statue is growing on me. Each time I see it, I like it a little more. How did you–"

Armstrong told him the story of how he'd met his wife.

"What was her name?"

"Sheila."

As Bartholomew started up the pickup, he called to Armstrong: "You could call the clinic 'Sheila House'."

49 | return of the prodigal son

IT WAS A LITTLE COLD TO BE OUT on the terrace, Samantha had to admit, even in the direct sunlight. But give it time; as the sun got higher, it was bound to get warmer. So she leaned back in the deck chair, turned a page of yesterday's *Wall Street Journal* (the only reading material readily at hand), and gathered the sweater a little closer at the neck. Staring out to sea, she tried not to think about where Gottfried might be.

Think about the good things, she told herself. Her father had come back. And had assured her that he didn't kill Haines. Also, he finally seemed to be back in his right mind—and maybe even a little the better for the wear. And so were she and Serena, for that matter; they were getting along now, which had never happened before. And—oh, where was Gosha? Was he all right? Did he need her?

Well, this had taught her one thing: She did not want to be separated from him again. Ever. No matter where he was, no matter what he'd done, if he came back, she was going to marry him as soon as possible. And they were going to be together for richer or poorer, in sickness or in health, till death did them part. Did absence make the heart grow fonder? You'd better believe it!

But where *was* he?

Off to her left, a gull circled upward, climbing a thermal. He (she assumed it was a he) seemed to be taking his time, adjusting his wings slightly to hold the updraft. He seemed to be—enjoying himself. Which surprised her. She'd always assumed gulls spent most of their waking hours working to find enough food to stay alive. And whenever they did stop, it was to fall asleep, exhausted. Though come to think of it, she did recall seeing gulls sitting around on pilings, basking in the sun.

A shadow from someone behind her fell across the newspaper. It scared her badly; all that shooting had taken place right here, less than a week ago!

She turned, shielding her eyes from the glare of the sun. The person was silhouetted by the sun directly behind, but she could still make out who it was. She let out the breath she'd been holding, and a great smile of relief spread across her face. "You came back! I knew you would!" (She knew no such thing, but she didn't want him to know that.)

Gottfried came around in front of her and sat down. Collapsed would be more accurate. His eyes were sunken and hollow, and he had a few days' stubble.

"You look awful, darling!" she said smiling. "Like you haven't slept in days."

"I haven't."

"Gosha, you poor thing, what have you been doing?" And she sat up and took his hands in hers, holding them, as if to warm them.

"I don't know," he muttered, "mostly driving."

"Where?"

"Just—around."

When he'd returned to their apartment, he'd gone through the messages on their answering machine. At the one from Serena about the murder, he began to think he might be a suspect. And the more he thought about it, the more certain he became; surely no one had a greater motive. Since she wasn't there to calm him down and reassure him, it only got worse—until finally he couldn't stand it any longer and got in his car. Afraid to check into a motel because his credit card might be traced, he'd slept in the car.

But when he woke up this morning, he'd decided he was done with running. He would come down to Eastport and face the music.

She looked at him, head tilted, a worried look on her face. "Gottfried, is there—any music to face?"

"You mean, did I do it?" he asked, laughing. "No, *liebchen*, I didn't."

Then she laughed, too, and hugged him, and started to cry and began shaking uncontrollably. And let him hold her and comfort her.

"Why are you crying?" he asked her softly.

"Because I'm so happy!" she blurted out, and realized that this must be what love felt like.

"What are you so happy about?" he said, rebuking her fondly. "My life is in shambles, my work is ruined, I've been betrayed by my father—your father—and you're behaving like a *kind* on *Heilige Nacht*."

"Oh, Gosha," she cried, hugging him, "it's going to be all right! Everything! It'll all work out, you'll see!"

For a long time they held each other. And she was right; the terrace was warm enough now.

Then Gottfried announced he was going to the police, to make a statement.

"I'll go with you," she said, standing up.

But he shook his head. "No. I'm going to do this by myself."

At the police station, Sergeant Whipple looked in the Chief's office, "Someone's here I think you'll want to see."

"Who?"

"You know a Gottfried Franc?"

"No, but I sure want to. Send him in."

Fifteen minutes later, a much-relieved Gottfried Franc exited the station. And the Chief, because Franc had only his fiancée, herself a suspect, to establish his whereabouts on the night of the murder, added his name to the list. But at the very bottom.

He had just circled the name at the top, when Brother Bartholomew arrived, to give him his evaluation of that person.

"Sorry, Dan, he didn't do it."

"Is this your–*blessed* intuition again?"

"I guess so. I had lunch with him. And you were right about his twigging to Haines being connected with the Hanson woman's death. But I'm sure he's not–"

"*Birdseye frozen peas!*" shouted the Chief, using his strongest substitute expletive. Then under his breath he asked the Blessed Mother to forgive him.

"Why do you ask her to do that?"

"Because she knows what I wanted to say!"

Bartholomew smiled. "Dan, all I'm trying to do is save you from embarrassing yourself."

"You mean, like last time?" said the Chief with a trace of irony. The previous year he had, against Bartholomew's advice and intuition, arrested what had proved to be the wrong suspect.

"I didn't say that. I–" he saw how close his friend was to losing his temper. "Look, just wait–two more days."

"Why two? Why not three? A week?"

Bartholomew held up his hands. "I don't know; just a hunch."

"All right," said his friend with a grudging smile, "go on, get out of here! But in case you think you've won, I've already put him under surveillance so tight, it squeaks. We'll just see what happens."

50 | the fifth dimension

BY THE FOLLOWING AFTERNOON (Thursday), things in the offices of Armstrong & Associates had pretty much settled back to normal—if anything could be normal, after the violent death of the office manager three weeks before, followed by a spectacular murder on the premises just a week before.

Clay Armstrong, after nearly disbanding A&A, was making a sincere effort to get his head back in the game, though his partner, Ed Forester, and junior partner (in six more days), Nigel Rawlings, would probably say that his priorities were still askew.

He certainly hoped so, thought Clay with a smile, as he paced from room to room. Something *was* happening to him— something strange, but good. He was changing. He didn't know what he was changing *to*, but he did know what *from*. And he had no desire to go back. He suspected that whatever was happening to him, Sheila—he stopped and looked up at her portrait—would approve. Too bad he couldn't have started changing before she—left.

In the two days since Brother Bartholomew's visit, the more he thought about his suggestion, the more he liked it: set up a center for the study and healing of clinical depression. And the thing he liked best about it was that, if his wife were alive, she would probably be more proud of him for doing it, than anything he had ever done.

That settled it! Sheila House was going to happen—as fast as it possibly could! And when Clay Armstrong set his mind to making something happen quickly, it usually made other people's heads spin. He chuckled out loud. And this time, he was confident his daughters would be a hundred percent behind him. Ditto, Ed and Nigel. Because he was not about to curtail the money-making engine of A&A; he was merely going to redirect a portion of its profits.

But A&A's modus operandi *would* be different, he realized, as he booted up his computer to get his vision into words. He used to take pride in being that shark that other sharks feared. No longer. Besides, where did it say in the rule book that nice guys *had* to finish last? What if one were also smart and quick and could see over the horizon?

His computer ready, he started conceptualizing. Though he used only two fingers, they were flying so fast that Ed Forester looked in to see what was going on.

"New concept," Clay told him.

Ed looked worried. "We *are* back on track with the Genome Project, aren't we? That's going to be the biggest score we've ever made!"

Clay rubbed his chin. "I've been thinking about that, Ed. I'm not so sure we shouldn't do it the way the kid wants: set him up, recoup our investment, take an extra year of profits, and then let it go."

"*What?*"

"You heard me: basically let him give his findings to the world."

"But that's *crazy!*" cried Forester. "I thought we were back to our original game plan!"

"Well, we are," replied the senior partner calmly. "I just don't think we should sell it the moment he cracks the code."

"But why not? You know that's when the short-term profit will peak!"

Clay wondered how to put it, so his friend could see where he was coming from. "You know," he said thoughtfully, "there's a dimension we've never considered: the moral dimension. If we give birth to a thing, enable it to happen, don't we have an obligation to ensure it's used for the greatest possible good?"

Forester stared at him like he'd lost his senses. "Clay! Don't tell me you're back in cuckoo land!"

The latter shook his head. "I don't think so. In fact, I've never seen things more clearly in my life. Look at the scientists who cracked the atom: sure, there was a wartime emergency. But how many of them spent the rest of their lives agonizing over their role in developing weapons of mass destruction?"

"How the Genome Code's used is *not* our concern!" Forester insisted. "*It never has been!* We get in, we get out, and we make some money in the process. That's A&A! Always has been, always will be!"

Clay shook his head. "Well, maybe it should be our concern. Cracking the Genome Code is going to be bigger than cracking the atom. It's going to be like Columbus discovering the New World." He paused. "Maybe our ability to direct hundreds of millions in venture capital—the power to birth or change entire industries—carries a moral obligation with it."

Forester looked at him a long time. "We're not on the same page anymore, are we, Clay?" he said with great sadness. "I'm not even sure we're in the same book."

"Never mind," said Clay, suddenly smiling. "We'll sort it out later. Meantime, I need you to do me a personal favor." He opened his center desk drawer and took out an envelope, from which he extracted the key he'd had made from the impression in the butter. "On the day Dorothy disappeared, I've reason to believe she put something in our safe deposit box at First Colonial in Hyannis—something meant for me. Something I now need. I'd go myself, but the EPD is surveilling me. They're supposed to be undercover," he chuckled. "I'm not supposed to know they're there. But they're so close that if I sneeze, they'll say *Gesundheit!*"

He handed Forester the key. "This is a copy of the key Dorothy kept." When his partner frowned, he added, "I know it's against the law for a locksmith to make a copy of a safe deposit key. Let's just say—a certain locksmith owed me a large favor."

His partner still did not look comfortable, so Clay said, "I've just gotten off the phone to Sumner Watson, the manager down there. He, too, owes me a rather large favor." He laughed. "I sound like a mafia don!" He went on in a hoarse, Don Corleone whisper: "Now the time has come for these favors to be repaid."

Forester didn't laugh. He didn't even smile.

"Anyway," sighed Clay, "I've given him a heads up that you're coming, so there should be no problem."

Two hours later, Forester returned. Empty-handed. "You were right: Dorothy did go there, and apparently did put something in the box on the afternoon she disappeared. But between the time you called and the time I got there, Watson apparently made some inquiries—and found that the police were investigating all circumstances surrounding her death."

He shook his head. "When I got there, he was extremely agitated. On the verge of calling the police, in fact, to see if they wanted to have someone present, when we opened the box."

Clay looked at him, alarmed, but Forester smiled. "I calmed him down. Said it was confidential but of no interest to the police. But we were happy to leave whatever it was right there. We didn't need to get into the box today."

"Did he buy it?"

Forester nodded. "Reluctantly. And only because, as you said, he owes you, big time." He smiled grimly. "Only now I guess it's *you* who owe *him*."

Clay did not smile.

"Oh," said Forester as an afterthought, "One other thing: He was really spooked, so if I were you, I wouldn't even call him."

"Thanks, Ed, I'm sure that's wise. We'll just leave that box alone for a long time."

51 | fitness can be hazardous

PART OF CLAY ARMSTRONG'S new slant on life was his new slant on fitness. His body was 65 years old. If he wanted to be 75, he'd better start taking better care of it. So after his "healing" he started a regimen of walking two miles a day. Every day, without fail. In fact, it quickly became such a part of his routine, that if he couldn't get it in first thing in the morning, he would be edgy until he could.

He did the walk down on the beach, which meant he got an extra workout at the end: climbing the 203 steps back up to the top of the bluff.

When he'd built the house in '81, the steps were set well back, cascading down into a deep, man-made cut in the bluff (which the EPA would never allow now), so that they truly resembled a wooden waterfall. But no one had foreseen the savagery of the No-name Storm and other "hundred-year" nor'easters, which had mauled the great sand cliffs like a giant cat. Sixty feet of the dune's face had been ripped off, and now the wooden waterfall was no longer protected by the cut, but extended out into space like an ancient rickety roller-coaster.

Twice, Clay had hired carpenters to buttress it, and before she died, Sheila had urged him to have the worst sections replaced. Now the whole waterfall needed replacing, once the Eastport Conservation Commission approved the new plan. But this they were loathe to do, and Clay had been forced to take the matter up with the Commonwealth's Department of Environmental Protection up in Boston. Meanwhile, going up and down the waterfall was increasingly dangerous to anyone who didn't know exactly where its weaknesses were. And perhaps to those who did.

Sometimes the press of business would force Clay to postpone his walk, but he never canceled it. Even if it meant doing it at night, like tonight (Thursday). With the flashlight from the kitchen closet, he gingerly made his way down the staircase, firmly promising himself that he would call his coastal engineer, Bill Walker, in the morning, to see how things were coming with the DEP.

Down on the beach, it was cold—but not too cold; just enough to keep him moving. The sea at night was vast, but not scary—almost comforting. As he walked, he went over the whole episode with Ed. Something there was not right, but he couldn't put his finger on it.

In the end he decided it was just their diverging points of view. Ed wanted him to come to his senses and return to their old way of operating. But that was the whole point: He *had* come to his senses! And having gotten a glimpse of what might lie over his personal horizon, he was anxious to keep moving toward it— whatever "it" was.

The shark may have had pretty teeth, Ed, but that's *had*, not *has*. He would have to have a long talk with his old friend in the morning.

He came to the steps and checked his watch as he started

climbing. And checked it again at the halfway point, where he was pleased to see he was under four minutes for the first time, which encouraged him to go for a strong finish.

Huffing upward through the darkness, he'd almost reached the top, when a form suddenly loomed out in front of him and pushed him hard against the railing, which gave way, pitching him out and down. Flailing wildly as he fell, he passed the halfway point in two seconds—and only then remembered to scream.

◆

Clay opened his eyes—or did he? It was so black, they might still be closed. Was he—dead? He tried to move an arm. It moved. Could dead people move? Of course they could! They went zipping all over the place—down tunnels, toward lights, into gardens. . . .

Whereas, he—could barely move. What *could* he move? His arm. His other arm. His leg. His other leg. His head.

"Mr. Armstrong? Sir, are you down here?" It was James. With a light.

"Over—here," he groaned.

"Oh!" exclaimed James, putting a light on him. "Thank God you're—"

"Alive?"

"Yes, sir," exclaimed James, hurrying over to him. "I heard the scream and came out, and saw the broken railing." He aimed the flashlight up—far up. More than a hundred feet up, to where the broken railing dangled.

Only then did Clay fully realize what had happened. And how extraordinarily lucky he had been. Directly below the broken railing was a pile of boulders. Had he fallen straight down, he would indeed be zipping down tunnels and toward lights. But whoever did it had pushed him so hard that he had fallen beyond the rocks, onto the steeply sloping sand of the bluff. He had missed the rocks by—he twisted painfully to see— less than five feet.

Now what? Could he—get up? He tried and winced; his back was out. But if that was the worst that he'd suffered. . . .

"Sir," said James, "I think you should stay here. I will go up there," he looked up the long flight of stairs, "and call 911."

Clay agreed. "That is unquestionably the wise thing to do. But—give me a hand here: I want to see if I can get up."

"I really don't think you should, sir. What if something internal is—broken?"

But Clay's mind was made up, and the old retainer knew better than to try to dissuade him. James helped as best he could, and together they got him upright, more or less.

Gingerly, Clay tested his mobility. The lower back complained mightily, but he could bear that. Slowly, one step at a time, they approached the wooden steps.

"Sir," said the housekeeper, shaking his head, "I'm not sure—"

"James," replied Clay kindly, realizing that the old fellow was also worried about his own ability to make the ascent. "Forgive me. Tell you what: We'll do this as if that were the summit of Everest, and this is the final ascent. Above eight thousand meters, you take one step, rest for a ten-count. Next step, another ten-count. You'll see: Slow and easy wins the race."

And it did. By the time they reached the top, Clay had decided to give James an immediate two-week all-expenses-paid vacation in Hawaii. Or London. Or wherever he wanted to go.

As soon as they were in the house, Clay called the police. Ten minutes later, a bright young female officer named Allen was at his door, taking down everything he could tell her. And then, everything that James could tell her: When he heard the scream, he went to the kitchen closet for the flashlight. It wasn't there; Mr. Armstrong must have taken it.

As he went to get the one in the front hall closet, he happened to notice something odd out the vestibule window, someone leaving.

Man or woman?

He couldn't tell. But he—or she—was on a bicycle.

52 | and then there were two

As the Chief pulled into *FW's* drive the following morning (Friday) and saw the old red pickup, he shook his head. Brother Bart had really saved his bacon! But how had he known to ask for two days?

James showed him to the master bedroom, where Armstrong was in bed, and Bartholomew was on a chair beside him. "It's not as bad as it looks," Armstrong greeted the Chief cheerfully, "but it was worse than I thought. When I woke up this morning, I felt like a truck had backed over me."

"Believe me," said the Chief with true compassion, "I know the feeling." He pulled up another chair. "Mr. Armstrong, I owe you an apology: I was sure you'd done it. In fact, I almost—well, never mind."

He came right to the point. "The reason I asked Brother Bartholomew to join me here is this: We're in a quandary, and we need your help. I think we can assume that Haines did Dorothy. But who did Haines? And nearly you?"

When Armstrong didn't answer, Bartholomew asked, "Do you think it was a man or a woman who pushed you?"

Armstrong shook his head. "It happened so fast. . . ."

Bartholomew turned to the Chief. "Can't we rule out his daughters? I mean, with Haines gone, there's no ARC, and everything reverts back to the way it was." He paused. "Unless– you're not having a problem with any of them about something else, are you?"

Armstrong shook his head. "Not that I'm aware of. Though sometimes a father hasn't any idea how much he's bugging his children." They laughed.

"Was there anything," the Chief persisted, "anything at all, with any of them?"

Armstrong thought a moment. "Only Samantha. She was upset with me, for having attempted to capitalize on her fiancé's life's work." He smiled. "If she could have seen me yesterday, taking her point of view! I was trying to get Ed Forester to see that we had a moral obligation to set excess profit aside and make sure Franc's discovery was made available to the world–" He stopped.

No one spoke. Or needed to.

"Gottfried Franc came to see me two days ago," said the Chief, careful to touch all the bases. He turned to Armstrong. "Does he know of your–change of heart?"

"All he knows is that the Genome deal is back on, as before. No one knows how much I'm now in sympathy with the way he feels–except Ed Forester."

The Chief passed a hand over his eyes. "Then we can assume Franc would have no reason to want you dead."

"On the contrary," chuckled Bartholomew, "it sounds like he's got every reason to hope you'll enjoy a long and happy life."

"Nigel Rawlings," said the Chief, moving them on to the last possible suspect. "He seemed to be freaking out at the prospect of the ARC closing down A&A. And I can understand: to be that close to a million dollars? With your whole future riding on it?"

Bartholomew frowned. "How does that whole business with his 'term of indenture' stand? Is he still in line to receive his 'golden payday'? I mean, it's this Wednesday, isn't it?"

Armstrong nodded. "As far as I'm concerned, that's the day he becomes a partner. He's certainly earned his million—and made us a few more, in the meantime."

The Chief frowned and looked out the window. "Here's a hard question: What if you were to die—but A&A was still in existence? Would he collect then?"

"You mean, from the corporation?" Armstrong rubbed his jaw. "Yes, he would. His agreement was with the corporation, not Ed and me." He winced. "You don't think that Nigel. . . ."

"I honestly don't know what to think," said the Chief. "But supposing Ed had a little chat with Nigel. Supposing he'd outlined his worst-case scenario of how A&A was likely to operate in the future, with the senior A, who'd already demonstrated he was loony enough to close the whole thing down, suddenly desirous of giving away the store, for the good of all mankind. Supposing—Ed convinced Nigel that with the senior A gone to his eternal reward a little sooner than expected, they could run A&A the way it used to run? The way it was running, when Nigel came on board?"

It was plausible—more plausible than any of them, including the Chief, expected.

All at once the Chief burst out laughing. The other two looked at him, astonished. "You know what each of them is going to tell me," he managed, "when I ask them what they were doing last night, when it happened?"

Bartholomew and Armstrong shook their heads.

"Watching *ER!*"

53 | sheila house

As the Chief and Brother Bartholomew were about to leave, Clay Armstrong asked the latter to stay behind for a moment.

"I've been giving a lot of thought to what we talked about, the last time you were here," he said. "In fact, I haven't thought about much else. I've decided to go ahead with Sheila House. In fact, I want to implement it as quickly as possible."

"Implement it?"

"Get it up and running." Clay sat up straighter. "The trouble is, I'm not sure where to begin. If this were a new business venture, I'd know what to do, but—"

"What would you do, if it *was* a business?"

"Oh, state the vision. Find out who the best people in the field are. And which of them might be persuaded to 'relocate,' if there were sufficient incentive. Find the right chief operating officer, and let him tell you what he would need in the way of staff, location, equipment, and funding."

Clay warmed to the project. "Then get it for him. And then, as soon as everyone's under contract, let the business community know there's a new player at the table."

He stopped and grinned at Bartholomew. "You're going to tell me I've just outlined what I need to do."

"Haven't you?"

The man in the bed laughed. "I guess I have. I'll have my favorite headhunter start rounding up the usual suspects. Meanwhile, I've got to get going on the vision statement, find a location, and start letting the right people know what's happening."

"Where will you locate it?"

Clay smiled. He'd already given thought to that. "I can't see any reason not to put it here, in Eastport. Over on the bay side, where it's more peaceful. Right on the bay, in fact. A couple of centuries ago, doctors were aware of the calming, restorative powers that came from locating a clinic or sanitarium beside a body of water."

"Makes sense," said Bartholomew.

"What's more, our bay has one big advantage over a lake in the Swiss Alps: It's never boring. Since high tide is six and a half hours from low tide, instead of six, you get a complete change of scene every week. You don't like having high tide on Sunday afternoon? Wait a week; next Sunday you'll be able to walk out a mile on the sand flats." He shook his head. "Could there be a better environment for healing depression?"

The monk smiled. "Almost as if it was arranged that way."

Clay was all business now. "I've got to find the property, lock in the staff, get an architect to do some visionary drawings, and then let the Cape—and the world—know what we're doing." He stopped and eyed his visitor. "I don't suppose you'd have any thoughts on that subject, would you?"

"I'm a monk," said Bartholomew with a shrug. "What do monks know about such things?"

Clay smiled. "You seem to know a lot about a lot of things."

"Well—you might let Holly Anderson help you with the PR. My impression is, she's got New York savvy for Cape Cod prices. Also, in a couple of weeks the abbey is having its annual fund-raising bikeathon, the *Tour d'Espoir*. Usually it's just for the benefit of the touring choir. But when we do our annual Fourth-of-July and Christmas events, we always name another Cape charity, like Hospice or Habitat for Humanity, to be a co-recipient."

He thought for a moment. "It's possible we could do that here. I don't have anything to do with decisions like that, but I could certainly present it."

Clay smiled. "How does it work? You ride so many miles, and people pledge so much a mile?"

"Right. We usually go for an early fall, three-day weekend and try to do 200–250 miles. But this year, because of scheduling conflicts, it'll be a one-day event. So we're going to do a Metric Century: one hundred kilometers—sixty-two miles—from Falmouth to Provincetown. And we'll be asking people to pledge at least a dollar a kilometer."

"All right," said Clay, making some rapid mental calculations, "let me sweeten the pot: If your ride could be combined and expanded—and I'm thinking of mega-promotion here, because there's so little time—and billed as the *Tour d'Espoir*/Sheila Ride. . . ." he grinned, "I would be willing to anonymously match *all* gifts. A ten-dollar-a-kilometer pledge to your choir would actually earn twenty, and Sheila House would gain a ton of positive publicity in the process."

Bartholomew stood up. "Let me talk to the people at home."

◆

Bartholomew talked to Anselm who talked to Dominic, and the two of them talked to Mother Michaela. She talked to the sub-abbot who talked to two of the clergy and the head of the foundation responsible for fund-raising for the choir. In two days word came back to Brother Bartholomew: You may inform Mr. Armstrong that he has a deal.

When Bartholomew went back to *FW* to inform Clay, the latter thanked him for putting him on to Holly Anderson. "She's shown me exactly what I need to do. Nine months from now, just about the time Sheila House will be fully operational, we're going to hold a symposium of the top people on clinical depression, not only in this country but around the world. And not only the doctors and the researchers, but also the best-selling authors and medical journal editors—*everyone*. Which means all the media will have to cover it."

Clay could see the symposium unfolding in his imagination. "We'll hold it over at Teal Pond," he mused. "Some journalists and editors will insist on paying their own way, to maintain ethical objectivity, but we'll subsidize it to keep the costs way down. . . . Who could resist a bargain week on Cape Cod in July?"

Bartholomew shook his head. "Mind-boggling."

"She likes your idea, too. The *Tour d'Espoir*/Sheila Ride could be presented to all the bike stores and cycling clubs, all the schools and hospitals, young people's groups and church activity groups—as a way to get behind a good new clinic that will be of great benefit to the Cape. We've only got a couple of weeks to get it all done, but she assures me it's do-able. The one thing that could kill us is the weather. . . ."

Bartholomew smiled. "Let me work on that."

54 | the path of obedience

THE FOLLOWING SATURDAY, two weeks before the ride, Brother Bartholomew was doing something he hardly ever got to do anymore—enjoying an afternoon of blessed quietude. All by himself in the Scriptorium, he was listening to a recording of French monks from Solesmes producing perfect Gregorian chant, and practicing calligraphy. With the vertical, crank-open window cracked enough to let in the unseasonably warm October air, he imagined that his high stool and work-table were facing a slit window in the high tower of a mountainside monastery in medieval Italy. Where monks had copied manuscripts for generations before him, and would be, for generations after.

Actually, he was doing something a little more challenging than forming graceful letters in careful, elegant lines. He was again trying his hand at illumination—the artful, intricate enhancement of the opening capital letters, with which monks had once adorned their presentation pages. The interwoven ribbons of color they had used utterly intrigued him, as it had

Columba before him. Bartholomew had first been drawn to the work when Columba had shown him enlargements of the illuminations in the ancient Book of Kells, and challenged him to discern how the old Celtic monks had done it. The more closely Bartholomew had studied the complex, even labyrinthine designs—"knot work" they'd called it—the more amazing they became. And they had produced them without a computer, or any technology, for that matter.

These illuminations, which must have taken months to work out, were the fruit of inspired, extremely patient monks who took anonymous joy in glorifying God in this fashion.

Moreover, they did it without ever breaking a line, much less a ribbon. Did they ever wonder if one day their handiwork would be admired by another illuminator? Someone who could appreciate the extraordinary care that had gone into their creation?

No, he decided, they weren't doing it for that. He recalled something he'd learned, when he and a few others from the abbey had been given a tour by candlelight of Canterbury Cathedral years before. At the time, the cathedral was under-going major renovation. In the process of replacing the lead roof, as they peeled back one section, they discovered a smiling face carved into one of the vaulting stone arches that supported the roof. Only this joyous visage wasn't on the underside of the arch, where it could be seen from the nave below. It was on the upper side of the arch, looking up.

Returning his attention to his work, he sighed and balled up another mistake, which he aimed at the tall basket in the corner—and missed. He envied the ancient monks their seemingly endless supply of time, so different from the situation of modern monks. Yet what he was *really* envying, he realized, was their perfect surrender.

His own surrender was far from perfect. What was it Columba had said, sitting over there on the other stool?

Bartholomew, your heart wants to surrender, even if your head and emotions and self-will—your soul—are set against it. But you have started on the path that will lead you there. The Path of Obedience is well-worn but not highly traveled.

He missed Columba and the quiet Saturday afternoons they used to spend here. . . .

Get back to work, he told himself. He started a fresh design—and felt a tail gently brush his leg. Bartholomew smiled—Pangur Ban always seemed to know when he was getting frustrated and needed a little distraction. He reached down and stroked the cat, until he purred and walked away, returning to his pallet, where he curled back up and resumed his nap.

Let's see, thought Bartholomew, if I take the blue ribbon here, and this time lift it *over* the yellow but *not* under the red, and wrap it around the foreleg of this little smiling griffin—

The pager on his belt vibrated. He almost ripped it off and flung it out the open window and down the Italian mountainside.

It was the Chief. Of course. Who else.

"I want you to meet me at Armstrong's in ten minutes," the Chief announced, when he returned his call.

"Dan, we just did that! I mean, can't you go alone?" No sooner were the words out of his mouth, than he realized he had hurt his friend.

"Look," replied the Chief curtly, "you think this is what *I* want to do right now? In the fourth quarter, with Air Force on our twenty-yard line?"

"Sorry; I'll be right there."

"Yeah, well, I wouldn't have bothered you, except Armstrong specifically asked that you be there, because there's a couple of things he has to tell us. And look, take it easy on him; he sounds a little stressed out."

The words stung. He's right, of course; I could use a little compassion, he chided himself, as he put his latest attempt away and cleaned up the work table. He was about to leave, when he remembered what Columba had told him once.

Compassion is not a fruit of the Spirit, Bartholomew. It is the wine of the Spirit. And the only way you get wine is by crushing grapes.

55 | a matter of diamonds

WHEN THE CHIEF AND BROTHER BARTHOLOMEW joined Armstrong in the library, they found him more than a little stressed out.

"I've misled you, both of you, from the beginning. I don't know what's happening to me, but I can't keep it inside any longer!"

"Keep what inside?" asked the Chief, who added, "This better be good. Because Air Force just scored."

Armstrong led them over to the piano and showed them the picture of Dorothy Hanson. "That Wednesday afternoon you were asking about? Haines looked at that photograph and mentioned how well she'd looked in that outfit. But since it was purchased in Antwerp, the only time he could have seen it was on the day she died."

The Chief shook his head, annoyed. "Why didn't you tell us? You knew we were grabbing at straws."

"You've got to understand: This was the man who saved my life! I'd never trusted anyone so totally!"

"Until you realized," Bartholomew calmly continued for him, "that he must have tortured Dorothy, to find out where the diamonds were."

"Yes," muttered Armstrong, his voice breaking.

The Chief looked at his watch; he might still catch the last ten minutes. "What's the other thing you wanted to tell us, Mr. Armstrong?"

The latter looked at Bartholomew. "Remember the key you showed me? The one I 'accidentally' dropped on the butter? Well, I made a copy." He reached in his pocket. "This copy."

He turned to the Chief. "I lied to you. I've known all along what that key was to: A&A's safe deposit box in the First Colonial branch in Hyannis. In fact, Dorothy and I used to argue about it. I said it ought to be kept in the office; she said that since she was the only one who used the box, she could keep it with her other keys." He smiled sadly. "When I tried to insist, she told me about driving down there once without it, which she was not about to do again."

"So that's where the diamonds are?"

Armstrong nodded. "That's what she was telling me, when she swallowed the key."

"What a brave woman," murmured Bartholomew.

Armstrong's eyes glistened. "I know."

"Did you know she had a cat?" asked Bartholomew.

"How do you know?"

"When you showed me her desk, there was a picture of a cat on it." He hesitated. "You know, if she was that loyal to you, you might want to keep her cat–I mean, if it needs a home."

"I hate cats."

Bartholomew smiled. "I used to, too. Funny how that can change."

"Are we finished here?" asked the Chief.

Bartholomew wore a bemused expression. "Sorry, but I get the feeling we're not." He frowned. "Something's nagging me, and I don't know what it is. . . ."

The Chief turned to him, exasperated. "Your intuition again?"

But Bartholomew was oblivious to him. "You indicated a moment ago," he said to Armstrong slowly, working it out as he went, "that the diamonds were still in the safe deposit box. But—you had a copy of the key. Why didn't you go get them?"

Armstrong laughed. "Because of your surveillance, Chief! It was as tight as a tick!"

They all laughed. "I did ask Ed to get them for me, though," Armstrong added. "He tried, but the manager was so skittish about the contents of the box possibly being of interest to the police, that Ed left them there."

All at once, Bartholomew stared at Armstrong. "Are you sure?"

Armstrong was speechless.

"Did he tell you that, before or after you went through the railing?"

"Before."

"Call the bank manager!" demanded the Chief. "Now!"

"The bank will be closed," Armstrong replied.

"Then call him at home. Or I will."

"I'll do it." Armstrong went to his office to retrieve Watson's home number, then came back and called. Watson's wife answered; he was on the golf course.

"Ask her if he's got a cell phone with him," said Bartholomew, momentarily thankful that it was not medieval Italy.

He did, and Armstrong was soon redialing. He had a brief conversation with the bank manager on the fourteenth green. Hanging up, he stared at them. "Ed did go into the box and left the bank with a small cardboard box."

"Bingo!" said the Chief.

"Motive and opportunity," murmured Bartholomew, not sharing his enthusiasm.

"What?"

"It's only what you taught me." He turned to Armstrong. "Why did he do it? I mean, I can see why he killed Haines. But why would he try to kill you?"

Armstrong smiled. "You should know better than anyone: I–something's happening to me. I've lost my killer instinct. I'm just not interested in shooting people out of the sky anymore. And he still is. It could be that simple."

"Well," exclaimed the Chief, "I'm going to get a search warrant and come down on Forester like a house falling in!"

Bartholomew rubbed his chin. "You sure you've got enough to put him away? There are no witnesses. No fingerprints. Nothing to place him near the crime. If you spook him, he'll just disappear. And with nine and a half million dollars in diamonds, he can *really* disappear!"

Thoroughly exasperated, the Chief said, "Well, what would *you* suggest?"

"What if–nobody lets on we suspect anything? But at the same time we keep the pressure on him. Put him under surveillance, and tap his phone, if you can get a court order. And have your people make it obvious that you're watching and listening."

Bartholomew smiled. "He'd hardly be surprised: It's logical that you would narrow it down to him and maybe Nigel. He'll try to remain cool, but it's going to be working on him, and after a while. . ."

Bartholomew was speaking almost as if he were watching Forester squirm. "When it really gets to him, he'll start thinking about bolting, even though he knows you'll be all over him, the moment he tries." He nodded with enthusiasm. "That's when he'll make his mistake."

"You're sure?" asked the Chief.

"As sure as I can be."

"All right, we'll do it. Let's go." And with that, he bid them adieu. With luck, he would be home for the last couple of minutes.

56 | the sheila ride

Saturday, Veteran's Day, the day of the Sheila Ride, dawned bright and fair. Technically it was the *Tour d'Espoir*/Sheila Ride, but so successful had the publicity blitz been that everyone now thought of it simply as the Sheila Ride.

Falmouth, like Chatham and Osterville, was one of the Cape Cod enclaves where old, heavy money had collected. Cotuit Harbor contained some of the most elegant sailing craft to be seen in New England waters, and houses and gardens created a century earlier reflected a painstaking appreciation of their surrounding landscape.

To readers of *Runner's World* and *Outside Magazine*, the town was best known as the site of the colorful and historic Falmouth Road Race that Bill Rogers and Frank Shorter once excelled in. But now a brand-new event was about to be inaugurated that promised to one day rival the legendary Falmouth Road Race.

Precisely at 10:00, the gun would sound, and the Sheila Ride would be officially underway. A little less than three hours later, the first elite riders would stream into Provincetown, where they would collect their souvenir T-shirts and water bottles, and lazily await the arrival of the thundering herd. All levels of ability would be present today, from Category II and III racers, to serious recreational riders, to fat-tired tyros who would be completing only the first ten miles or so.

Whether or not the abbey's prayers had anything to do with it, the weather turned out to be all anyone could hope for: sunny and mild (upper 50s), with a wind from the southwest—which meant that it would stay warm, and they would have a tailwind the whole way. Perhaps because of the clement weather, registration was stronger than expected. By ten minutes to start time, some 227 riders had logged in, with a couple of dozen last-minute arrivals waiting not-so-patiently in three lines at the registration tables.

A banner across Main Street marked the Start line, and the scene in the road behind it was one of happy chaos. At the front, so no one could get in their way, were the racers and elite riders with $3,000–$4,000 exotic bikes of titanium or carbon fiber or cast aluminum. Their bikes weighed under 20 pounds (not counting water bottles), with tires no thicker than a finger and inflated to 140 pounds per square inch.

Putting in at least 200 miles a week in the saddle, these riders wore serious lycra outfits that bulged nowhere, and had thighs that looked like the trunks of small trees. Their headgear and eyewear was the latest and lightest, and when fully accoutered, some resembled Darth Vader's light-hearted cousins. There were perhaps thirty of these, and they were not going to have fun today. They would be pushing each other to the limit, and punishing anyone who tried to match their speed. As they rode, they would tell themselves that no matter how much it hurt, it had to be hurting the other guys at least as much. And with that thought firmly in the forefront of their minds, they would try to hurt themselves a little more.

Behind the zero-body-fat cadre (A Group), came the fast club riders (100–150 miles a week). They, too, wore Lycra, but they did not look like multi-colored stick figures. Most belonged to cycling clubs that rode together regularly, and while the first group might average 22 or 23 miles per hour on their 75-mile Saturday morning and Wednesday afternoon rides, these fast club riders were down around 17–19 miles per hour for 50 miles.

Behind B Group came C Group (80–100 miles a week), a little older, a little slower, a little thicker. And today they would have the most fun. Because they were sufficiently trained to go the distance easily, and would carry on conversations as they rode, having nothing to prove to anyone, least of all themselves.

In the end, the main difference in these three groups was in mindset. If someone in A Group got a flat tire on their Saturday ride, the others would wave goodbye and maybe shout, "See you next week!" If someone in B or C Group flatted, everyone would stop and stand around chatting, while he or she changed the tube. It was a chatty group underway, too, and at their high-cal breakfasts.

Behind them came the rest, ranging from weekend warriors in varying stages of fitness and commitment, to the out-for-a-lark gang who came in all sizes, shapes, and flavors. Some would be riding hybrids, some fat-tired bikes, and some on equipment so ancient that the Smithsonian ought to have sent an acquisition scout. These larkers would have fun, too, up to a point—which usually came between 10 and 20K out. Some would gut it out to the first rest station (22 miles) and a few would push themselves to the very end—and pay for it all weekend, with rubbery legs, aching calves, and sore seats. And perhaps never get on a bicycle again.

In B and C Groups were 26 riders from the abbey. There was the Dawn Patrol, led by Pete Zimmer and Warren Schubert, who could average 21 plus in a fast-pace line. And there were the Old Fudds, led by Ban Caulfield, who couldn't. (But who still remembered when they could.) There were the Tan Tornados from the Friary, led by Brother Bartholomew (18–20 mph), and even three Sisters from the convent who called themselves the Flying Natanyas. Each group had its own jerseys, which made for a certain amount of corporate hubris.

There were two groups from Eastport Cyclery, the more fun (albeit a bit slower) group being the Eastport Neversweats, led by Lauston Williams, and featuring Eastport denizens Dina Mark, J.D. Jack, and Carol Rich. Even the EPD was represented by Arnold Buchman and his wife, Ginger.

At Clay Armstrong's insistence, Armstrong & Associates was represented by Ed Forester and Nigel Rawlings. They did not ride together, however. Forester on his white Colnago was up with the elite riders where he did not look out of place, while Nigel on his yellow Canondale was back with larkers, where *he* did not look out of place.

At two minutes to ten, there was so much adrenalin coursing through the waiting riders that it felt to Bartholomew like they were standing an inch off the pavement. At precisely 10:00, the starting gun went off, and the elite riders started to roll, clipping in, shifting up, and departing in a pink haze of testosterone. Then B Group got underway, and C Group, and gradually, all the rest.

Zimmer and Schubert's Dawn Patrol found themselves riding in the draft of the first riders to depart. "Hey, Pete! Look at your computer!"

Pete did; it said 31 miles per hour. "Man, I don't believe this!" he cried. "I can't go this fast!" Everyone grinned; they were all having similar experiences. And then they swept into the first bend. "Hold your line! Hold your line!" came the cries, and suddenly bikes were flying everywhere, with a disastrous pile-up in the midst of the fastest riders. Demolition Derby, thought Bartholomew, who had warned Ambrose and the others from the friary, to ride outside the pack or *peloton*, just in case something like this might happen. They had gotten through all right, and so had Pete and Warren, but there were a dozen A Group riders who would be nursing severe road rash or worse.

After an hour and a half of hard riding, they rolled into Hyannisport and the first rest stop. The little waterfront village was so quaint it almost made your teeth ache. Thanks to the Kennedy compound, it was the best-known community on the Cape. Visitors invariably tried to nose their cars onto the causeway leading to the compound, only to be turned back politely by security guards. It was doubtful that the compound's neighbors appreciated their proximity. One inviting front lawn bore the sign: "Don't even *think* about parking here!"

At the waterfront parking lot where the rest stop had been established, there were banks of portable toilets, awnings for shade, and tables laden with huge vats filled with water and energy-replacement drink. Other tables had bananas for the zero-fats and Dunkin' Donuts for the extra fats. And everywhere were volunteers in red shirts, trying to be helpful.

Bartholomew, with Ambrose behind him, pulled in with the first of the B group to arrive. Pete and Warren were already there, along with forty or so other riders. Everyone was exhilarated, sharing experiences, grateful to have avoided the debacle in the first bend. The decibel level rose steadily.

Just then, Bartholomew noticed something out of the corner of his eye. Ed Forester, his white Colnago leaning against him, stood with his back to him, on his cell phone, holding his hand over his other ear and trying to make himself heard. Bartholomew slipped up behind him, downwind. Closer, closer— close enough to catch what he was saying.

"—about 1:30. Tell the pilot to have the plane warmed up and standing by. And both of you be in it. I just want to throw the bike in the back and get out of there!"

He closed the little flip phone and returned it to the right back pocket of his jersey. Bartholomew backed up and quickly turned, so Forester would not realize that he'd been standing there.

But he was not quick enough. For a moment their eyes met. Then Forester jumped on his bike and stomped on the pedals for a rapid exit. Too rapid: He ran into one of the red-shirted volunteers, and they both went down, sprawling on the parking-lot pavement. On impact, Forester's under-the-seat bag opened and spilled out a spare tube, a spoke wrench, tire spoons, chain separator, allen wrenches—and a long, odd-shaped, metal tool.

Hurriedly Forester scooped it up and re-stowed it, before anyone could wonder what sort of tool that was.

But Bartholomew didn't wonder; from his days in Viet Nam, he knew. It was the slide action of an automatic pistol.

57 | the taste of blood

WATCHING FORESTER GET BACK on his Colnago and take off, Brother Bartholomew whipped out the cell phone he'd borrowed from the Friary (but had not checked to see if it was fully charged). He called the Chief's home and got Peg.

"Dan's at the Stop & Shop," she said cheerfully, "stocking up for the holy war."

"Holy war?"

"Notre Dame's playing Boston College this afternoon."

"Peg, this is an emergency: Tell him I've got the goods on Forester, but he's making a run for it. Right now! He's in the Sheila Ride, and he's using it as a cover—" The phone went dead.

Bartholomew quickly scanned the crowd. He saw Ambrose about to enter a portable toilet. "Ambrose! Saddle up!"

"But I've got to—"

"No time for that now! Get Pete and Warren and catch up with me! Hurry!" And with that, he jumped on the old Peugeot and charged up the road.

He figured Forester had a two-minute head start on him. That didn't sound like much, but at 21–22 miles per hour, it was enormous–provided he could catch him at all, which was doubtful. But if Pete and Warren and Ambrose could get up here, working together they might just be able to overtake him. . . .

He looked in his rear-view mirror; no sign of them. But he was passing other riders, and now a fast B Group pace-line was passing him. He jumped on the back, his front wheel no more than a foot from the rear wheel of the last rider in the line. By taking advantage of the draft created by the rider in front of him, he could save a third of the effort required to move at that speed. But riding in a pace-line required maximum concentration: If the wheels ever touched, one or both riders would go down, and at that speed, bones were likely to be broken.

All Bartholomew was concentrating on right now, though, was not being dropped off the back. This group was averaging 23–24, and it was all he could do to hang on.

The sudden boost did have its pluses: He fully expected to catch sight of Forester soon, probably on the long, undulating hills approaching Wellfleet–unless, of course, Forester had managed to jump on the back of a similar express train.

On the downside, this pace-line he was in now was going to make it almost impossible for Ambrose, Pete, and Warren to catch up to him–that is, if Ambrose had even been able to find them.

And now another thought struck him: What did he think he was going to do, if he *did* catch Forester? Knock him off his bike? Make a citizen's arrest? In 'Nam he'd been a corpsman, not a combatant. And while he'd learned a fair amount about saving men, he didn't know Thing One about incapacitating one. And what if Forester pulled that gun on him? No, he didn't have to worry about that; it would take him longer than two minutes to re-assemble it.

They were on an upgrade now, and Bartholomew was fading. He should have pounded down liquids at the rest stop, filled his bottles. But how could he know that this—any of this—was going to happen! His flare-up of anger was another sign that he was close to bonking. And his thighs were burning with the extra effort to stay connected. He had to face it: The needle was on the wrong side of empty. Another tenth of a mile and—

"Hey, Brother Bart! Man, you're flying!" Startled, he glanced to his left. It was Pete! With Warren pace-lining behind him! And Ambrose! And even Ban Caulfield! A burst of joy fire-hosed away the despair of a moment before. He wasn't alone anymore! He'd been so preoccupied, he'd forgotten to check his mirror.

"So what's happening?" asked Pete, who was in such good shape that he could match his speed with little effort, even though he was on the front, pulling the others in his draft.

Bartholomew, on the other hand, was finding it hard to carry on a conversation at this pace. "The East Bluffs murderer?" Breath. "He's up ahead." Breath. "On a white Colnago." Breath. "Using the Sheila Ride to cover his get-away." Breath. "Headed for the P'Town airfield." Breath. "Trying to make a 1:30 flight." Breath. "You got any water?"

Pete had filled both his bottles at the stop, and he passed one to Bartholomew. Who dropped off the pace-line to drink it, as he pedaled. Then, refreshed, he got on the back of Pete's line.

After half an hour of hard riding, they had yet to catch sight of Forester, who must have caught a pace-line himself. Up ahead was the strip mall beyond the Wellfleet stoplight that was the site of the last rest stop before Provincetown. There were the drink and food tables and portable toilets, and the red-shirted volunteers, and perhaps a dozen riders—not as many as before. They'd been going so fast, they'd passed all but the elite riders and a couple of dueling B Group pace-lines.

Letting Warren take the lead, Pete drifted back to Bartholomew. "You want to skip the stop?"

"No." Breath. "Let's take on water." Breath. "He won't stop." Breath. "And when he hits those hills in Truro, it's going to cost him."

"Okay," said Pete, who then accelerated to the front of the line to let Warren know.

They roared in to the stop, did flying dismounts, and rushed to the drink table, chugging sports drink and filling their bottles.

Ambrose came up to Bartholomew. "Bart, I'm sorry; I've just got to go to—"

"It's okay; I was going to ask you to do something anyway: Get hold of Chief Burke, somehow, somewhere. Tell him Forester's up ahead of us. He's got a gun and almost certainly the diamonds, and he's heading for the P'town airfield, to make a 1:30 flight to Logan."

"Brother Bart!" yelled Pete. "We're ready when you are!"

Bartholomew looked at Ambrose. "You got it?"

Ambrose nodded.

"Okay," Bartholomew cried, "let's go!"

As he took his place at the back of Pete's line, he checked his computer. The pit stop had taken one minute, 18 seconds.

Maybe it was the adrenalin. Maybe it was the sports drink replacing electrolytes. But Bartholomew was feeling stronger. Strong enough that when it was his turn to pull, he was able to hold their average. And they had the hammer down! Zinging along at 27–28 on the flats!

Up ahead was a line of four A Group riders. With Pete on the front of their line, they caught them. And pulled alongside. Both groups were pedaling furiously. Max focus, no talking. And slowly Pete's line opened daylight on them.

Bartholomew grinned. For a moment he could hear the strains of Mendelssohn's overture to *The Barber of Seville* on the soundtrack, and could imagine a Cinzano truck in front of him, with the driver holding out his arm with three fingers extended, then four. . . .

"Is that him?" Warren cried from the front of the line. And far ahead of them, going up the last of the Truro hills, was a group of three. The rider on the back was on a white bike.

"Could be!" gasped Bartholomew.

Warren, who was riding at close to his sustainable peak, now went anaerobic. The others barely managed to hang on—except Ban, who dropped off the back, totally spent.

They were closing. A few more minutes and—*psewb!* Warren's tire flatted, and he pulled off the front of the line. "Go ahead!" he shouted to Bartholomew and Pete. "You can do it!"

Bartholomew was on the front, Pete behind him. He gave it his all, going so hard that he could taste blood in his mouth. But he managed to close the gap to less than a quarter of a mile.

Pete pulled past him. "Let me take it," he grunted. "You're going to need it at the end." Which would be soon, for they were now on the straight flat, as Route 6 approached Provincetown.

But now Forester—and it was clearly him—had seen them. He left the two men he'd been riding with, and broke away in a desperate solo sprint.

"Oh . . . no . . . you . . . don't!" Pete yelled, and he, too, began sprinting, with Bartholomew hanging on for dear life. They passed the two riders that Forester had been using. They were now doing 30—and 31—but Pete was unable to close the gap. Finally he went anaerobic, pulling Bartholomew to within a few hundred feet. But it cost Pete all he had, and shaking his head, he pulled off the front.

Forester looked back and saw who his lone pursuer was. He sprinted again, pulling away from Bartholomew, who simply had nothing left.

But neither, apparently, did Forester. Not having stopped for water, he was riding ragged now, wobbling, obviously close to bonking.

But it didn't matter; he'd made it. The airfield was coming up on the left. And there was his connecting flight, out on the tarmac next to the runway, port engine turning, waiting for its last passenger.

If I can just hold on, thought Bartholomew—*poing!*

He knew that sound and knew what it meant: He'd just popped a spoke. He gave a quick glance down. Sure enough, the rear wheel—but unless it got caught in the chain, it would slow but not stop him, though his quarry was now pulling rapidly away.

Forester swung into the service road entrance to the little airfield, ignoring the sign that said "Authorized Personnel Only." Up ahead, out on the tarmac, was the twin-engined plane his accomplice had chartered, the hatch open and waiting, the starboard engine idling.

And then suddenly, coming up the road behind them, was a white Bravado with its siren emitting a piercing two-note scream. Forester saw it and panicked. He suddenly sprinted, past the waiting plane and out onto the runway. He took a last look, to see how far behind his pursuer was—and failed to see the ancient DC-3 approaching from the opposite direction, flaps down, wheels reaching for the runway.

Bartholomew saw it, horrified. "Look out!" he shouted. Forester heard him. And turned—too late.

There was nothing the DC-3 could do. Its wheels were rolling on the asphalt, when suddenly out of nowhere a cyclist was directly in its path, where a moment before the runway had been clear for landing.

Frantically the pilot tried to veer right, but it was too late: The port prop swept into the cyclist. There was a thumping, grinding sound, and blood splattered along the port side of the plane, as it completed its landing.

Brother Bartholomew reached the scene, just as the Chief was getting out of his vehicle. He looked and then had to look away, or be sick.

As the overcast parted, something on the asphalt flashed in the midday sun. He forced himself to look back. Out of the broken seat tube of the white Colnago's twisted frame, diamonds had dribbled–a lot of them, glittering on the black pavement.

"There should be 31," said the Chief matter-of-factly.

"I'm sure there are," replied Bartholomew. "Just as I'm sure that the ballistics of the disassembled automatic he's got with him will match the slugs taken out of Haines."

In the waiting aircraft, pilot and passenger strained to see what had happened, like rubber-neckers slowing their cars as they passed a turnpike accident, hoping to see victims–and then wishing they hadn't.

Groaning, the pilot averted his gaze. But not his passenger. Lena Haines calmly took it all in. She could even see the diamonds–*her* diamonds–that now would never be hers. Instructing the pilot to take off, she fixed her gaze on the person responsible, the pursuing cyclist conferring with the Chief of Police. So *that* was Brother Bartholomew!

Trembling with hatred, she vowed that one day–no matter how long it took, or how much it cost–she was going to bring him down.

epilogue

ON THE FOLLOWING SATURDAY, Mark Rogers and Tina Gray were joined together in holy matrimony, in the first wedding to be held in the abbey's new basilica. It was a glorious setting, with rays of midday sun streaming in through the south-facing clerestory windows. But it was also a little overwhelming, like being married in Westminster Abbey.

Mark and Tina had picked Mozart's Coronation Mass, and the choir's jubilance lifted everyone's hearts to the rafters. Hearing that music, thought Brother Bartholomew, who could not stop grinning, one could almost imagine heaven joining in. Columba had once told him that the veil between heaven and earth was especially thin at weddings and funerals. The funeral part had not surprised him; he'd long had the sense that it was granted to departed souls to linger if they wished, to say farewell to friends and loved ones.

But it had never occurred to him that it might also be true of weddings—until now. He laughed aloud, at the awareness that along with the angels accompanying the choir, Columba and other former members were present, sharing their family's joy.

Across the aisle, even Ban Caulfield was smiling. The bride was wearing white—which meant what it once did. And Ban was not wearing red, as in a scarlet letter A. He had gone to see Mother Michaela, told her the whole thing. And seeing that his repentance was deep and likely to be lasting, she forgave him. And sent him to Father Andrews, to make a full life confession, and receive absolution. No one else in the abbey family needed to know what had transpired. Should he tell Betsy? Perhaps one day, said Mother Michaela. When and if God so led. But now, as she was in no way responsible for what had happened, it would only hurt her. But—and here she had fixed him with her gaze—if anything remotely akin to this ever happened again, he could be certain that whatever he did in secret, God would see shouted from the housetops.

Ban shuddered and smiled; it was good to be back. He told that to the face of Christ, who was looking down at them. At him. Never again, he said, meaning it. And in truth, not once since that night had his thoughts wandered to Saralinda—

Who was, at that moment, gliding down the bike path, suitably clad in white windbreaker and leg warmers. Beside her was a novice rider who had only recently taken up the sport, and whose acquaintance she had made a few minutes earlier. . . . He had a fancy bike, a yellow Canondale, but he was a tyro, all the same. In fact, he still hadn't figured how to use his gears to optimum advantage. "Keep your cadence up," she advised. "That'll shift the load to your lungs, not your legs. Otherwise, they're going to be like wet spaghetti tomorrow."

"Okay," said Nigel gamely. "Only—what's my cadence?"

Also keeping his cadence up was Dan Burke, who was at the moment helping Notre Dame beat Rutgers. They didn't need much help, he thought, mopping his brow. But on the other hand, they weren't playing in the shadow of the golden dome; they were in New Jersey, and you could never tell what might happen if the home team got emotional. He'd better stay with them for the entire second half.

In the past, he would have been burrowed into the living-room sofa with a six-pack of Guinness and a bottomless bag of Doritos. But this afternoon he was down in the rec-room, riding a stationary bicycle and drinking from a tall plastic bottle filled with sports drink, periodically replenished by Peg, who didn't even mind that he was dripping sweat on the carpet.

In New York, Serena had taken her son, G. Gordon, to a Dorothy Parker festival. A lot of the people had gone to considerable pains to look very smart—Flapper skirts, marcelled hair, and cigarette holders. But while Serena had donned a cloche hat, that was the extent of it; she felt DP would have approved.

In *FW*'s library, the oldest Armstrong sister and her fiancé were on stools at the chart table, going over plans for his new lab, making up lists of what he would need, and the brilliant geneticists whom he would invite to join his team. "*Our* team," he kept reminding her. For he had refused to consider the project, until she'd agreed to be administrative director.

Late that evening, her father (whose preferred bedtime reading had once been the *WSJ*) was absorbed in John Grisham's *Testament*. And for the first time in five years he had a companion in bed. Which he was having trouble getting used to. When he had gone to see Dorothy Hanson's mother, to assure her that all her needs would be taken care of, she said that the one thing she felt bad about was her daughter's cat. They did not allow pets where she lived, so she'd placed him for adoption with the Animal Rescue League in Brewster. "They're wonderful people there, but not too optimistic about finding him a home. He's no kitten, though his being a Maine Coon helps, and he's friendly as all get out."

Clay had never owned a cat (or a dog, for that matter). But in a way, it seemed the least he could do for Dorothy. So he called the Rescue League and said he'd take the cat.

He took it into his home. But not into his heart. At least, not at first, even though the cat followed him from room to room. That annoyed him at first, until he realized that whenever the cat didn't follow him, he began to wonder where it was. And what it was doing. It seemed they were going through a period of adjustment. The tall one had to adjust to the fact that the small one refused to sleep anywhere but on his bed. And the small one had to adjust his position, every time the tall one moved, to get back into the crook of his knees—the best sleeping place of all.

MR 01 '01

Mystery
Manuel, David

DATE DUE			

GAYLORD M2